DRAGON DREAMS

To: Dean family. Good Neighbors Enjoy the read

CHARLES SCHWEND

Karls "Chuck" Schwend

Black Rose Writing

www.blackrosewriting.com

ISBN: 978-1-935605-16-4

PUBLISHED BY BLACK ROSE WRITING

www.blackrosewriting.com

Printed in the United States of America

Dragon Dreams is printed in 12-point Andalus

Dedication

This book is dedicated to my wife, Dolores, who persevered the many nights of an empty bed, and the sleep robbing noise of a clicking keyboard with a sprinkling of choice words when the word processor, or my brain, were not working just right. Only with her support and comfort was the "Dragon Dreams" novel completed.

I would also like to thank my member peers of the *Highland Writer's Group* and the Edwardsville *Write Place Writer's Group* for their constructive criticism. Also deserving are the many individuals who pointed out plot and period problems.

Especially deserving of my appreciation is Reagan Rothe, Black Rose Writing, for publishing my novel.

THANK YOU ALL.

Preface

At the onset of human chronology, when Neolithic ancestors of the Chinese civilization were prevalent, and before the great Mongolian migration began, a Caucasoid race, ancestors of the Uyghur, found their way out of the Tarim Basin in central Asia, across the continent, stopping on an island now known as Japan. The Japanese call this heavily haired race "Ainu".

The Ainu were the first to embrace the martial arts as a way of life, a model for the later Samurai to emulate. Their skills of combat won them the position as the first Imperial Guard to the Emperor. Their weapons assimilated into the Japanese culture.

When the ruling Japanese began to methodically eliminate the barbaric Ainu, a secret society—"The White Ninja", was organized to counter the genocide, and preserve their vanishing race. The potentate of these mythological protectors of right and keeper of their accumulated knowledge is called the "White Dragon".

In 1956, an American teenage sailor, Web Drache, is thrust into this turbulent confluence of myths, races, cultures, and mysticism. Web becomes the leader select of the White Ninja by default, from an old man, the reigning White Dragon.

The old man hates the Americans who killed his entire family, all but one young woman, his great granddaughter, at Hiroshima. By mandate of the White Ninja's ancient traditions, he must prepare this young unwilling sailor, his rescuer, who he feels is unacceptable for his exalted station.

Web must deal with the mercenary forces of the Black Ninja, without the benefit of martial arts training. He soon learns to survive by his wit.

As Web travels the Far East and the United States, the old man prepares his young successor with a regimen of mental conditioning, through his only available method of contact – dreams – 'Dragon Dreams'. Web soon doubts his sanity, not understanding what has happened to him, and is not fully convinced that his legacy is really honorable.

Chapter
ONE

October's crisp evening air created billowing clouds of vapor from my breath, while walking along the narrow high road from the Naval Air Station to town. It did not take long for the pungent smell of the benjo ditches (open sewers), on both sides of the road, to overwhelm my sense of smell and taste. The odor of Illinois pig farms smelled nothing like this. As the city grew near, the music and revelry reverberated in my ears. Local working girls surrounded me outside the first nightclub demanding my time, and money. I knew I wanted to see the city and its landmarks, especially the Kentai Bridge that I have heard so much about, before enjoying the nightlife. Shouting "No-No" to the women, above the din of the strip, I continued on my way. I thought back to the warning from the old Navy Chief. "Web, maybe Japan surrendered, but the Kamikaze did not. They are lurking in the shadows, waiting to slit your throat. Their oath is to fight for their emperor god to the very last man. Their agents are everywhere, waiting their opportunity. Their mothers, wives, daughters, sons, and friends will promise anything to get you back off the main streets and into the maze of back alleys and dead-end paths. I have heard that they will submerge you alive, to the bottom of a benjo ditch with weights, feeding their rice paddies with your rotting flesh. The working girls of the street will love you for compensation, and when you are finished, exhausted, and finally asleep, will slit your throat with handmade blades fashioned from the lid off the tin of coffee that you paid them with for their service."

The old timers of Navy Patrol Squadron Nine (VP-9) enjoyed putting me on, while explaining all the horrors and pleasures of 1956 Japan to this novice sailor. It was humiliating, trying to act the old seasoned salt, and realizing I was not fooling anyone but myself, as I tried to regale my shipmates with imaginary stories of lustful liberties taken in foreign ports.

I must have wandered for several hours, enjoying a few drinks in the local clubs, seeing the revered white snake pit of Imazu, Iwakuni (In Japan all white animals are held in high respect.), and the RTO (Railroad Train Office), before getting good directions to the Kentai bridge, an ancient serpentine arched bridge. I had only seen this type of view before in pictures. To think that this bridge has been in constant use for four hundred years was impressive. It looked like a sea dragon, with its multi-humped body slicing through, and over the river Nishiki.

Trying to cross the structure, a staggering group of drunken American Marines blocked the way. They ran into an old man walking cautiously, leaning on his cane, and a young woman at his elbow, helping him. Knocked to the bridge decking, the young woman uttered a short scream, as the old man fell through a temporary barrier where the bridge railing was under repair.

The woman called out "sosofu!" (Great-grandfather!), as a weak cry came from the falling frail man. Breaking through the ice, his head submerged, and then popped up like a cork.

I froze. No one reacted, as if nothing happened. The screams of the young woman, and the barely audible calls for help from the old man ignored. *What the hell...* and like a dumb fool, not thinking how deep the water might be, or how cold, I ran to the break in the rail and jumped.

Dropping to the freezing water it came to me, *I am a stupid idiot. I am not responsible for that old man, or these people.* Here I am risking my life for a man from a culture that only a few years before, was an enemy to my country. It was too late to use second thought as a precaution against my impulsive action.

The thin ice broke under my feet, and every inch of my descending flesh went numb. The pain was excruciating as my muscles cramped while plummeting through the icy water. I thought it was strange that my life did not flash through my mind, as people recount of their near death experiences.

Hitting the bottom of the shallow river, the top of my head still exposed to the freezing air, my face surfaced and I trod water. The opening I made in the ice was right next to the hole the old man created. He was thrashing around and still holding his cane. What a surprise -- he hit me with that damn cane. *He is frantic and does not realize what he is doing.* Remembering my Red Cross training, I submerged into the icy depths, turned him around to face the opposite direction, grabbed him by the waist, pulled him under the surface of the water to subdue him, pushed up from the bottom and clutched his head, from behind, in my arm. Every muscle in my body was screaming in pain.

The old man yelled at me between his coughing and spitting, scratched at my arm with one hand and tried to strike me with the cane in his other. Swimming was impossible in the ice-covered water, so I bounced up and down, submerging -- pushing myself up from the bottom, breaking the ice from beneath. The old man started to hold his breath every time I submerged, sputtered and screamed out words that sounded like obscenities, while trying to gasp for air whenever I surfaced. My feet finally found firm ground, while my head and shoulders were above the ice. Beating on the surface ice with my free arm, I broke open a path to follow, until I was able to stomp it down with my feet.

The young woman and a small group of vocally excited locals converged on the bank of the river. They surrounded the old man. Someone threw a blanket, or something, on me that smelled worst than an old horse blanket. Everyone was jabbering -- nothing was coherent to me, until I realized the young woman was speaking English, thanking me, and speaking Japanese to the old man all at the same time. The flushed cheek old man was still vehemently cursing me, his eyes bulged and face contorted with hate and contempt.

A passing cab stopped. The young woman pushed me into the front seat, and the still cussing old man into the back seat. She quickly jumped in beside the old man, and yelled instructions to the driver. The taxi accelerated with a jerk, pushing me back against the seat.

If I had only stopped at that first night club with the street girls, and acted like a normal sailor, I would not be in this mess. I knew that it must be getting late, and since enlisted personnel are on Cinderella liberty (liberty that expires at midnight); the possibility of being AWOL came to mind.

The liquor drank wandering through town, the drone of the engine, the fumes from that foul scented thing around me, the blast of hot air from the heater, the soothing, consoling voice of the young woman in the back seat, and the grunts and curses from the old man, soon lulled me into a light sleep. A bump in the road woke me, while the lights illuminated an area of strewn rubble. An old demolished rock building, maybe the old Kentai Castle that I had heard so much about.

The roughness of the road vibrated up through the tires, stiff suspension, and firm seat, brought me out of my twilight snooze. Darkness obscured the landscape until the turning cab swung the headlight beams across a wooden structure, with a gray patina, built onto the side of a rocky cliff. The stormy wind shook the small taxi, and the rhythmic gusts pushed the vehicle into a semblance of a rocking ship at sea.

The young woman reached across the old man, opened the door and pushed him out. Wrapped in an unorganized pile of rags and cloth he stumbled out. "Come -- Come," yelled the woman. The thought that I should go back to the base flashed in my head. The cab driver was gesturing with his hands, telling me "Go -- Go.". *Oh, what the hell.* I thought, I was most likely already in trouble, but it's Friday night and I do not have duty tomorrow.

I opened the door and the cold freezing wind took my

breath away. I followed the woman and old man, and braced myself against the elements. I could not believe that frail old man was walking erect, and steady in this blustery gale.

The building looked solid and massive from the taxi, but reaching the recessed front door revealed a wooden structure with smoked glass panes instead of clear glass. The front entrance was made of sliding doors and more smoked panes, held in place with thin strips of wood. A wide overhang roof protected the entrance from the weather. The young woman opened a sliding door, and then pushed the old man inside. Reaching back, she grabbed my arm, pulled me inside, saying "Come. Come." I watched them pull off their shoes, putting on slippers that were inside the door. There were no other slippers. Reaching down I untied my wet shoes; slipped them off, and followed the young woman and old man into the interior. Inside, the furnishings were sparse, but cohesive, clean, with a high polish – but still cold.

The old man was still grumbling, his intense steely face looked at me. Their heated conversation came to an abrupt stop. The woman motioned to me and said, "Come with us –– where it is warmer," leading us to the back of the structure, to a solid wood wall. The old man balked, resisted the young woman's direction, but she appeared to be very determined, and coaxed him forward.

In the dimness of the room, I saw her push on a small panel, and the wall slid open revealing a stone arched passage leading to a large cave. Standing in amazement, I looked around, gaping, not realizing they were already in the next room, until the young woman called to me, "Come. Come." Hesitant, I followed them into the cavernous room, and heard a soft whirring sound behind me. The wall closed behind us, and I no longer heard the wind.

Chapter
TWO

A huge fireplace illuminated the room through a hearth opening so large you could walk through it standing upright. The fire cast long ominous dancing shadows across the floor. The walls were rough and hewn from solid rock. The light did not reach the high dark ceiling.

I became apprehensive and guarded, as similar scenes from horror films seen, came to mind. The woman seated the old man and me at opposite ends of a large wooden plank table near the fire. The old man still grumbled, glared at me, snarling in his native tongue. The woman poured us each a small cup of hot tea from a pot that sat on a metal shelf in the fireplace.

By the firelight, I saw she was young, beautiful, slender and well poised, not like the women I had seen earlier in the streets of town. Her walk was graceful, like she floated across the floor. My eyes locked on her. I wished for her eyes to make contact with mine. I must have seemed rude as my eyes took in every detail of her body, every gesture, every facial expression.

Speaking sternly in Japanese to the old man with an assertive tone, and then looking at me, making solid eye contact, she said softly. "Warm yourself by the fire. I will be back with dry clothes." Her soothing voice captivated my senses. A trance like cloud covered my thoughts. I could feel my uneasiness ebb, and felt safe. She left through a door in the wall, to the left of the fireplace.

I looked back to the old man, and saw a skin tone lighter than normal for a Japanese man. I also noticed a different expression come onto his face, just as menacing – but worse. He must have been reading my mind, observing me watch her every move. He was starting to intimidate me and I wondered if I did the right thing, not going back to the base.

I felt my skin start to crawl and goose bumps rose under the old man's scrutiny. The young woman returned with an armful of clothing, placing them at both ends of the table. She started to help him change from his soggy clothes, stopped and looked at me. I was reluctant to change in their presence.

The old man, in a more forceful voice, talked to her in a mocking tone while nodding toward me. She spoke sternly, and stopped him in mid-sentence. She walked back to me, placed her left hand softly on my forearm. I mentally saw the electrical force, generated from the contact of our touching skin, spark into fireworks. Looking into my eyes, she motioned with her right hand, pointing to the right corner of the room and said "Change."

Wanting to believe her smile told me more, but knowing the need for common sense, I brought myself back to the real world with a mental reality check. There was no way that a woman, who looked like a goddess, could be more than casually interested in someone like me. Reality checks can puncture a temporarily enlarged ego.

Picking up the bundle of clothing, I slowly walked to the corner where she gestured. A four-paneled screen stood around a table and chair, and a small shelf on the wall. It felt good to get that smelly old rag and wet clothes off.

None of the clothes fit. The huge wrap-a-round shirt hung from my shoulders and the pants were more like a long bolt of rough cloth, tailored to fit a giant gorilla. I wadded everything around myself, tying the ends in a square knot befitting a good sailor.

Stepping out from behind the screen, I had walked halfway back to the table when the old man looked my way and started roaring with laughter, while trying to talk to the young woman. She was also smiling at me, almost to the point of laughter. Hand covering her mouth; she could not stop the giggles that should have embarrassed me. I could tell she was trying very hard to control herself.

Being the brunt and focus of their amusement, knocked a couple of rungs out from under me. Trying to maintain my dignity, I returned to the table acting as though his laughter, and her smile, had no effect on me. My acting had no effect on his superior smug demeanor, whereas she had a more concerned, softer look about her.

Her smile was different. He noticed the smile and the look she gave me, gruffly spoke to her and she left. Again, I began to feel nervous. Her presence had a calming effect on him. He seemed a lot larger, much larger than when I first pulled him out of the freezing water.

He refilled his cup and continued sipping tea, not offering any to me, but occasionally looked my way with a new, more belittling expression. After a few minutes, she returned, floated across the room with a green porcelain pot, and two small matching cups. She spoke softly to the old man, placed the first cup in front of him, then brought the second cup down to my end of the table, sat it before me. "Sake." She said.

She did not drink, but spoke to the old man in a much softer voice. He was, from the tone of his voice, arguing again. She abruptly stopped the conversation with him, snapping her head away. She turned her attention to me, and asked sharply. "What is your name?" Her sudden question and tone of voice caught me off guard, or maybe it was the sake.

I answered, "My name is Drache, Web Drache. I am from the naval base (when I said that, I knew it sounded stupid - where in the hell else would I be from). Where am I?" I asked.

Looking at me as if I was delirious, she said, "Yokoyama, Iwakuni - This is the house of my great-grandfather. He is thankful to you for saving his life. He is also under obligation to pass onto you..."

The old man jumped up, stopping her in mid-sentence with a shaking raised fist, and shouted in perfect English "I pass nothing to him. He is an American, a race without honor. His pitiful attempt to help disgraces me; it would have been honorable for me to drown rather than relinquish to his pathetic gesture of rescue. My head bows in shame in the house of my ancestors. The old ones will never allow me to pass in death with honor. There is only one way for me to make appeasement. Bring me my ha-jitatsu (ceremonial hara-kiri knife) and leave me."

She shouted back at him in Japanese. Her heated verbal attack took him by surprise, his shoulders dropped and he slumped down into his chair. Looking at me, she said, "My great-grandfather must follow tradition. He must follow the traditions of Izumo. He is obligated and has no choice but to follow his kyoshoku, the instructions of his ancestors that have been adhered to by his family for over two thousand years." She walked over to me, and stood inches from me. The closeness forced my eyes to take in the whole of her face, memorizing the sparks that danced in the dark depths of her eyes, her nose, the flair of the nostrils, the smooth lips bordering a gentle - delicate mouth, her chin, the translucence of her beautiful light clear skin, the wisp of hair across her forehead, and her perfectly formed ears.

I felt shaky, as though I was trembling, weak in the knees, and tongue-tied. Her sweet breath smothered my senses. It was hypnotic. Looking up into my eyes, she continued talking. "I will leave. The words my great-grandfather will speak are not words for a woman of the family. Do not be afraid, he speaks sharply, but he will not harm you. Listen to my great-grandfather. Listen very hard. He will impart much wisdom to you, if you are receptive to the word of the Ryu Hakujin."

What in the hell is this Hako whatever, was the thought of the moment, when the woman, slowly and firmly said "Great-grandfather! I will leave you; you know what you must do." She left.

I looked for a way out. The old man had a deranged look. I gulped down my cup of sake.

"Sit - Sit down" he shouted at me. I sat. Staring at me with his dark penetrating eyes, he spoke to me in a low, deliberate, and intense voice - "I am the Master of the White Ninja. I am the Jonin (the leader or high man) called the White Dragon.

This guy really thinks he is special.

"Centuries ago, a feudal lord, a daimyo, a black hearted man who wanted to rule the world, gathered his samurai, a following of rabble. They studied the martial arts and called themselves Ninjutsu Kuro - The Black Ninja. They performed their evil deeds at night, under darkened skies. They were murderers. They practiced a deviant form of bungei, a martial art, void of honor or the principals of decency, and led by a renegade mercenary.

This evil man, and all his descendants, had wanted to rule Nippon (Japan), and replace the laws and ways of life set down by the Legendary God-Emperor Jimmu, who first ruled this land. They were a secret organization who ruled the night, terrorizing the land for over a thousand years. At first, nothing could stop them. They killed all who they thought could gather a following to repulse their evil force. Their goal was at hand. Nevertheless, there were other elements at work - The White Ninja. To suppress the evil Black Ninja, my ancestors created the White Ninja. We have countered most of their attempts successfully. Today the struggle continues. Our minds and hearts, our main weapons, tempered with the wisdom of my ancestral lineage, and the superior martial arts knowledge of the Ainu, the original Caucasoid inhabitants of Nippon, known by you as Japan. They were white like you. From the White Ainu came the descriptive color in the White Ninja, and the White Dragon.

They were a superior race, and that was why the massive tide of invaders from the Asian continent, my other ancestors, and the ancestors of the Japanese race, had to eliminate them. The ancients called the Ainu barbarians, like you Americans. However, they were the warriors from which the samurai adopted their martial art skills, and assimilated their weapons. Instructions from the ancient gods of Tibet, the land of the Ainu's ancestors, were passed from one generation of master sword makers, to the next, always keeping the knowledge of their arts within the realm of the White Ninja.

Their legends of creation melded with the new conquering people, blending until the source of each entity is untraceable. My ancestors were the first imperial court's guard, and the emperor's personal warrior samurai.

Emperor Jimmu called on Izumo the dragon protector of the Sun god to train them in the ways used to protect the gods since the predawn of time. Dragon Izumo took the family elder to a secret cave, in the Iga Province, to instruct him in the ways of ancient warriors, and make him receptive to the ancient teaching and philosophies.

Since that time, to the elder passed the secrets, and position, Master of the White Ninja – The White Dragon. I am the last elder, the last male of the family. I am the last White Dragon to fight the evil dark ones. I have you, the Americans to blame.

I have only my great granddaughter, a surviving twin. If only she were ..." he sighed, "but I can carry no hatred for you. By tradition and ancient mandate, no harm may come to you. It is sad. You are an American. Americans have no honor, no mental discipline; they are barbarians, not receptive to the true ways of life. You are not an acceptable recipient ... but I have no choice."

I sat dumbfounded. The hairs on the back of my neck raised with the anger I felt. *Who the hell does he think he is?* He must have escaped from some loony bin. Deciding it was in my best interest to humor him, and bide my time to get out of this strange place. I have to get back to the base. Looking up at the old man I said "That's interesting, and I'm sorry for being unacceptable, but ..."

"Stop – do not patronize me" yelled the old man. His eyes still locked on my mine, painfully penetrating, but I was unable to break away from his gaze. He continued. "I am sorry. I may be a little overly caustic toward you. Let me get you a better drink." He broke his gaze away from me, bringing relief from the burning sensation behind my eyes and forehead. He turned and went to a cabinet to the left of the fireplace, struggled to his left knee, opened the door, and took out a bottle and two gold colored cups. Getting up, he returned, placing the bottle and cups on the table in front of me. He went to his chair and pulled it over to the side of the table across from me. His face was much softer, projecting a new reassuring and calmer demeanor.

The bottle he placed between us was a clear, very ornately carved decanter, with a golden wire filigree inlay, that formed an intricately designed dragon's head, surrounded by swirling mists, with a sun above its head. The cups were heavy but delicate to touch and sight. The lip curved and rolled downward for a quarter of the way around the rim.

He poured a clear drink into my cup. "This is better," he said.

"Where is your drink?" I asked suspiciously. There was softness in his voice.

"I cannot drink this, it is too strong for an old man like me, but I can join you with sake." He poured from the warmed sake pot into the golden cup nearest to him.

I picked up my cup and cautiously smelled the drink. It had a fruity citrus smell. I took a sip; just enough to wet my lips, allowing it to tease my taste buds. The clear liquid was very sweet, and made my stomach warm, but did not have a bite to it. It was extremely smooth and mellow. We sat looking at each other, sipping at our drinks. When my cup was empty, he refilled it, stood up, and walked to the arched entrance across the room.

He lit a long slender torch and walked around the sides of the room, lighting previously unseen lanterns suspended on chains, hanging from brackets high on the walls. I continued with my drink. The additional light revealed a cavernous room with a high arched stone ceiling. Weapons covered the upper half of the walls, most all of which I had never seen before.

I recognized some as archery weapons, spears, swords and knives of every description, axes – all looked medieval. There was also some type of uniforms, banners, beautiful tapestries, flags of every description, and large metal medallions, or shields that I could not identify. Slowly I became conscious that my cup was again empty. My eyes were getting heavy and I was getting extremely sleepy. The last conscious vision I remember was that crazy old man walking toward me, through a swirling white cloud, followed by something that looked like a dragon's head, half hidden in milky fluff, talking of the White Ninja, and the White Dragon. I must have fallen asleep and was having a nightmare.

Chapter
THREE

I felt the warmth of the sun on my face before consciously waking. My left hand was sore from a cut across my palm. I could not stretch out my fingers, for fear of tearing the cut apart. "Damn."

I looked down the road to the main gate. It took two wobbly attempts to stand up. My groggy walk down the road to the base was interrupted when a cab full of agonizingly loud and screaming shipmates damn near ran me down. "Web – come on. We'll give you a lift back." A smashed, grotesque face decorated the cab window. It was my friend Mitchell.

I pushed my way into the tangle of half-awake bodies suffering from a long night of heavy drinking, and smelling terrible from vomit, bad breath and B.O. I had to shake Mitchell awake before asking, "Where in hell were you guys last night?"

He peered at me through half opened, bloodshot eyes, and began talking to me with a foul smelling mouth. "The group was arguing how far south the local train went before it turned around and came back."

"Well, how far does it go?"

He looked up at me again and mumbled, "It doesn't come back." He told me that the group spent the entire weekend with the Executive Officer (X.O.) of the squadron trying to get back to Iwakuni.

Not believing what I was hearing, I shouted – "The whole weekend". "What day is it?"

Mitchell sarcastically said "Monday morning, duffus. What did you do this weekend?"

"Nothing" I replied softly, knowing he would think I was out of my mind if I told him what happened, or what I thought really happened.

The X.O. and the rest of the group followed in another taxicab. Stopping at the main gate, we waited for the second group, to avoid any problems with the Marine gate guards. It was Monday morning, and none of us had overnight liberty. The X.O. got us through the gate and onto the base. Later in the morning, we had to go before the Commanding Officer (C.O.) to explain ourselves.

I acted as if I was with the group and X.O., nobody said anything different. We figured he could not do much to us enlisted men, without doing something to the X.O., and we were right. The C.O. gave us a royal reaming, and sternly warned of treading on thin ice. I started shaking when he said thin ice, but regained my composure when he looked at me like I was nuts. He walked over to me, getting close into my face, and spoke in a low threatening voice. "You men had better shape up, or you'll not be around. We have places to straighten out people like you. Now get out. X.O. – stay. I have some words for you."

Telling anyone what happened that weekend would have been a mistake, knowing no one would, or could believe my story. Not knowing what happened, my mind completely blank, from Friday night to Monday morning scared me at first, but as time went on the experience gradually stopped preying on my mind. *I know that this sailor is not going back across that bridge again.* Nevertheless, I could not get that beautiful, mysterious and captivating girl out of my mind. It was as if our minds linked. It was a little eerie. She was constantly in my thoughts, always in my head.

Mitchell and I regularly went on liberty together, but mindful of the C.O.'s warning, I had been staying on base for the past week. Mitchell had been bugging me all day to hit the beach with him. "Good God, its Friday. Byron has to get his teeth out of hock. Come on, we are not going to get into any trouble. We will just go into town, he will get his teeth, we can stop and get a bite to eat, a few beers, and come back to base early. What do you say?"

"I don't know, that Byron is a wild man."

"Don't worry. He just wants someone with him at the hockshop. He's a little leery of that Mama-San." Mitchell said reassuringly.

"O.K., O.K., but I'm keeping my nose clean. The C.O. has been watching me. Every morning when I bring him his coffee, he lays a heavy eye on me. Asking me all kinds of questions – What did you do last night? What time did you start the coffee this morning? Are you writing home? He was kicking out questions one after another. It gives me the willies. You would think he was watching me for my mom or someone."

A crude, wild man, Byron had blonde hair and a body covered with a curly mat of black hair. He would hock whatever he could whenever he needed money. If he had nothing left to hock, he would leave his false teeth for collateral on a loan, which he did at a local pawnshop ran by an older toothless Mama-San.

Taking a cab into town, Byron, Mitchell and I stopped at the hockshop to redeem his dentures. Byron could not locate his uppers and lowers in the display case. "Shit. Can you see them? I can't find them anywhere." Mama-San opened the back room curtain and shuffled in. "Where's my teeth?" Said Byron excitedly. "There not here."

Mama-San stood silent, giving him a big toothy grin, and then turned her back to him. (In Japan it is not polite to put in or take from your mouth without first covering it, unless turning from eyesight.) She removed his dentures, wiped them dry on her apron, and handed them to him.

Her use of his dentures did not faze him. Paying her, he then calmly walked out the door, to the nearest bar. Ordering a bottle of *Asahi* beer, he rinsed his teeth and popped them into his mouth, clicking them together to seat their fit. Mitchell and I looked at each other, laughing.

"Hey, you guys want a drink?" yelled Byron.

"You have to be joking," answered Mitchell. "We're going to get some food." (Eating local fare is taboo.)

We walked to the intersection known as *four corners*, as a freezing November drizzle slicked everything not covered. We decided that a platter of fried rice, from the sidewalk eatery diagonally across the intersection, was the food and place of choice. Mitchell took off like a shot, running across the intersection. Halfway through, a three-wheeled truck, made like a motorcycle, with a wide rear axle that supported a small box bed three feet by three feet, ran over him. They are awkward looking, not very heavy, and very maneuverable. Mitchell must have run right in front of the on coming truck.

I could hear the whoosh as he was run down, watched in horror as the small truck bounced over him, squeezing his lungs, forcing all the air from him. Thoughts of loosing my best friend flashed through my mind. From a muddy pothole in the middle of the heavy traffic, came a barrage of cussing that only another sailor could appreciate. I did not know if he was cussing because he thought the truck driver was incompetent, or if he was mad at himself for doing something stupid; like running into heavy traffic.

He stood up in the muddy puddle of water, with steady rain falling around him, trying to wipe off the diagonal tire tread marks that ran across his chest and legs. I ran out to him, to see how badly he was hurt, and found an unharmed, unrepentant jaywalker, madder than hell, refusing to get out of the traffic, while he cussed out the world for his misfortune.

I could not stop laughing, which made him all the madder. I coaxed him from the intersection, away from the traffic and the blasting of horns, into the sidewalk cafe. He grumbled throughout the meal about ruining his clothes, the bruises he knew would pop out the next day, and the inept driving skills of the local drivers.

The cafe was very small with every inch of space utilized for maximum use. The grill and a narrow workspace in front of a cabinet covered wall were twenty feet long by six feet wide. There was just enough room to squeeze by a row of stools under an eating counter. In reality, it was more like a low roofed chicken coop, with seats and grill, from end to end. However, the food was marvelous. The fried rice with baby shrimp, slivered grilled scrambled egg, mixed with green onion, rice, and other mystery ingredients made a mouth-watering meal. Everything was prepared on the grill, served on a large oval platter, with soy sauce, and a bottle of local *Asahi* beer. My stomach full, I stretch my arms and legs, noticed the line of waiting customers, waiting for seats to empty. Looking over to Mitchell, I said, "We had better get back to the base."

"Sure, sure," he answered, but, stepping out the door, seeing that the rain had stopped, he finished his sentence. "I think I'll stay out in town for a while. You sure you want to go back?"

"Yah, I'm sure. I'll see you tomorrow." Disappointed with his decision, I turned and started walking back to the base, watching for a taxi. It was a two-lane road, and cars could not pass on it with oncoming traffic. When I was halfway back to the base, walking on the shoulder of the right lane, I looked up, and saw two sets of headlights coming toward me. Looking over my shoulder, I saw another set of headlights coming from behind me. I knew I was in deep shit. Holding off as long as I could, and wishing for someone to stop, or slow down, I apprehensively watched the headlights come closer, and closer, but at the last moment, I had to jump. There was not enough room for three cars abreast and me on that road. There I stood, armpit deep in the human waste of the benjo ditch.

Oh man, does the stench ever rise fast, burning nose and eyes, when that floating scum is disturbed. As I crawled up the muddy, steep, slippery dirt bank, I wondered how those three cars made it past each other on that raised narrow road. I was lucky again. I must lead a charmed life!

The Marine guards manning the gate, who normally were very close – up in your face, and meticulous, would not allow me near them as I tried to show them my identification. They backed away and waved me through. Passing cabs would not stop as they normally did. I walked the distance to showers located in a cold cinder block building adjacent to the old kamikaze quarters, our barracks.

Chapter
FOUR

It was after the squadron rotated back to the Naval Air Station, Alameda, California that I started having weird dreams. I could only remember bits and pieces never complete images - mummies, treasures, weird looking weapons, and me as a martial arts expert. It was good remembering what little I did. My self-esteem bolstered, I saw myself rise up from that nerd self-image.

California was a completely different world compared to Illinois, with strange customs, and another language - like a foreign country to a small town boy like me. I turned eighteen, and on top of the world. Mitchell and I still bummed together on liberty, and met many interesting people.

One Sunday afternoon, I went to Oakland by myself, needing to be by myself and relax before the heavy Monday workload. I was not looking forward to having duty on Monday. The late night post watch on the tarmac was always damp and chilly. It was downright scary out there alone, with the strange noises, shadows, smells, and the nightly heavy fog.

I went to a movie, a western with John Wayne. I enjoyed the film and felt relaxed, but hungry. Leaving the theater, I looked for a place to eat. Turning down onto a street, I found a four-lane entrance that ran into a large parking lot behind a business district opposite of the theater.

Thinking I could walk through, to the next street, to catch the bus back to the base, *I can grab a quick sandwich at the club on base.* The entire block-long building was solid with no way through. Walking around the perimeter of the parking lot, I spotted a passageway and hoped it would lead me through the complex to a street. Entering the hole in the wall and turning a corner, I encountered two tall, husky brutes beating a smaller and older man. Before I could react and run for help, the nearest thug grabbed and threw me against the wall. His huge fist knotted the front of my shirt. He growled to his friend "This is our lucky day, two for one." Dropping his face down close to mine, he spitted out, "Give me your wallet or I'll break your scrawny face." He followed that statement with a swipe to my face with the back of his hand, knocking my glasses to the ground.

"O.K. - O.K." I mumbled. Scared stiff, my head got all tingly. My body started shaking; a deep animal like growl came from deep in my throat. The sound terrified me, as if I had lost control of my mind and body. My newly energized hands came up and slammed my assailant away from me. My right hand shot up with my thumb extended and rigid, penetrated deep into the soft tissue between his throat and jaw, his whole body convulsed, becoming limp. My foot kicked solidly into his groin. The air spouting from his mouth sounded like a punctured balloon. My left hand held him up by his shirt, while my right hand swung from my left to right. My exposed fingernails cut the skin of his throat. My right hand slapped against the wall rebounding back in a straight line, straight to his throat.

My thumb and index finger extended in a U-shape, and I felt them penetrate his throat, through the skin cut by my nails, clamped tight, jerked back, tearing his throat out with a horrifying, gut wrenching, sucking sound. I could not believe I was doing this. I had no control of my actions. My attacker silently collapsed to the pavement, and my focus turned to the other mugger, who was unaware of his partner's fate.

He enjoyed himself, laughing and making high pitch sounds of pleasure while kicking his victim, who was laying on the ground in a fetal position, begging. "Please stop. Don't hurt me anymore. You can have anything you want. Please." Stumbling forward a few steps, I kicked him in the groin from the rear. The thrust raised him off the ground a good twelve inches. Before his feet returned to the ground, my two hands were coming together to slap his ears. The air pressure from my hands ruptured his eardrums. It sounded like popping corn.

As he crumpled, I grabbed his long greasy hair and the back of his leather vest, and smashed him into the solid block wall. His head made a sickening hollow thud as it flattened against the wall. Reaching down and grabbing his exposed shirt, I yanked the tail out of his pants, and wiped the blood off my hands. I picked up my glasses and checked them for damage. I was pleasantly surprised that they were undamaged. Then, with trembling hands, put them back on. The comprehension of what just happened hit me. Tingling sensations pulsated at the onset and ending, of a period of numbness that came over me.

Shaking violently, I helped the other victim up, brushing debris off his coat. He stared at me with a horrified expression. Stuttering, I blurted out "No -No-No-one has to know of this. O.K.?" I had no idea why I said that. It just came out of my mouth.

He mumbled a hollow sounding "Yes."

"Are you all right? You're not hurt are you?"

Stiff arms wrapped around his chest. Holding his sides, he whispered. "I'll be all right."

I ran down the passage, gasping, my chest heaved, sucking in air from the mental exertion as much as the physical. I turned toward the bus stop when it came into view. It seemed like hours before the bus came, but in reality only took minutes. The mumbler did not come the same way. My body involuntarily shook on the ride back to the base. I tried to rationalize what just happened during the ride back to base. In my mind, the whole episode appeared like a fuzzy nightmare. My thoughts wandered through the possibilities of arrest for murder, thrown in jail, and on and on. Arriving at the main gate, I felt that my actions were in slow motion, like a zombie. The guards scrutinized my ID and liberty card twice, before waving me through the turnstile. My heart pounded fast and hard. I thought my face reflected my secret.

That night my recurring dream returned in its entirety for the first time. There was that crazy old man again talking about that Izumo thing. That damned Dragon Izumo.

The old man in my dream started in his smooth articulate monologue. "You have begun the first of ten visits, learning experiences with Izumo. I am surprised you have reached this level since you Americans have no honor. You must listen and master the knowledge of level one before entering the next encounter. Each phase of knowledge is double the one before. I am sure you will not go far. You Americans have no discipline and have no focus when mentally tasked. Do you remember me telling you that the Master of White Ninja passed from generation elder to generation elder, and that my family, all of the heirs to this position, died in Hiroshima? The White Ninja dynasty is no longer viable. There is no longer an heir to the White Dragon, but Izumo lives.

Ancient teachings, order that the knowledge must pass to anyone, even an unfit person such as you from a self-destructive degenerate race, if that person saves the life of the Master. This knowledge can pass only if the recipient is receptive, honorable, and capable, both physically and mentally. I do not believe you have these attributes. I will attempt to transfer the knowledge since not being of your race, I am an honorable man, and must follow the teachings of my ancestors and that of Izumo.

Do not attempt to find my granddaughter Minkoto. If you return to my homeland, searching for her, my ancestral home, or me, you will not be successful. I feel dishonored, due to my inability to pass my station to a blood heir. Izumo's followers cannot acquire his knowledge. Only to blood male heirs, and you, who risked your pitiful life to save mine.

Be forewarned that if anyone identifies you as the bearer of Izumo's knowledge, you will lose that knowledge. The identity of the bearer must remain secret in order for it to be effective. If you fail any of the ten levels of knowledge, all levels acquired will be lost to you, and you will return to the bumbling American fool you are.

You are entering your first level. You must learn the knowledge of this level from observing Izumo. Visualize actions taken and remember them. You must be able to absorb the knowledge you need, visually, mentally and physically. If the Black Ninja is ever encountered, you must think what they think, and know what they know, and anticipate their every move before they do. This a Ryu Hakujin, a White Dragon, must do.

You will not consciously remember these instructions, or any other level of instruction, until you master your final test. However, you will remember my visits with you. Izumo comes. Sweet Dreams my young naïve American." Darkness came with a sinister laugh.

I could hear Harry James, getting louder and louder. Damn, reveille woke me, my bunk was soaked with sweat, and I felt drained of energy. The previous day's events, followed by last night's dream, hung in my head. I was a good candidate for the funny farm. A million thoughts flashed through my mind, all at the same time. *I am going to jail. I am a menace to society. How can I trust myself to mingle with people? How could I ever be with a woman? What kind of a life could I expect now? How did this happen to me? Why, why did this happen to me?*

As the thoughts ranged from going to jail, to asking myself why, I felt faint, lightheaded, nauseous, and all the other sick feelings a person could experience.

Mitchell bounced up from his bunk. His feet slapped the floor with an accompanying annoying laugh, and yelled. "What's the matter Web, you look green around the gills. Hah – you're not able to take the nightlife - huh? Get a move on. You will be late. Say, have you seen my khakis?"

I pushed all thoughts of the tormenting dream from my mind. Looking around I took in a visual inventory of his clothes haphazardly scattered around. "All I see is your jeans and chambray work clothes."

Mitchell gave me a dumbfounded look "My Khakis!" Speaking slowly and over-pronouncing each syllable. "You know what I start my car with - you dumb shit."

"I don't know why you people from Boston have to speak in near-English. Car keys - Car keys, is what you are trying to say. Not Khakis." Laughing, I cleaned up, dressed and went to the chow hall. Mitchell was on my case all through breakfast for not knowing and speaking proper English.

I did remember the old man visiting me again while at NAS Alameda. The following March I received orders, transferring me to an aircraft squadron in the Philippines. The intervening time softened the perceived threat to my remaining sanity left by the violence. I was starting to be able to relax again.

Chapter
FIVE

I am going home to Illinois, for a well-deserved thirty-day leave before shipping overseas. Flying home on a space available military flight, I could feel an excitement as the plane landed at Scott Air Force Base, near Belleville, Illinois. Trying to thumb a ride home to Highland, thirty minutes north, a state trooper stopped. "Hitch hiking is not allowed in Illinois, Sailor. Where ya going?"

"Highland."

"Get in." The state cop commanded. "I'm headed that way. Is Highland your home?"

"Yes."

"What's your family's name?"

"Drache, I'm Web Drache. I'm home on leave before going back overseas."

"Where are you going back to, Web?"

"No, I was in Japan. Now I'm going to the Philippines. I'm not going back to the same place." I said.   Our conversation was light talk, nothing in particular. He drove through Lebanon, Trenton, and pulled into Highland. Nothing had changed. I could see the pastures of the old Schmidt pony farm where I worked as a kid. Everything changed slowly in a small town like this. I was home. A feeling of safety, a security of mind and soul came over me. After more directions, the trooper pulled in front of my house.

"Well Web, I hope you enjoy your leave, and your new duty station."

"I'm sure I will, and I really appreciate the lift officer." I looked over, opening the car door, and saw my mom coming out the front door of the house with a worried look on her face. As soon as she recognized me, she rushed over to hug me.

"What's my baby doing home? (She still thought of me as her little baby. I think mothers do that to keep themselves feeling young.) I just knew you would be walking up the sidewalk sometime this week. I was watching for you."

I did not tell anyone I was coming home, but my mother always knew. How mothers always knew was a wonder to me. *How do they do that?*

I waved to the officer as he drove off. He must have thought me a little kid, my mom hugging me like that, making over me like a young teenager. Why I had turned eighteen, and have seen a good part of the world – a seasoned traveler, I thought.

All my old friends are gone, moved away for a job, or left town with no forwarding address. I spent time with my brother Don, drinking a beer or two in the evenings – nothing exciting. I was getting bored with the monotony of it all, but the dreams were not coming to me.

I had two more days of leave before heading back to the West coast, and felt confident that my worries and concerns were over. I had beaten this Izumo – White Dragon thing. I was feeling good and sleeping sound with no nightmares and no more violent episodes in my life. I decided to go bar hopping that night. Let my hair down and get with it. My brother Don agreed to loan me his new red Chevy pickup.

Later that evening, after dropping Don off at the corrugated cardboard plant where he worked, I started with a few of the local bars to whet my thirst for social contact, adventure, and fun – whatever comes my way. Predictably, I drank too much, and found myself in some dank, dark, scuzzy bar down off the slues of the Mississippi River.

The bar lizards showed their years of being rode hard and put away wet. A gaunt drunk, ugly, tall, redhead, dressed in bright green shimmering shorts and halter, slithered onto the stool next to me, and started in, trying to bend my ear. "Are you looking for a good time – a party honey?" Jeez – the dribble of her voice made the whole side of my head wet from the dampness of her putrid breath.

Her dull, lifeless, green eyes could not focus on me, the pupils looking all over the place, but not at me. I was repulsed at the thought. "No – I'm not up to that tonight, maybe a rain check? I haven't had enough to drink yet." I replied with a courteous smile, trying to be halfway nice.

With an indignant stance, she yelled at me. "Whatsamatter – you too good for me – Jim, Jim, Come here. This uppity son-of-a-bitch thinks he's too good fer us." Red was waving toward some six foot something. A huge, round bag of backwater slew dump, and the closer he got, the bigger he became.

"Shit – get away from me lady. Did I ask you for anything?" I was trying to get some distance between that red-on-the-head matchstick and myself, when Jim's huge fat hand, with thick sausage like fingers, tried to crush my shoulder.

"What's tha matter – ya don't wanna pay, Red? You play – you pay!"

"No – I did not play with anything and I'm not paying anything." I wanted to stress that there was no involvement with that red headed bar floozy. I was wrong again. He shoved me off my seat, with the flat of his pizza pan like palm. I hit the floor with the stool landing on top of me.

"You damn smart-ass tightwad, I'll teach you to cough up when you owe Red." With that, the blob kicked the stool off me, and kicked me in the hip. The blubberous mountain picked me up halfway up off the floor, and with the force of a bulldozer, shoved me out the open door into the parking lot. While sliding in the muck, I planned my getaway to my brother's pickup. I did not make it. The blob did not move like a bulldozer – more like a large racing car with a humungous engine. Six inches from the pickup door handle, a ton of problem hit me between the shoulder blades. The pain went up my neck and down my spine like a newly exposed tooth nerve. The truck door would not open. My hand would not work. My fingers would not follow my brain's electrical commands.

I felt my feet slide away as my body sunk into the soft wet earth. Trying to get to my feet, Jim kicked me in the shoulder. "Get up you turd." I was trying to get up when fat Jim let loose with a kick to my chest. The word "shit" was escaping from my mouth, turning into an sshhh sound, like an air hose cut in half, when my body started shaking; energy was rushing to my arms. I heard that animal like growl, and I heard Jim laugh – but not for long, no, not for long.

My hands were palm down in the muddy dirt, the energy in my arms snapped them straight and rigid, my body rose up into a crouched upright position. I saw a blur and ducked my head. Jim's massive arm swung over my head. My open hand shot out with its heel striking Jim's nose. He hesitated, grabbed his nose, covering his face with both hands. Leaping up into the air, my cocked foot kicked out, striking Jim's chin, and he went down for the count. Out of the corner of my eye, I noticed the bartender holding out my glasses. "Get out of here, someone called the cops," he said.

Looking him in the eye, I nodded in acknowledgment, said "Thanks," turned and opened the truck door.

I was in the pickup, started the engine, and was back out on the road before my mind, or breath, caught up. Only vaguely knowing where I was, it took some time before making it back to the main highway.

It was midnight, thirty minutes late, as I pulled up in front of the plant to pick up my brother. "Where the hell you been. Look at all that mud," exclaimed my brother as he slid behind the steering wheel. "See if I'll let you use my truck again." I knew he was not serious, but he had to go through the oral drill for my benefit. It was then I decided to start back to San Francisco the next morning instead of the following day. I was not looking forward to sleep, knowing what would be visiting, knowing WHO would be visiting me in my dreams.

My brother asked if I wanted to bum around for a while, he was not sleepy, and wanted to wind down. "Let's find a couple of girls." My exhausted look gave him my answer. In less than fifteen minutes, I was back in my mother's living room, looking out the window, watching my brother drive off. I was trying to think of reasons for not going to bed.

My mother was looking at me, and said – "Are you stiff, you're not standing right."

"I'm O.K. Mom; I slipped and fell before I came home. I think I'll go to bed."

I was looking up at the ceiling, thinking to myself, that I had to get some sleep. Trying to visualize blackness, trying to make my mind go blank, all the while knowing what was coming. My body entered that semi-sleep state, dreaming that I was fighting off that same dream. In my sleep, the knowledge of the inevitable has permeated my subconscious.

Here comes that damn cavernous room with the spooky walls. There was that wispy white haired crazy old man, pompous, with that look of superiority. He was staring down at me. "Once again you surprise me, American. You made it to the second level. However, have you learned from your experiences? Have you acquired honor, or have you stayed adamant in your American way of life? Now we must get on with your lesson.

Regrettably, I cannot pass onto you the martial arts of the White Ninja – that would take years – a lifetime – and we only had two days and three nights to pass the philosophy of Izumo to you. This knowledge should prepare you, if you are receptive, to become a White Ninja. Not a complete White Ninja, but you may achieve a level of completeness if you reach the tenth level.

Bear in mind that being a White Ninja is a mental state. You must master the tenth level, becoming a full White Ninja, before achieving the status of Master of the White Ninja, becoming the White Dragon. Martial art excellence is secondary, a little insurance to ensure supremacy over the Black Ninja, and others like them. I do not think you will need this!

I do not believe you will reach the tenth level. Only a physically toned body can replace me. You must be aware of the fact - the outcome of all martial art engagements, are decided in the first few seconds. Those short seconds will determine if you live - or die.

Look at you, puny, soft - no muscle tone, 134 pounds, glasses - Aaarg - I must be wasting my time. To continue ... to achieve the third level you must know right from wrong. At first, this may sound simple. Consider this: everything has a right to time and space, to fulfill its natural purpose. All creatures, all water, rocks, stars, everything, even the Americans who destroy everything around them.

Do not judge. You must learn to evaluate. To learn mental dexterity, to understand all things, and become attuned to forces and elements of the world. You must recognize the purpose of the inanimate. Only when this is accomplished can you start to begin on the journey. To learn how a White Ninja thinks, you must learn who, and what you are. You must find and know yourself.

One more thing I must stress upon you, my great-granddaughter Minkoto wishes for your return, after you achieve the tenth level. She sees something in you that I cannot. I must tell you, I command you, YOU CANNOT. YOU MAY NOT ever return. Hah! I should not worry. You will never reach the exalted position that comes after the tenth level.

I see by what you have done to generate this visit that you have learned not to kill or maim unnecessarily in the blind fury of rage, and not use your powers needlessly. Only to use what is necessary to protect others and yourself. In each visit, I will remind you the importance of no one knowing the powers you may possess. If anyone recognizes what you are - who you are, you will become ineffective. If anyone recognizes you before you reach the tenth level, or, if you fail in attempting a level, you will lose all your powers and you will remember nothing, nothing at all. You will not remember the names Izumo, White Ninja, White Dragon, myself, the visits, nothing.

Once identified, even after the tenth level, your adversaries will be on you like maggots on rotten flesh. Now rest, as the remainder of this visit will be subliminal as are all Izumo's visits. You will know the secrets passed in his visits, only as the needs arise. The times of enlightenment will be at Izumo's discretion. Now sleep – sleep– sleep – slee ..."

Waking up was tough. The sun was up. My strength drained. Damn, just like before. I was lying in a pool of sweat. My mouth dry. Knowing I was too beat to travel today, I rolled out of bed, dressed and went to the kitchen, where mom had breakfast waiting. Good old mom, what would I do without her?

Grumbling good morning, I shuffled into the bathroom to clean up. I was brushing my teeth when mom came to the door commenting, "You must have had a rough time sleeping, rolling and tossing. You were mumbling words that I could not understand. What language were you speaking in your dreams last night? It sounded oriental. Was it Japanese?"

Looking up after spitting into the sink I said "Oh Mom, I don't remember my dreams, that was just mumble-jumble. I cannot speak anything from over there. Only a few slang words. I wasn't there long enough to learn anything." After finishing in the bathroom, I went to the kitchen table and told mom I would be leaving the next morning, on my way to the Philippines. I began the rest of the day loafing around town.

While at the park, sitting up against a huge oak tree, the thought came to me that everyone in town seemed different. Not all the people in town could change. After some deep dwelling on the thought, it came to me – they did not change, I changed. My perspectives have broadened from travel, experienced new cultures, heard other viewpoints and rationales, and seen new places. Yes, and that old man spewing outlandish, unbelievable dragon drivel, does not invade their dreams and disrupt their sleep either. I knew that feeling sorry for myself would not help me, or my mental state.

I went over every word remembered from my dream, or visit, or whatever. Coming to the old men's reference to Minkoto stopped me dead in my tracks. Her name brought back all the visual images and smells tucked away in my mind. I smiled, daydreamed, and fantasized.

My thoughts went back to the beginning of that first night, flashing forward, stopping when I studied her by the light of the fireplace. How poised she was. How delicate. Her expressions when she became demanding of the old man. How she made me feel inside. How she made my gut feel like it had not tasted solid food in a week. How she made my knees weak. How could such a beautiful, and sensual woman, come from his bloodline?

I sat, relaxed, under that massive oak tree, thinking of her. The old man's warning not to return materialized in my thoughts. That warning was a challenge. Who in the hell does he think he is telling me what I can and cannot do. We will see what opportunities lay ahead. We'll just see.

Chapter
SIX

After boarding a military, space available flight at Scott Air Force Base (AFB) Illinois, and flying all day, we arrived at Travis AFB, California. It was early. There was a lot of time to kill before reporting to Treasure Island Naval Base for transport overseas. Giving my buddy Mitchell a call, I told him my status, and prospects for liberty.

That first evening was spent settling in, getting blankets, a bunk, and getting the lay of the land; where the chow hall was, what transportation was available and to where, how they selected working parties - important, need to know information like that. The second item on my agenda was calling Mitchell again, to let him know he could expect to see my smiling face the next afternoon at Naval Air Station, Alameda. He had better get the half day off.

That night I experienced the best night's sleep in weeks. No dreams, no sweats, just total blankness and eight hours of solid rest. The next day found me on a navy bus to Alameda. Everything looked like it did before going on leave.

Mitchell had changed into his civvies (civilian clothes) and looked ready for liberty as I yelled out "Sure hope that old 49 Ford still runs."

"Like hell," he replied. "That sweet running chunk of heaven will still be cruising when you're long gone." Passing through the main gate, I could tell from his words and tone of voice that he knew it would be a long time before we chummed together again. I had a sense of foreboding, a heavy feeling of something valuable slipping away and we would never see each other again, a friendship turning into memories with no future.

On the road, driving along, we enjoyed ourselves, listening to the current hit tune *Red Sails in the Sunset*, trying to decide what to do. Hitting the bars was out of the question, me being underaged. Mitchell was now legal, but this sailor was not going to sit in a car waiting for a drink, while he was inside enjoying himself. We decided to go to Richmond, to see what trouble we could get into. We had dated a couple of girls that lived there, but they were nowhere around. It was a Wednesday night and nothing was going on. Mitchell bought a six-pack of beer and we headed for a drive-in movie that was showing *Sayonara* with Marlon Brando and Red Buttons.

Since Mitchell bought the beer, it fell on me to get the popcorn and snacks. It was best to wait until the movie started, then the refreshment stand would be empty. Mitchell felt he had to pick a spot way out in the boonies, because of my age and the beer, and it was a long walk to the stand.

If I took a straight path to get the popcorn I would not hear the movie, as the speakers would be inside the cars, so I was following the circular line of empty car slots listening to the speakers on their stands. Nearing the center lane, I noticed a van parked farther out, sitting alone in a large empty area. It was shaking and rolling. Chuckling to myself that there must be a couple of huge people in there getting with it, I turned down the center lane following the smell of fresh popcorn.

Returning from the refreshment stand with two large bags of popcorn in my arms, I turned at the end of the center lane toward Mitchell's car. Involuntarily, I glanced over to the van with a smile. *Must have been a quick one,* I thought. The van seemed to be standing still. It looked lonesome sitting out in the dark all by itself. There was a lull in the soundtrack from the movie, it was quiet, all quiet, until I heard a faint cry, a muted, pleading cry of a girl, or young woman. "Help! No! Let me go. Please, stop." It was coming from the van. There it was again. "Please help, somebody, make them stop," Then another voice growled. "Shut your trap bitch, what did you expect, a church social date."

Shit! Shivers came over my body, and I set down the two bags. I mentally prepared myself for the dreadful, inevitable transformance. The shivers produced large goose bumps, the hair on the back of my head stiffened and stood out, my ears itched, and the vibrating hair tickled my neck. My body experienced waves of unexplainable sensations. Taking off my glasses, I placed them between the two bags so they would not get lost, and an audible low growl came from my throat while running toward the van in a shallow crouch. My energy level shot up above anything I had ever experienced before.

The closer I came to the van, the clearer the voices became.

Circling to the side, I peered through a teardrop window. The interior was bathed in a dim red light. A young girl was held down by two large grease balls, big flabby guys, while a third creep, whose nude frame would make an artist cry, was removing her underpants, pulling them down slowly from her knees. Her jeans and torn bra lay on the back of the driver's seat. He was laughing gutturally as she lay whimpering. Her face expressed exhaustion from a long struggle. The two slobs holding her down were jeering and encouraging the third idiot on with lurid suggestions.

There was no plan in my mind. No thought. No emotion. No caution warnings to temper my actions. My nerves were following electrical impulse commands from a brain other than my own, or from an area of my mind where I had no control. Slamming my fist against the driver's door twice, I pivoted and sprang to the rear of the van. Yanking the doors open, I grabbed the shirt collars of the two animals that were holding down the girl. They were totally off-balanced as I pulled them backward off their knees, smashing their heads on the sturdy step bumper. They did not have time to call out, or make a sound. Two hollow cracks penetrated the night. They slithered to the ground like the snakes they were. The third gutter-rat, who had moved forward to check out the noise at the driver's door that interrupted his pleasure, spun around to face me. He was in a semi-crouch. His naked hairy body was ludicrous to behold. The girl was dazed and still on her back between us. He lunged at me as I was picking up a loose tire tool that was lying near the back door. I was holding the tool point up, when he stumbled over the girl, falling toward me. He reached out to me, but missed by inches. He did reach the pointed tire tool. He made a funny hissing-like sound, laying face down. The hissing turned to a gurgling cough, then silence. His body trembled before turning still. The girl was struggling to get out from under his dead weight. She sat up twisting around to look over her shoulder. She was weaving, trying to get her balance. Holding herself up, she looked at the back of his neck with the twelve inches of bloody steel rod sticking up out of him. Her body shook, and drool ran down from the corner of her open mouth, across the bottom of her cheek. Looking at me with a blank, unseeing dazed stare, she uttered a thin screechy sound that might have carried ten feet. Her eyes rolled up and she slowly collapsed, settling quietly on the van's padded floor.

After quietly closing the back doors, I walked around to the driver's door, opened it, turned on the headlights and emergency flashers, closed the door, and returned to my two bags of popcorn and glasses. The whole episode seemed to be a detachment from reality. It was as if I was watching a movie, seeing myself as an actor following a script, and not experiencing the emotions that would normally be associated with a real event.

Getting back to the car Mitchell reached out from behind the steering wheel. Grabbing the bags of popcorn, he yelled, "Where in the hell have you been. Hell, the popcorn is cold."

"I stopped to watch the people crowded around a van back there." Leaving when the movie was over, we noticed a police car, an ambulance, and a small crowd of people, around the van setting way back by itself, but no longer in the dark. Its headlights were on, and emergency flashers still blinking on and off, out of sequence with all the other flashing lights in attendance. It reminded me of a musical light show, and might have been enjoyable, if not for the knowledge of what the pulsating lights were in score for. I was trying to escape the thought of what would invade my sleep tonight.

Mitchell drove me back to the transient barracks at Treasure Island. Our vocal attempts were muted by my inability to fully process was he was saying. He would try to engage me in conversation, while I replied in one or two syllable responses.

Arriving back at the barracks on the base, I showered and flopped exhausted in my rack. Why is this always happening to me? Why can't I control this? Does my presence generate this violence? This stuff does not happen to Mitchell or other people I know. Am I a Jonah?

I knew that denial, not accepting the visits from the old man was not in my best interest, but I also knew acceptance would make my sanity ever more questionable. Questions swirled in my mind, searched out answers, anything that might sound plausible, as I slowly drifted into that foreboding semi-conscious pre-dream state, portal to Izumo's visits. "Again you surprise me" the voice came from the bowels of that misty rocky cavern that was now so familiar to my dream life.

The old man's image was pushing away the whitish, foggy, translucent curtain of swirling mist, coming ever closer. How does he do that? He's not walking. His feet do not touch the floor. The closing image stopped, as always, when it was twice life-size. Is that an ego, or what? His eyes stared through me, as if my presence was not important enough to acknowledge, and he spoke in a laughing, humiliating tone. "There may be hope for you yet, American. Your feeble presence made me forget that anyone, and everyone, no matter how insignificant, has purpose, can contribute positively to a socially orientated world. You must be a bad influence to make me forget. My last visit with you was not that long ago. You must be eager to ascend your ladder of progress, to achieve the fulfillment of the tenth level. I do not have anything of personal consequence to tell you during this visit. Everything will pass into your sub-conscious, into that depository you call a brain. Hah. HO-HO."

He takes great pleasure, flaunting his belief that Americans were like barbarians, while his ancestry was civilized, with a history of culture, the enjoyment of finer things, the ability to understand all the mysteries of the world, and the capability to cull out the dregs of the human race. I think he was deluding himself. That whole country over there, including the old man, must surely be brainwashed.

He continued. "Since we do not have time for martial arts training, you must start developing your own training. Once again, you must visualize Izumo's actions. Go over the movement and rhythms of your body. Feel how your force interacts with, and changes the force of everything around you. Everything must be in balance: Yin and Yang; Conscious and sub-conscious; Physique and diet; Exercise and rest; everything. Study carefully. One day your life and my legacy will depend on your attention to detail and mental acuity. You must prepare yourself. There is so much to learn, and not enough time to learn it. You will find that the more you learn, the more you realize you do not know. You must pay attention. You must absorb everything; there is no time to waste. Now sleep, sleep, sleep, Izumo comes."

Consciousness was coming over me; someone was shaking me, "Are you all right man? You're talking in your sleep. You scared the hell out of me"

"Yeh, Yeh, I'm O.K." I muttered over a thick tongue, and through a dry mouth.

The voice continued "Man are you ever sweaty, are you sure you're not sick with the flu or something?"

"Noo ..." I said, "I'm O.K."

"Well, go back to sleep. Get your rest so you will feel better in the morning," said the hazy far off voice, as I returned to a deep sleep.

There she was - Minkoto. What is she doing my dream? "Web-San. Quiet! My great-grandfather does not know I am here. I must talk to you. You must return to Iwakuni. Great-grandfather needs you. Only you can save him from the Black Heart Ninja. He is an old man with weakened powers, and his pride prevents him from calling you back for help. You are the only one who can save him ... you are the only one". Her image started to fade back into the mist. Even in my dreamland state, I could hear myself shouting "Wait - Minkoto. Wait." However, she was gone.

It was morning. I was exhausted, as expected. Opening my eyes, I could see a burly, hairy, giant of a guy swing his feet out of the bunk next to mine. "How are you this morning? You scared the shit out of me last night. Were you sick, or having a nightmare?"

Struggling to sit up, I mouthed out the words. "You wouldn't believe me if I told you." A visual take of the stranger, and his demeanor, told me this guy was not going to give up or be quiet.

"My name is Lee. Lee Lanzer, but everyone calls me Tiny. Are you sure, you are O.K.? You look a little weak and wobbly to me?"

"Well I feel fine Lee. My name is Web Drache, and everyone calls me Web."

Tiny laughed, "You're funny. Come on, get up, I'm hungry. You want to come along."

"Yah, sure." I grunted, getting up, looking around trying to re-orientate myself to this new environment.

Later in the day, early afternoon, I was on a charter transport plane, over the pacific, heading for Hawaii, Midway Island, and the Philippine Islands. I sat in the seat, my head back, feigning sleep, while trying to go over Minkoto's visit last night, trying to figure out how I could possibly return to Iwakuni. It was hopeless trying to concentrate; Tiny was apparently going to talk the entire trip. It was when we were first boarding the plane he told me he is being transferred to the same aircraft squadron I was going to. VU-5A, at NAS Cubi Point.

We landed at Clark AFB, Angeles City, Philippines, after an agonizing long trip trying to block out Tiny's voice. It was hot, sticky and smelly.

Ordered to stay in the terminal, Tiny and I waited impatiently. A scheduled circuit flight would take us to our squadron at the Naval Air Station, Cubi Pt., by Olongapo City.

That afternoon we landed at the Cubi Point terminal. Luckily, the hangar housing VU-5A was just across the ramp. Looking up, Tiny and I took in the mountain jungle crowding the airstrip on one side, and the bay on the other sides. I could hear monkeys screaming, birds screeching, and those damned starving skeeters and bugs, after my exposed skin like I was their ten-course meal. Picking up our duffel bags, we started to hoof it across the ramp, to the squadron duty office on the second floor of the hangar.

Looking out the office window, I saw some scroungy looking aircraft. "What are those?" I asked the sailor on duty. He was only wearing a tee shirt, and standard white pants. I had no idea what his rate and rating (military rank and specialty) were. He looked up at me as if I was the dumbest person on the face of the earth. "Their B-26's, made by Douglas, but since the navy doesn't have B-26's, we call them Jig-Dogs, JD1's."

What in the world am I in for, I thought, and looking over I saw Tiny looking around with that big goofy smile of his. It was dark by the time we finished checking into this outfit, and I was beat. The barracks were on top of a jungle mountain, and a wild drive up the mountainside took us to the top. Arriving we were assigned to a bunk and issued sheets, a pillow, and of all the dumb things to have in the tropics, two wool blankets. There are no glass panes in the windows due to the typhoons - no glass breakage. I just knew this pungent place was at the bottom of the list of places, a normal person would want to be.

Chapter
SEVEN

Morning! I did not see Tiny, everything was looking better. Several of the squadron personnel introduced themselves to me, and gave me their best advice on what to do (most of which revolved around the local women), where to go (most of which revolved around the local women), and how to get there (most of which revolved around the local women).

There were only forty-five men in the unit, including the C.O. - a Commander, and three butter bar Ensigns. We had four aircraft, a pilot for each aircraft. My assigned job was a desk job, but I would be doing everything. I was the only enlisted man in the Maintenance/Operations/Technical Library/Aircraft & Pilot Logs office.

I did not do the work from the Administration/Personnel Office, or the Supply Office, but I would look up all the oddball parts numbers the supply office could not find, or match up. All other office work came to me. I'm a lousy Airman, replacing a 3rd Class and a 1st Class Petty Officer. What the hell was going on? The men I was replacing gave me a five-day training period, and then were gone. I was on my own. After a month, I realized no one really knew if most of my work was right or wrong. Over a period of several months, I picked up the accuracy and speed to prevent major problems. During this period, Tiny's nickname became Baby Huey. He was not the brightest person but very good natured, and a good asset to the squadron. After six more months, eight other men from my previous squadron joined me in this *McHale's Navy* outfit.

Nine months after coming to the Philippines, strange things started to happen. Relations became strained between the United States and the Philippines. Organized crime was becoming entrenched in Olongapo, attacking the U.S. military. We received warnings against traveling alone due to the rapidly increasing number of crimes and violence. The Philippine politicians were fighting to take possession of the military bases, and the military reservations.

Philippine–American relations were rapidly deteriorating. The area surrounding NAS Cubi Point and Naval Station Subic Bay was a military reservation, under the control of the U. S. Military. The word was out that this area, including the city of Olongapo, would return to Philippines control.

I took refuge from the political and criminal craziness that was running rampant in Olongapo, by spending my time off, at the main pygmy village, only venturing into town when necessary. I was a loner, my nights spent in the jungle, at the edge of town, or in the deepest and darkest shadows of the streets. I was apprehensive of the possible consequences to confrontation.

I visited the head chief of the seven Zambales nigreto pygmy tribes, a wise black man, physically standing four feet tall, who in my eyes stood eight feet tall. He had yellow gnarled teeth, lean, muscular, black kinky hair, and a face with deeply etched lines, grotesque by Western standards.

The perceptive chief, aware of my powers, and more knowledgeable of their application than I, took me under his wing and tutored me in the ways of the jungle, and of the people that lived there. He was a spiritual man of nature, who learned the ancient laws of right and wrong from old legends, folklore passed down by the shamans, the storytellers of the jungle tribes, and passed some of his knowledge to me. I was a welcomed member of the jungle dwellers and given the name *Protector of the Night*

No wind stirred. The tribe's people were suffering from the humid stifling heat. The chief and I sweat, sat in his nipa hut, and discussed religious ministers, priests, shamans, medicine men, and the like, when I made the point that showmanship and the art of entertaining was necessary to be successful in these vocations. He disagreed. He felt those chosen people are destined for their life-roles at birth; some by birthright, others ordained by a higher authority. I proposed that I could delude his people into thinking I was a chosen one, and had magical powers.

Standing in front of the chief's residence, I saw a breeze move the tree tops off in the distance. Without thinking of the consequences, I raised my arms and in a slow, deliberate, and loud voice shouted. "Wind come! Wind come!" And the wind came. The nigretos looked at me with awe, but did not say anything.

The old chief gave me a knowing smile and shook his

head. Laughing he said. "Play like that may return to you in many ways."

When the distant treetops stopped swaying in the breeze, I raised my arms, and shouted. "Wind stop! Wind stop!" The tribe's people again looked at me in awe, talking among themselves, and gesturing toward me.

That night, the chief's elevated nipa hut was comfortable with a cool breeze blowing across pallets placed on the floor by the open paneless windows. I woke late in the morning. While eating our breakfast of jungle fruit, a group of tribesmen hunters came and asked me to stop the wind. They were distressed; the wind was blowing harder, making it hard to hunt monkey and wild cock in the swaying tree branches.

The chief with a big grin on his nodding weathered face motioned me off saying, "Go! Go, stop the wind." Standing in the tree clearing of blowing dust, feeling like a real idiot, I held my arms up high, waiting for the distant treetops to stop moving and bending, while the tribesmen prance around me, shouting for me to stop the wind. During a lull in the wind's intensity, their stomping feet intensified the cloud of dust that choked my breath and dulled my sense of smell. A re-directed wind cleansed the air of dust, and carried a new scent that rejuvenated my nostril's power to taste the air, the smell of a nearby pigsty. The acrid airborne ammonia, mixed with other heavy odors, burned my nasal linings, and pulled tears from my eyes. My performance was over. My hands dropped from their gestural embracement of the sky to tend my watering eyes. Humiliated, I did not stop the wind.

I was trying my best to save face with the chief's people, when off in the distance, rifle shots cracked. The tribe went into a panic shouting, "The evil ones are here." "The slavers are going to capture us." "The cannibals are to going eat us."

In an instant, the village clearing emptied as they melted into the jungle. The chief and I jumped to the ground and entered the jungle's edge, making our way toward the sound of the gunshots. Two hundred yards into the jungle, the chief and I observed Huks (terrorists) rounding up the men who had been building a fish trap. The heavily armed Huks, lined the men in single file, and tied them together by their necks with ropes. The chief retreated to his village, to assemble a war party while I followed the Huks, leaving a trail of bent branches, for them to follow.

I followed the captives, parallel to their trail, and heard sounds of whipping followed by anguished cries. Crawling in closer, I saw a guard beat an injured fallen captive, near the middle of the file. He was being beat on the back with a slivered bamboo whip.

As the slivered, unbound end of the whip struck the fallen man's back, the sharp edges sliced into his flesh. His screams were unbearable for me to hear. Silently, I approached the guard, and reached him, as the whip was poised for another painful blow.

The whip pulled from his hand; he turned to face me with a look of disbelief on his face as the whip slashed. The flesh of his throat parted, his life's blood flushed from his body. His gushing blood spurted to the ground, flowed down his neck and across his chest, as the bound captive nigretos pulled him down and dispatched him with his own knife.

I cut the ropes from the fallen, flogged man's neck. The forward group was told to continue along the trail as if nothing happened, while the rest of the men and I took care of the rear guard. The pygmies disappeared into the jungle as they were released, making their way back to the rear guard.

There were four rear guards; all bunched together, talking and laughing amongst themselves. The escaped pygmies fashioned deadly pointed weapons, but before I could tell them to take prisoners, they silently killed the guards. Their mutilated bodies looked like a grandmother's pincushion. A pygmy vengeance was something terrible to see.

Regrouping the small men, I told them. "We need live prisoners to interrogate. We must find out who is behind this genocidal warring, and we must punish their leader." By this time, the chief and his assembled group returned with their weapons in hand. The chief was worried about my safety, and possible identity compromise. He told me to return to the village. They would engage their enemy.

It did not take them long to finish the skirmish, but no prisoners returned with them. The chief said he could not restrain his men once the engagement began. The heads of the slain Huks were impaled on poles held high as symbols of their victory.

After the tribal celebrations, the chief said to me, "I have informed the authorities of the Huk activities, and how they enslave my people, but the politicians will not spend the money to help us. They do not see us as people, but something to hide from the world. In their eyes, we do not have a good world image. And our friends, the Americans, cannot help unless our cowardly politicians ask for their assistance. Help not properly asked for, would violate the treaty between them. If we had to live on the promises of the government, we would all be dead. We must feed our young, fight our own battles, and continue our own history. We have the weapons, taken from our enemies killed in battle, hidden away. We will train our warriors in the use of these weapons, and will bring the respect and honor of our world back to my people, when the time is right. We will force the government to acknowledge our heritage and rights. The people of the jungle are warriors, people of trust and honor. We are the allies of the Americans, not those city dwellers who call themselves Filipinos. We will rid ourselves of those animals that have such a low regard for life. Many men from all the tribes come to join us, to train, to bring together all our knowledge. We will not be taken advantage of. No, not again, never again to be used like animals of burden."

The sun was setting; the nigretos were celebrating their victory with food and wild tales of their unwritten history. All night long, I had noticed a line of young women filing past where I sat, all with the look that makes you feel warm all over more than anywhere else.

Leaning over to the chief, I asked him, "Why are those women looking at me like that? Who are they, and why do they walk past in a line?" With a laugh that did not sound human, he said that it would honor him and his people, if I would infuse my bloodline with that of the tribe.

Taken aback, I related to him of my true love, Minkoto,

and my need to return to her. "This" I said, "would not be an honorable thing for me to do. Any children born would not come from a love between two people. They would not know their father."

"I will be their father, and the whole tribe loves you. How can you say there is no love? Take a close look at their faces. Feel the touch of their souls on you like the kiss of the wind." Said the chief. "Yes, I understand your feelings for someone from long ago, and so far away." Hesitating, while looking into my eyes, said. "You do not look well. I will summon two young women, not yet with a man, to administer to your needs during this night." The cagey chief selected two beautiful young, lighter skinned women that were like amazons in comparison to the rest of his people. He knew they would be a great temptation to me. Statuesque and very attractive, they were the result of American G.I.'s that lived with the tribe during W.W.II.

During the night, Izumo visited me. The foreign mumbling frightened the two women, but they stay and bath me with cloth rinsed in fresh cool water, to help reduce my dream sweating. The nigretos have a high regard for dreams and their influence on life. To them, dreams are a portal to the gods, a way for them to acquire direct counseling in a time of need. The two women thought of me as one who has access to god's ear, and to bear a child from me would bring them honor and respect from the tribal people. Trying their best to wake me, to arouse me with their charms; they failed. For in sleep, my mind, heart, and soul lingered elsewhere.

In the morning, Sunday, the chief, his personal jungle

medicine man and the tallest, the most becoming of the two women that stayed with me the previous night, took me to their secret place of worship. It was the source of their village water. It fell dancing in a beautiful, misty waterfall, from a spring through a hole in the side of a jungle cliff, into a pool of effervescent bubbles and swirls.

The chief told me to refresh myself in its water. Stripping to my shorts, I started to dive in when the chief stopped me with an outstretched arm. He said sternly, "We drink this water; we do not wash our bodies in it. We bathe there." Pointing to rocky depressions to the side of the stream, where the pool at the base of the falls overflows, making its way to a smaller stream that went around the village, and where the women washed clothes.

The chief noticed black and red blisters covering my legs. He told me, "That is not good. My physician will cleanse your legs of that poison." The medicine man left us to go into the jungle and after ten or fifteen minutes, returned from his herbal forage. He ground his plants and roots, and washed my legs with the first concoction. He shook his bag of chicken bones, singing incantations. After a short period of silence, I thought he was done, and then he rubbed a second cold slimy muck on my legs. The contact of the cold poultice startled me, caused me to jerk my legs away from him. His laugh was very similar to the chief's, loud, gravelly, and honest. I have to admit, it felt good after it covered my legs.

The chief told me that this place was the source of their life. A holy place. "This is where we know our god lives. He is the giver of life." He asked me if I have a god. I spent the better part of the day, explaining Christianity to him, as I knew it. As we finished examining our religious beliefs, he told me that we have identical beliefs, with the same god having different names. I agreed. Later that night I went back to the base and hit the sack.

Monday morning I woke early, feeling fine. The leg blisters were completely gone. Stopping at the dispensary (sickbay), I told the medics that they were trying to cure my legs for months, and it took an uneducated witch doctor to do it. I do not think they believe me.

My new role in life was becoming increasingly more comfortable. The natives from the surrounding tribes, referred to me as the "Protector of The Night," my tribal given name. My visits from Izumo have progressed from a state of apprehension to eager anticipation. My need for sleep diminished. The base did not conduct bunk checks, though we do not have overnight liberty. Cinderella liberty was not enforced. This gave me the opportunity to function in the protection of darkness, defusing confrontations, protecting fleet sailors who do not know the area, customs, dangerous places, and dangerous people. A reward was on my head by the criminal element. I understood it was dead or alive. They could not pinpoint me. I had learned my lessons well.

Particularly challenging were the local martial arts groups that search for me every night. Their attempts were rather transparent. Many times, other sailors or marines would face down my minor adversaries, and I got credit for their actions. I could not ask for a better cover than the confusion surrounding my description and identity. Sitting back, listening to stories of my real and fantasized feats, I quietly kept a mental tally of mine and other's efforts.

I became adept at playing the role of a pencil pusher, a skinny, bespectacled, average person, not drawing attention to myself. I enjoyed the tales people told of encounters with, and the heroism of the *Protector of the Night.* Many talk of personally knowing this defender of the innocent, who travels in the darkness of the night, while others will swear they hear him in the jungle, always searching out evil and wrongdoing. I think that the great protector was often confused with the monkeys and other wild creatures of the night.

Chapter
EIGHT

I needed a mental retreat and went on an R & R (Rest and Relaxation) trip to Baguio, an ancient city high on a mountain peak, where the legendary gold and silver mines are. I visited a village of Igorots. They are proud, tall, handsome, slender and very agile. They are also headhunters. The government had been vigorously curtailing their head hunting activities, coercing cooperation with threats and rewards. Americans did not need to fear them, as they only harvested heads from the Filipino.

Typically, a young Igorot male, will take a Christian's head and present it to the father of the woman he wants to live with, as a sign of his love and sincerity. The more important the person was before losing his head, the higher the girl's father regards the gift. If it was a good head, properly taken and prepared, and from a person with a status high enough to match the value put on the daughter by her father, the suitor could assume parental blessing.

Standing off to the side of their village, admiring the wooden life size statues the Igorots artists created, a weathered faced old tribesman, who noticed my change of attention to a fog bank descending over the area, told me that the bank was a cloud, a gift from one of their gods to refresh them. That many times they could look out from their village, down over the cloud tops, and see their god riding the cloud. Their god had not shown himself for some time. They felt the tribe must have angered him, and he left them to fend for themselves, without his protection.

The cloudbank rolled in, and what a refreshing relief from the heat it was. The moisture condensed on my exposed skin running in little rivulets down my neck, sides and arms. Remarking how wonderful it must be living here, smiling, I leaned over to ruffle the hair of a small child, who was roughing out a future work of art. She looked up at me and began crying. I picked her up and tried to console her with gentle hugs and soft words of comfort.

She could not understand me, nor I her. The elderly Igorot looked at me intensely from head to toe. "Are you the one who walks the jungle at night?"

I looked into the elderly man's sorrowful eyes. "Why do you ask?"

The old man told me. "The little girl's father, and others, are captives and forced to work in a gold mine that was not very productive. The Moro's from down south, came north in large war parties, and captured the women and children of the village while the men were away hunting. The Moro's hold their wives and most of their children hostage on the east side of Basilan Island, the southernmost island of the Philippines, to force the men to do their bidding. They work in twelve hours shifts down deep in the ground. They told us they would sell our women and children to the slave mongers, or trade them to the savage cannibals who do their bidding, if we do not obey them. Igorots are warrior hunters, not miners. We cannot work and live underground.

We cannot strike out against the Moro's because they are too far south, and we have no way to get there. We need help. No one in the government will listen to our cries for help. We need the Protector of the Night. He would help us if he knew of our need."

A look across the village, showed the children were not smiling or laughing, and the men walked with heads downcast. Turning to the old man, I saw the water running down his face was not cloud moisture, but tears. I spoke softly, "Yes, surely he can help. Can your people wait a few more days while something can be arranged?"

"Yes," He said.

"Good. If you do not hear from me in three day's time, take at least fifty of your best warriors with their weapons, to the village Aringay that sits by the edge of the sea directly to your West. Someone will meet you at sunrise on the fourth day, a Saturday. You will recognize them as my agents when they give you my name *Drache*"

I left Baguio within two hours, back to Cubi Point Naval Air Station, and reserved the Cubi Queen, a cabin cruiser that rents out for R & R and fishing expeditions. I offered to throw a hunting and beer party for *Fearless Mike*, My Navy Seabee friend, and his crew. "The party will be on the east side of Basilan Island. All you need is your group of about thirty men, their combat gear and transportation to Aringay village."

Mike looked up at me, and his eyes rolled up in their sockets. "You gotta be shittin me. You got someptin goin on, don't you?" His smiling mug told me he was highly interested.

"Yep" I said, "And your men will have more fun in two days, than they would get in a month in Hong Kong."

With a crackling laugh, "You're on." he replied.

I talked the operations officer into flying me down over Basilan Island, with the excuse that I wanted to see where my new girl friend's family lived. A favor in return for me logging in all that instrument time he needed, but did not have. He said he needed the extra flight hours anyway. That afternoon we were over that southern island, he was piloting his Jig Dog (JD-1), while I checked over the charts.

Ensign Beset looked over to me and asked. "Where does your girl come from?"

"What girl" I realized I made a potentially major mistake, but I did not think he heard me over the noise of the engine and air turbulating over the cockpit canopy. "Oh ya, my girl – down somewhere in a village that's not on the map. She said it was on the East side of the island, on the beach." I said, feeling guilty about my lie.

"Drache, Are you nuts? Those are Moro villages. Don't you know about them?"

"Yep, but she's different" again swallowing the lie down my dry throat. "There they are, this is it, fly low over it." We spent a long twenty minutes flying over the village, while I drew a map, showing the huts, the war canoes – large dugout canoes with outriggers, jungle trails, and a river that flowed to the sea, isolating the village at the end of a peninsula. While exposing a roll of film of the entire area, I shouted to the pilot, "Boy this is great, this will really impress Bessy." We turned back, and returned to base, mission accomplished.

After we landed, I took the film to another friend, *Chinook* an eskimoan from the Aleutian Islands. He worked in the Air Intelligence section of Commander Fleet Air Philippines Headquarters (COMFAIRPHIL). He volunteered to go along, when told of the mission.

"My family tells stories, of how the Russian sailors would make sport of shooting our people in the water as they hunted the Arctic sea in their frail craft. They enjoyed watching the hunters slip under the surface of the frigid, deadly water. Yes, I will be more than happy to go along. I hate abusers and killers of innocent people." After telling Chinook my plan, we agreed to meet on the Cubi Queen, Saturday morning, four hours before sunrise.

That evening I called on Mike and gave him the full story. Mike smiled and said, "I hate those amok animals. Last year we were down there to repair some inland roads for the Philippine Government, as a good gesture, and those bastards went *amok* - crazy, killing two of my men. Do you believe we could not do anything about it? The powerhouse families control the court system, and leans toward the good old boy process. Going nuts, what they call *amok*, is a legitimate defense in those southern islands. My men would love a payback; I do not have to ask them. I gave Mike a copy of the photographs and the map. We made our plans.

Friday morning, Chinook and I went to the armory to check out weapons. "We're going after big game." Said Chinook.

The Ordnance man on duty looked at us "You can take whatever you want, but you have to bring back the brass. I have to go to the back and start locking up for the weekend, so list what you are taking and sign for them before leaving. And remember, I know everything that's here. Sign for everything."

Walking over to the small-arms/personal weapons cage, we took a visual inventory of what was available. We did not have a prepared shopping list, but our eyes lit up when we saw the grenades. Giving each other an arched eyebrow glance, we filled an ammunition pack with grenades, and clips for Chinook's rifle.

I picked up an issue .38 special in a shoulder holster, with two boxes of ammo. Leaving, Chinook asked me "Is that all you're taking? You can't do much with that."

Putting the pistol into the pack with the grenades, I told him, "I'll use one of my own personal weapons."

Early the next morning Chinook and I pushed off in the Cubi Queen. We had her rented for a week. It took four hours to meet up with Mike and his crew. We loaded the Igorots onto a high-speed search and rescue craft, at the Aringay village. Mike told me, "I borrowed the boat from a friend at the repair facility in Subic Bay." His sheepish grin led me to disbelieve him, but I was not above taking whatever was available at a time like this. I follow my own priorities.

Mike, Chinook, and I went over our plans again, to ensure proper synchronization. I swore them to secrecy. Other than the three of us, no one was to know all the overall details of this operation. As far as the men knew, this was a legitimately approved military action. One that never happened, should someone inquire. On paper, we were all on an extended fishing trip, with our guides navigating our craft.

As soon as the boats were loaded, we started our rescue mission. Mike's men and the Igorots were eager for retribution.

The second morning, before dawn, we were lying low, just off the beach by the Moro's village. Mike and his men dropped off the Igorots at the mouth of the river, and silently poled up stream, to stop any escape off the peninsula. We planned to have a hundred percent success in this operation. Chinook had left earlier to check out the village defenses. He returned distressed, tears running down his face. He told me that a small group of cannibals were at the village. They had roasted one of the young hostage girls, and some of the remains were still on the spit over the fire. The cannibals were drunk, passed out; no guards posted, but Moro's religion prohibited the use of alcoholic drink, and they were early risers. "We must be cautious. They are stirring," warned Chinook.

Chinook saw the .38 cal. Special strapped on my left shoulder, and looked at the grenades clipped to a belt over my right shoulder. His gaze dropping to my white rope belt, sash and machete. "What the hell is that? You can't be serious?"

"Don't worry about it." I replied, acting like my mind was concentrating on the map of the village. "Let's go." We made our way over the side to the boat's emergency rubber raft. Silently, we paddled our way to the beach and landed with less than a minute to spare.

Our diversion, at the far backside of the village started with shots fired intermingled with hollow thumps followed by exploding mortar shells. From the river to the side of the village came Igorot war-shrieks, sounds that could curdle blood. The village came alive with stumbling half-a-wake warriors. The Moros were disorientated, disorganized, and headed toward Mike's men, the source of the mortars. The Igorots saturated the Moro's flank with fusillades of poisoned arrows, forcing them from a forward, to a left oblique advance, toward a cliff jutting up and over a rocky beach. Mike and I separated as we headed toward the compound and buildings, where the hostages were confined. I looked through a crack between bamboo poles in the back fence, and saw the red coals under the remains on the spit. Upwind from the fire, I gagged, trying not to vomit from the pungent, sweet smell of burning human flesh. Two guards at the open entrance of the compound fell from Mike's deadeye shooting. The cannibals were stirring, getting up from their tight sleeping circle.

It took five grenades, thrown into their midst, to flatten them before they could spread and find cover. Mike was receiving fire from the building. He ducked for cover. The compound wall was made of bamboo tied with hemp vines. I cut the bindings and shifted the poles to the side, then squeezed through. I drew my machete before moving toward the back of the building. The women and their babies were in one bay and the children and childless young women in another.

The hostages cried and begged for released. A Moro aimed

his automatic weapon out the window looking for Mike, shooting random rounds. I picked up a rock and threw it through the opening into the middle of the first bay, and ducked. The startled women and children, screamed. I counted to five, and then peered in. The guard had turned to see what caused the ruckus and then turned his attention back to the window.

The women and children continued to scream as I jumped through the opening. Swiftly crossing the bay, I held the machete at ready, firelight reflected sparkles from its razor edge. The guard sensed my presence and pulled in his weapon, turned his head toward me as my machete passed through his neck. A light ringing sound filled the air. His body went limp, slumping to the floor with two soft thuds. His head slowly rocked back and forth with an ever-diminishing roll. The open eyes stared up into the darkness above, fixed in their sockets. I could not locate any other guards, and began to cut the captives free of their bindings. The first two women released, quickly took the offered bayonet and sheath knife from the dead guard, to assist me in freeing the others

After all the prisoners were free of their restraints, and without speaking to each other, they ran out into the compound. Carrying lengths of rope, the bindings removed from themselves, they attack the dazed and wounded cannibals. Quietly, void of expressed emotion, they tied their captors. One by one, stretching them out with the ropes tied to their arms and legs, they then slowly dragged them onto and over the red-hot bed of coals. One by one, they met their death in the burning coals. I could not force myself to stop them. I had seen the pile of bones from their earlier feasts. Their painful, begging screams filled the air for hours, penetrating the thick surrounding jungle, a warning, and promise of retribution to the few that escaped.

Mike and his men in their frontal attack, and the Igorots from the flank, forced the remaining Moro's onto the cliff overlooking the surf, to hide in the rocks. Mike's sharpshooters were unable to put them in their sights, but the Igorots, sat in the cover of a run off ditch, and shot volley after volley of arrows up where their trajectory brought them down in a saturating rain of death on the Moros.

Only soft cries and moans came from their rocky shelter. The Igorots, armed only with their long knives, scoured the rocks for living Moro. After a few faint pleas for mercy, and an occasional curse of the damned, only the sound of the surf remained. A mind and soul soothing sound to ease the pain of death's sights and sounds. A mental escape mechanism to refocus the mind, a diversion to avoid the sanity drain that follows violent combat. A device that most mentally whole combat veterans knew.

A quick muster of Mike's men and Igorots revealed no casualties. It took the rest of the morning to give first aid to the few wounded, look after the hostage's needs and load them onto the rescue boats. Some of the Seabees will have to return with Chinook and myself on the Cubi Queen, to leave room for the women and children on the Search and Rescue craft. There were many happy reunions of loved ones, and some sorrowful gatherings, recounting the horrors of lost family members. It took another two days to get the Igorots back to White Sands beach, and for the rest of us, back to Cubi Point.

After returning to Cubi Point, on every alternate Saturday morning, I found a small gift, usually a woodcarving, inside my secret cave's entrance. These carvings, made with special, ceremonial quality, resembled me. I had no idea what part my image played in the Igorot's ceremonies. I only kept a few pieces, placing the rest in a crescent moon shaped opening, on a rocky ledge in the cave.

The late afternoon sun heated up my office like an oven. I had just finished checking an errata sheet for some aircraft technical manual changes when the Commanding Officer came into my office and remarked, "The last administrative inspection team commented that I must be working you too hard Drache. They were amazed how much work comes out of this office, and how good it was. They suggested that a little R & R might be a fitting reward. Oh yes, you will also get a striker (an unskilled trainee) in to train, in case you decide liberty is better somewhere else. So, how would you like two weeks in Japan?"

A vision of Minkoto, and the request to help her great grandfather, flashed in my brain. Without hesitating, I blurted out "I'm packed, when do I go?"

The skipper laughed. "Wait - hold on. We have to get your new man trained to take over your duties. I have to make some arrangements with another squadron in Atsugi, Japan to host you."

Transportation arrangements and orders preparations took a week. I do not think that the skipper knew how much I appreciated these orders. It is free basket leave. How lucky can a person be?

Chapter
NINE

It was a cold, damp, October morning when I arrived at Atsugi. I reported to base personnel, and had my orders modified, allowing me to continue onto Iwakuni. It took two days, but I made it. Eager to find Minkoto, I rushed to complete checking in.

Everything appeared to be the same, and yet different. The buildings in town looked the same, but everything else felt changed. I hailed a cab to take me to the Kentai Bridge. After a short, slow and tortuous ride of anticipation, I arrived, paid the driver, got out and looked around. I crossed the bridge and flagged down another cab. The driver gave me a blank look when I described the wooden structure built into the cliff.

"Castle ruins." I shouted to him. Another American sailor was standing nearby and heard me shouting. He approached and asked if I was looking for the Kentai Castle. "I guess so, I don't know."

The driver shouted back to me "Kentai Castle - Hai (yes).

"I jumped into the cab "Hiacko Hiacko." (Faster - faster). I was in a hurry, and the road was bad with many obstacles. It took forty-five minutes to get there. It was not the right place. The driver saw my disappointment, and kept saying, "Castle, castle." I looked at it shaking my head no. I paid the driver and waved him off.

I looked around the outside of the remains of a large demolished rock castle, resting on a hilltop. Nothing looked familiar. I sat down on a large limestone boulder, bent over with my chin in hand. I had no idea what to do next. *Guess, I'll start looking around* I told myself. Getting up to leave, I spotted the cliff in the far distance. It was farther down the road, and on the other side of the mountain. *What is wrong with me that I did not see it?* My spirits soared, I started down the mountainside road in a jog. The house was getting closer. There were the massive timbers. The wood had that gray patina. My heart raced with anticipation. *It will not be long now.*

Approaching the front door, broken glass panes and trim startled me. The area was unkempt, and the grounds in a state of disrepair. The sliding door was hard to push open, its track dirty and stuck from lack of use. This was the place; everything was the same as that first cold night, on my first visit. *What is wrong?* Walking through the room to the far wall, I pushed on the panels. Nothing happened. Trying to remember how Minkoto triggered the door, I pushed the panels every possible way, but my efforts could not find the right panel. I could not get through to the cavernous room.

Someone yelled to me. I did not understand. I saw a large man standing in the door, holding a long thick staff. He was menacing. I forced myself to relax and speak in calm English – "I'm sorry I do not understand Japanese. Do you speak English?"

He did not change his stance and motioned to me with his staff, to come toward him. With slow deliberate steps, I approached him. I was ready for any sudden moves. His demeanor cautioned me and made me distrustful of him. His assessing eyes betrayed his recognition of my prowess. "Who are you and what do you want?" he demanded of me, in perfect English.

My gut was tightening, I was uneasy. Everything was moving too fast. I did not completely comprehend what was happening and forced my body to relax while my nerves and muscles were winding up. I was anticipating a target to focus the built up charge of energy. "My name is Web, and I am looking for an old man and his granddaughter, who told me that if I ever come to Iwakuni, I should see the Kentai Bridge, and visit with them, because they knew the history of the area. I was given directions to this house and told they lived here."

"No one like that has ever lived in this house. Go. There is no one like you describe." He said. I watched his eyes, his brow twitching, the pupils darting back and forth, his gaze dropped, tightening his grip on the staff, and I knew he lied. He was now watching my eyes. He knew what I knew. He slowly backed out of the doorway, out onto the circular drive. I matched his every move, step for step, until I was just under the roof overhang. In the cold, crisp October sunshine, I could see this was no ordinary Japanese man. I am five feet eight inches, and he was four or more inches taller.

He stopped and his body tension eased. He was relaxed, cradling the staff over his right shoulder. He held a devilish grin across his ugly face. A slight upward flicker of his eyes gave him away. I jumped back as a blur of a figure flew down from the roof, landing twenty inches in front of and facing me.

The figure off the roof had a three-foot club with a round ball on the end, and a wicked looking blade sticking out of the ball. It looked to me like an American Indian war club. My body did not always get the violent shakes anymore, maybe a detectable quiver, but the growl was deeper, projecting out with a concussive force. My deep growl took the jumper by surprise. He swung the club down in an arc toward my head. I stepped back six inches, grab the top of the ball on it's down swing, pulled it towards me, and down where my foot pushed the weapon down to give it an uncontrollable speed, driving the blade into the ground. He was completely off balance, and trying to regain his posture, to strike again. My right fist came up, from pushing down on the ball of the club, hitting him under the bridge of his nose. I heard the cracking bone and felt it break free, penetrating his skull's bone mass, into his brain. He was dead. It took a milli-second for his brain to process his death.

As he slumped to the ground, my right hand grabbed the handle of his club, letting it fly straight to the idiot with the smirk on his face. He was trying to get the staff off his right shoulder when the blade of the tumbling club struck, penetrating through his staff, pinning it to his shoulder like a large nail. He went down, writhing on the ground.

"What kind of dumb shits are you?" I stepped over the dead carcass in front of me and jumped on the tall idiot. His smirk replaced with a grimace of pain. A yank on the club's handgrip produced a cracking sound of the collar and shoulder bone breaking that vibrated up the handle to my hand. I threw the club, and the split staff, off to the side. Hitting his broken shoulder with my closed fist produced a violent shaking from his pain. Grabbing his grubby clothes, I shook him. "Let me ask you again, where is Minkoto?"

"Who are you? What are you?" came from his mouth twisted in pain. My gaze locked onto his dilated eyes. His English was not so perfect now. "You will never find Minkoto; she is spoken for and given." His hand started to move.

I hesitated long enough for him to withdraw a blade from under his waistband. The end of the blade was four inches up away from his body when I shoved it back down through the side of his stomach into his kidney. He knew he was dying. Leaning over I Looked into his eyes and said "Ryu Hokujin kuru (The White Dragon comes), I am The Dragon of the White Ninja."

His eyes opened wide. He was muttering "NO – NO – NOOOOO ..." in disbelief as his eyes turned dull. He was dead.

I looked around with uncertainty. *What the hell was going on?* I got up and walked over to a small stream by the path; washed my hands, splashing some of the cold running water onto my face. I left everything air dry, and walked to the road. I walked on the shoulder of the road for over an hour before a cab with some sailors came by and offered me a lift back to the bridge. Naturally, I accepted. It was late when I got back to the barracks and still had to clean up and unpack. That night my anticipated visit appeared.

The old man floated up to me "Welcome, Web Drache. You

have surpassed all tests. You are now Jonin, High Man of the White Ninja. On your shoulders alone ride the responsibilities from the Dragon Izumo. You are the only one to carry on the traditions of the White Ninja's realm. In your heart and mind is embedded all that is Izumo. The expectations of you are great. The more you achieve, the more humble you must be. When in doubt, listen to your heart and your mind. Do not let emotions trick you. Of all things, you are White Dragon first. Everything else is secondary to the order of what is right. Go and let the Sun God Izumo be at your right side and his Dragon protector at your left. Go! Become whatever you have to be."

Chapter
TEN

I woke early, refreshed, and energetic. I knew Minkoto must be in great danger. I went to the library for the quiet space and analyzed what had happened. *Where can I find Minkoto?* Since I was on unofficial R & R, I was free to follow my own pursuits. Going back to town, I went to the Kentai Bridge. Sitting at an open-air sidewalk restaurant by the bridge, I ordered oolong tea with sake, a drink that Minkoto had introduced me to, and slowly sipped with the image of Minkoto in my thoughts.

I paid my bill and walked down to the middle of the bridge. It was late afternoon and my course of action was still not set. I did not know what to do, or where to go for advice. Standing, leaning against the rail, I saw a graceful slender woman approaching from the North.

It was Minkoto. She did not see me. Her eyes were downcast. She was crying and drying her tears with a handkerchief. Waiting until she was five feet from me, I softly spoke her name "Minkoto."

She froze, looked up with immediate recognition, and in one leap, in my arms. "Web." She cried out. Her crying more pronounced, as she held me tightly. Standing there in each other's arms, we did not speak as we embraced. Taking her arm in mine, we walked back to the open-air restaurant.

I Nodded toward an isolated table and pulled out a chair for Minkoto to sit. "No" she said, "We must not be seen together. My friend's house is near, and safe from prying eyes and ears."

We walked through a maze of back paths, fences, and gates. We came to a large enclosed courtyard with a tori-styled gate. Inside the wall, a heavily beamed house stood with a covered porch surrounding it. The ancient house looked like a once wealthy family owned it. The garden was rock, gravel, small bonsai trees on raised platforms, and short leafless trees. The chill in the air disappeared as the fence shielded us from the wind, allowing the sun to warm us.

Minkoto called out. An elderly couple emerged from the building and happily cried out her name in acknowledgment. We removed our shoes and the old couple ushered us in. After a quiet exchange of greeting, their attention turned to me. Minkoto told me the long depressing story of how her great grandfather's archenemy, the Black Ninja, penetrated house defenses while they slept. "He had no chance, no time to call on the forces of old to bolster his aging skills. Six of the black hearts were on him before he could arm himself, or sound an alert. The Wind of Izumo came after his death, to carry his spirit soul to his ancestor's realm. I was bound and gagged, placed in a heavy bag, and taken to a distant place."

Minkoto paused, as the elderly couple rose and excused themselves. Waiting until they left the room, she continued.

"There, a man, whose family was so evil that the name was forbidden from the tongue and ordered forgotten in the land, was waiting for me. Emperor Mutsuhito, the Meiji, exiled his ancestors to the Ogasawara Gunto Islands in 1868 when they were defeated in their attempt to overthrow the emperor. They have returned with all their evil intentions. Their leader has a forged letter of bethrothment, from my dead father, promising me to him for marriage. The letter is a false contract."

Minkoto stopped to wipe her tears. "This marriage is needed to legitimize his claim to power. I will die before I allow this to happen. With my death would die the recorded bloodline of the Kikkawa family of Yamaguchi-Ken as connected to the ancient Ainu people, the white ones of the north. However, my great-grandfather's life will not be dishonored, and the Kikkawa family will continue to thrive. It will continue with you Web-San. You are Kikkawa. When you were in your dream state and before knowledge passed to you, my great grandfather, after examining your mind and heart, found you an honorable being, a suitable receptacle for Izumo. He mingled Kikkawa blood from his right hand to your left. You are blood Kikkawa. He adopted you with an ancient ceremony, but it was not a recorded ceremony for the black hearts to see. They must not know who, or what you are."

Minkoto continued with tears running down her cheeks, "And when great-grandfather saw me secretly observing you in Iwakuni, he realized then, what was in my heart, what had happened. He found you one evening, put you into the dream state, and cautioned you against coming back, coming back for me, because he knew we could never be - your blood is his blood and his blood is my blood."

The old couple returned with tea and rice cakes. Again, Minkoto paused to wipe her tears. "I will go into hiding where it is safe, where the black hearts cannot find me, until they are no longer a threat. You and I must leave on different paths, until we meet again. We must leave. This must remain a safe haven for us."

I did not have time to ask questions, my heart was pounding, my mind was swirling. In the same instant of time, I had found my love and lost it. We passed through the gate, and walked different paths. I was not alert; my mind was reeling with the information revealed to me.

A tall Japanese man approached me with a flower in his hand and a smile on his face. He looked like he wanted to say something to me, or ask me a question. I was not alert, not at all. Everything went black.

I woke with a start, and my head was pounding. A rough cloth across my face burned my eyes; there were streams of tears running from my irritated eyes and down my cheeks. I heard loud boisterous laughter, jeering, and muffled high pitch screams. The volume of noise was overwhelming. The sounds were echoing, as if I was in a large metal tank.

Trying to collect my senses, I mentally checked my condition, my bindings. I was not physically hurt. I was helpless, hands tied behind my back to my feet, bundled on the floor by a narrow gutter next to a wall. The air smelled of oily smoke, dampness, terrible food odor, and sour body perspiration. I could not loosen the rope from my hands and feet. There was a slimy substance in the gutter.

I shifted my hand and feet, smeared the oily goop into my socks and onto my ankles. The attempt to free my hands from my feet was not successful. Struggling, fingers stretched out, I untied my laces, and slipped my shoes and socks off my feet. Smearing more of the gunk onto my bare feet allowed me to slip off the bindings. My feet were free. I swung my hands under my feet, brought them to my chest, and then twisted my arms and hands at the wrist, the bindings loosen and my hands were free.

I heard a tremendous outburst of laughter. I lifted my blindfold off; my eyes adjusted to the light, focused in on a group of five laughing men - watching me. With terror, I saw Minkoto chained to the opposite wall. She was naked to her waist. Burns covered her body. She was dirty, black streaks smeared down her, as if she was drug through mud. She was moaning through a dirty red cloth gag. Her head hung heavy from her shoulders. The room's content focused. This was a chamber of torture. This did not happen in real life. This had to be a nightmare. A swift kick to my gut told me this was no dream. I leapt to my feet. My reactions were slow. My audience was still laughing. Trying to regain control of my senses, I put my hand on the wall for balance. Still they were laughing. A fat ugly man walked over to Minkoto, lifted her head by her chin. He looked at me with a sickening smile, cupped her breast in his hand, and squeezed hard. She inhaled sharply with a gasp, in pain, as he squeezed her waist with his other hand. Leaning over he bit her ear. She cried out. The blood trickled down her neck. He laughed like a crazy person.

Her eyes were puffy but opened wide when she heard me softly call out her name. She saw me standing. Her bleeding lips moved, but I heard no sound from her mouth. Rage built up within me. The sound of the growling welled up inside me from down deep, drowning any thoughts I had. They were still laughing, but not for long--no--not for long.

Two of the four remaining men in the group swaggered toward me, still laughing. As they closed the distance between us, I kept my gaze cast down, until I saw their feet. I clicked the nails of my ring fingers against thumbs. Raising my eyes and field of vision, I saw they were looking to the source of the sound. They were still laughing when my hands shot up – thumbs extended upright, gouging deep into their eye sockets. Before they screamed, my thumbs find matching eyes. Everyone stopped laughing as the two fell to the floor, screaming, their eyes held, trying to hold back the pain.

The last two men of the group shouted something that sounded obscene, moved toward me, one behind the other, with a newfound caution. I bent down, and with my left hand pulled a knife free from its scabbard attached to a writhing, screaming body at my feet. Slitting his throat, I passed the blade from left hand to right, focused my eyes to aim, and threw. The first man, my intended target, ducked. The knife traveled for another four foot, and silently sliced into the throat of the second man in line, who did not duck. My eyes locked onto the spear the approaching man held with both hands, he lunged, I sidestepped, and the spear snapped sideways striking my side.

I knew the pain was there but the controlling power inside me anesthetized me against it. He pulled the spear back to ready for the fatal lunge when my fist that was following his retreating spear, struck him in the face, knocked his head back, and his body went off-balance. He hunched over. My body sprung off the wall, my right foot struck up, smashing his larynx. As he settled to the floor, I grabbed the spear falling out of his hands and rammed the handle into his open grimacing mouth, forcing it down the choking, gasping, throttled gullet. I felt the flesh inside his scrawny neck tear, as I push it down, again and again.

The first man who attacked me was still squirming on the floor, trying to get up. The swinging spear produced a loud crack from his head, as the heavy bladed spear struck the side of his skull.

The fifth man that was torturing Minkoto was coming toward me with a knife in hand until he saw his cohort stop moving. He turned to his right and tried to make it through an open door when the spear severed his spine. No noise came from him, his body made a hollow flat thud as it fell to the floor, and his right hand tried to pull himself, and then quivered to a stop. I saw what he had done to Minkoto. She had blood from stab wounds, pouring down the front of her body. His knife had repeatedly penetrated deep into her lungs and abdomen. I heard myself scream "No."

Running to her, I knew no medical help was close enough to save her. Shackles released, I held her in my arms and lowered us both to the floor, where I tried to comfort her. "Do not talk. Rest. I will protect you."

Her eyes were staring deep into mine. "No I must speak. My blood is your blood. My love is your love." She whispered. "You are Kikkawa. You are honorable. My great grandfather and I are greatly honored." The words slurred from the blood welling up in her mouth. "The values of our family now rest in your protection. They must be held safe for new generations." My falling tears washed the grime of her ordeal off her face.

She coughed, blood trickled from the corner of her mouth. I heard the air from her lungs, bubbling, pushing boiling pink foam out of chest wounds. Bright red blood flowed from other wounds. Hissing air escaped from her neck wounds, and made sucking noises as she tried to talk. Each sound produced stabbing pains as my heart clinched up with spasms. My mind and body numb from knowing I was losing Minkoto.

Minkoto struggled to speak. "The Trove of the Kikkawa is held in a secret chamber beyond the chamber, where you first dreamed in the passing of knowledge. Find it, learn its secrets and guard it well. I must go now, Great grandfather awaits me ...”

I leaned over her face, gently placed my lips on hers, felt her trembling lips. I pulled my head back a few inches and looked into her eyes. "Good-bye Web-San." A breath escaped her mouth, gently caressing my face. Her face rolled to the side and she was still. I heard myself shout. "I love you. You cannot leave me." I cried all night holding her in my arms.

A pain in my side woke me. Minkoto's cold, stiff body was still in my arms. I heard myself tell her how much I love her, how she will always be with me, always in my mind. Anger welled up in me, why did a god, any god, take her from me. She was innocent, as our love was innocent. Nothing good could come from this unwilling sacrifice. Blaming everyone, everything, and myself, for my loss, I gently laid her body on the floor.

My attention turned to the second man to come after me. He was moaning. I kicked him in the side. He cried out in pain.

I pushed him over with my foot, and knelt down; grabbed him by his dirty, oily hair, and questioned him. "Where is your master?"

Moaning, he asked, "Who are you?"

"White Dragon of Izumo – Dragon of the White NINJA. Where is your master? Where is that bastard black heart?"

With a weak voice, he uttered, "He is at the castle." I shook him, my hands around his neck; I wanted to ask more questions. He slipped into unconsciousness, or died, I did not take the time to find out which.

I returned to Minkoto, picked her up, and found my way up a stairwell, through a door into the morning sunlight. My eyes hurt from the brightness. Scanning the landscape for help, no one was in sight. In the distance, I saw the familiar cliff. I struggled to reach the Kikkawa home and did not realize how weak I was. I had to stop many times, to rest, pausing to tell Minkoto that she would be home soon, home with her great grandfather.

Stopping to catch my breath at the front entrance, I slid the front door open, crossed the large room, and found the panel triggering the passageway through the wall. It closed behind me. I found the switch next to the door and light filled the chamber of knowledge. I walked to the large wooden planked table, placed Minkoto on it, and walked to the wine cabinet when I could not find water. I poured wine into a goblet, took a towel and cleansed her. She had a peaceful, serene expression on her face. I did not know where to place her. I did not know where her great grandfather lay.

I sat next to her, cried and kissed her hand. Images from the past two years filled me, slowing and stopping at her appearance. I studied each vision of her in detail. Her smile, sparkling eyes, the graceful walk, the determination and set of her face when she was angry, the playfulness when she looked at you from the corner of her eye, and I put my head on the table by her side, feeling lost, with no purpose in life or reason to live. I wanted to be with her, if not in life, then in death. My thoughts clouded, and drifted randomly through fits of sleep.

Chapter
ELEVEN

I slept, and the dreams of knowledge surfaced to my semi-conscious mind. The old man visited, giving instructions, reinforcing previous training. This visit was different; it was as if his mental force became the electrical source of renewed metamorphic life. A newfound energy in my body, in my brain, was making me over into something different, someone new.

Hours later, I woke. I covered Minkoto with a tapestry pulled off the wall. I knew what I must do. I searched the wall until I saw a sword in its cradle. It was not a thick heavier samurai sword, but a lighter, more graceful, slender, and very old sword.

Covered with nicks, cuts, and scratches, with the dragon under the sun etched into the blade, barely visible from over two thousand years of polishing. The scabbard and handle were made of sandpaper rough white shark skin. The handle was large for my small hand, but the grip, confident and firm, fitting like an extension of my arm.

From deep in my subconscious come the old man's words "With heart, mind, and body, I will protect. I am yours to command." Raising it above my head caused a hum. A vision came of an artisan folding the white-hot steel blade thousands of times, strengthening it, alloying it with rare powdered elements, and tempered in a long, shallow, narrow trough, jade green with gold handles. I knew where my power came from and what I must do.

Raising the cabinet top opened a hidden shallow cavity that held a jade jar with a gold lid containing clear sweet smelling oil and two white silk funeral robes emblazoned in gold thread, with matching headbands.

I could not read the symbols, but I knew what they meant. IZUMO. I washed myself with the same wine and towel I used on Minkoto, then oiled and dress myself in the larger white robe with the gold thread. I removed the tapestry from Minkoto, oiled her body, and dressed her in the smaller funeral robe. The tapestry rolled, and placed under her head for a pillow. I kissed Minkoto good-bye.

With renewed purpose, I crossed the distance to the castle, entered the ruins through a heavy wooden door. A stairway led upward to a sunlit opening to a courtyard. The courtyard contained five Black Ninjas, dressed in brown, as their master watched from an elevated decking. He spoke in a language not recognized, but I know what he was saying. They were waiting for me.

He shouted to me in English, pointing to me. "I was told earlier that you and your dog of a mistress escaped from my game room. We will find your Americanized whore to fulfill her purpose in life, bowing to my wishes. You have come to entertain me. My men are awaiting you. Your death will bring pleasure to me; and to my warriors – practice and exercise." I drew my sword, and the sound of its withdrawal turned into a loud hum, like a tuning fork, as it sang to me. I felt the presence and guidance of ancient Jonins, the knowledgeable ones, and a lust for revenge, for a lost love, coursing through my blood. The battle was a blur. The courtyard covered with the pieces of five bodies, covered with brown cloth, splattered with red blood. I looked up, my eyes searched for that black villain. He had made his escape. I knew we would meet again.

I stopped at the Kikkawa house, to kiss Minkoto again, for the last time, and search the chamber of knowledge. One of the metal medallions hanging on the wall had the Dragon embossed on it. I followed its gaze to the corner of the room.

There carved in a round stone in the wall was the sun, shining down onto a pair of hands shaped in a V. I pushed on the stone carving of the sun. Part of the wall slid back and to the side, revealing an opening to another large room. There standing guard were line after line of men, dressed in white silk burial robes emblazoned with gold thread, all mummified but one, the old man. *All their knowledge culminates in me. Am I worthy of it? Can I carry it? Can I build on it to pass to another?* I did not think I knew how to pass the knowledge to another. How could I? No one had told me how, and I did not know where to look to find out.

I returned to the chamber of knowledge, lifted Minkoto and placed her body into the niche next to her great grandfather where she belonged. She was the only woman in their presence. There were no more empty niches. *What should that mean to me?*

The dark burial chamber looked like it narrowed at the far end. Striking a flint spark onto a torch burst it into flame and illuminated a light switch on the wall. I turned on the lights, and returned the torch to its deep-cupped receptacle. Walking to the back of the room revealed another narrow, smaller, blank rock wall. On the wall is one torch bracket.

I went back to the room entrance, ignited the torch, and returned to the back of the room placing the torch into the holder. The flickering light cast a shadowed depression on part of the wall. I push in the depression with all my strength, but nothing happens. I looked closer at the wall again. The depth was greater on the left side of the depression.

Placing both hands in the depression, I pushed to the left, the wall slides back. I removed the torch from the holder and entered the new chamber. I followed the wall around the smaller chamber, lighting torches as I came to them.

One wall was solid with books and manuscripts stored in open square wooden boxes sitting on their side, on shelving supported by a twenty-foot long reading table. A table at the other wall held charts and maps of the ancient world. Coins I did not recognize overflowed stacked chests, wood boxes of jewels, and small golden figurines placed on a pattern game board, like a chess game.

On the walls were works of art and drawings that I did not understand. I was surprised at the lack of dust. Everything was clean. Time was lost as I tried to read and analyze what was there. It took hours before it came to me that I understood the words and symbols. I did not take anything, but carefully returned everything to its proper place after examining it, then retraced my way out. The wall opened before me and closed behind me.

I changed back into my street clothes, walked to the road toward Iwakuni, to the base, clutching a white handled white sheathed sword and the uniforms of my new station found in the cabinet.

A taxi stopped. Resting in the cab, everything that happened crashed in on me. With tears running down my face, it took all my mental strength to keep from wailing. I walked across the Kentai Bridge, and another hailed taxi took me to the main gate.

The gate guards waved me through without noticing my red, bloodshot eyes, asked. "Did you picked up some souvenirs?"

"Yes" and I continued walking with a slight limp, trying not to show I held an injured side. My bruised, raw and throbbing right hand from where I had gripped the sword's sandpapery rough finished handle ached.

Washed and changed, I reported to the squadron duty office. "Drache, Where in hell have you been? We've been looking for you for the past two days. You're wanted back at your squadron in the Philippines. Get your ass back to Atsugi."

I told the duty officer. "I left some personal items back in town that I have to get." I returned to the safe house.

They did not want to talk to me. I told them some of what happened. "Minkoto is dead. Her death will be avenged." I arranged to send them money to purchase the Kikkawa home, so they could live in it. They told me the history of the old Kikkawa home. "Very few know that it was the original residence of the daimyo (lord) of Iwakuni back in the seventh century, and given to an unknown, reclusive, member of the family when the daimyo relocated closer to Iwakuni."

"The most recent resident of the old Kikkawa house was a mystery to the townspeople," They said. "Until Minkoto came, after the terrible war, to live here with an elderly relative no one can remember seeing before her arrival."

"There is still that mystery, in that no one can place the old man or Minkoto in the Kikkawa lineage. All Kikkawa were trained in the martial art *bungei,* but they were a very private family. It was said that Kikkawa is not their true name. Their real name is lost in ancient times, when it changed to confuse old enemies.

We have heard that the Kikkawa bloodline can rarely produce females. They bought female babies, schooled to be proper wives, and trained in proper ways. Some were married into powerful families binding them together in an alliance, following old family customs. They normally tried to acquire the girls at birth, to be raised by a traditional segment of the family, to school them in the ways of the socially elite."

"It was also said that a branch of the Kikkawa family tree had bad blood, when the Kikkawa were shamed and dishonored by the discredited lineage. There were many rumors, not spoken aloud outside private walls, never where people gathered. Other's ears and eyes are everywhere. It is not as bad now as it was years ago, before we became westernized. Today, you should still be careful what you say about powerful families when you are in groups of people, or in the throngs of shoppers. It is wise to be more cautious, than a little careless."

I swore them to secrecy. The black ninja must not know Minkoto is dead. I answered their questions. "She is with her great grandfather. All arrangements have been taken care of."

What they had told me, did not set well. I had thought the old man as honorable, not as they had described. I pushed all that nonsense out of my mind. Minkoto's memory must remain pure, for what else do I have. I know they are of the same blood. I would never tarnish her image.

Chapter
TWELVE

Two days later, I arrived at Cubi Point, Philippines. The memory of what happened never leaves my thoughts. The old man has not visited since the night after Minkoto's death. Life existed in a mechanical daze, focused thoughts impossible. Several weeks pass without me realizing it. Living in a semi-trance, I knew my life must go on.

Sitting in a club, drinking a San Miguel serbesa (beer), I listened to the surrounding conversations. The Protector of the Night has not been active for three weeks. Crime and attacks against the Americans are on the increase. *Yes*, I thought, the focus of their conversations must resume his deeds. Criminal activity interrupted, people are feeling safer at night. The base commanders dropped the caution warnings to their men going to Olongapo. Times are again peaceful. Oh, there were squabbles, arguments, and still crimes of passion, but the safety element for the organized criminal was gone. Early mornings, when sleep comes to me, welcomed visits by the old man and Minkoto, mostly sweet Minkoto, came.

It was evening and I had just returned from a trip to

Manila. I stopped in town to purchase and eat, large yellow mangos, when from behind the market place an excited, shouting group gathered. Two men dressed in black, in a nondescript jeepney, abducted a young girl and headed north out of town. They shot a local police officer at the outer checkpoint. The fear of returned Chinese white slavers was foremost in their conversations.

I went to my secret place, an old abandoned storage cave from the Japanese occupation days, and changed into my clothing of the night. I picked up my faithful sword, felt the comfort of vibration, and heard the reassuring familiar hum.

I scaled the base perimeter fence where it snaked through a dense patch of jungle, and headed around Olongapo, taking a jungle trail made by the Zambales Pygmy's, a short cut. Halfway to the checkpoint I came across two pygmy men in the path who were returning from a late hunt. They fell to their knees with heads bowed down.

They would not look into my face. The aborigines thought of me as a moon god, the Protector of the Night. There was no fear, as they knew that I protected and helped them. They told me of evil men dressed in black, who terrorized the jungle tribes, using them for unwilling sparring partners to practice their martial arts, killing some with weaponry practice. They were afraid to take me to the evil one's enclave. They told me the location and its security. I told them I would ask their gods to give them plentiful hunts.

I made three circles around the compound to verify that the information was still valid. The security system was infrared activated batteries of powerful crossbow panels with backup mechanical trigger devices in case of power failure. I worked for an hour modifying the triggering devices around the ring.

Penetrating the ring was easy. The security guards armed with automatic armalite rifles (AR-10s), checked in with their base unit using hand held two-way radios every fifteen minutes. I could not have eliminated all the guards in that short window of time.

I shadowed myself through their lines of vision and worked my way to their inner circle of security, the wall. Lower leveled light illuminated their inner perimeter. On close examination, the wall was heavy wire fencing overgrown with the cover of dense jungle vines. A vibration of the woven fencing panel would trigger a section of bamboo-powered arrow-bolts with a grid of bamboo poles mounted on jeep axle springs.

I silently laughed at the crude design, and rolled under the bottom of the fencing, carefully, and silently, scrutinized the building in the center of the fenced field that was two hundred feet across. After studying the building from all sides, I waited my opportunity.

There was one guard at the entrance. A stack of barrels and trash hid me, opposite the gate guard; I waited until the lights of an approaching vehicle flashed across the guard hut.

When the truck came to a stop, I rolled under it and held onto the frame, lifting myself off the ground. There was the normal small talk from the men in the truck, but it rode on a background of erratic muffled noises of panic, restrained scuffling, and forced nasal noises. The truck drove to the front entrance of the building, instead of the parking area where I thought it would stop. There was another guard at the main door. The men in the truck were drinking and laughing. A girl's scream followed the sound of tape ripped from skin. One man bragged to the guard "This one makes five, and is she ever wild. She'll be good entertainment." The two men from the truck dragged the bound girl into the building as she struggled against their grip on her bound arms. The guard from the main door followed them in. Once inside, she screamed again. All I could do was wait. No noise came from the building for thirty minutes.

The gate guard had dropped his cigarette. It burned slowly to gray ash, in the dusty road, as he dozed in a roughly made chair leaning against the guard hut. Dawn would be coming soon and it was time to make my move. Crawling out from under the truck, I made my way up the steps to the side of the main door. Slowly releasing my sword from its scabbard, it talked to me with a quiet hum. Softly stepping inside, my senses intensified. I recognized the pungent odor of cheap rum. One guard was sitting next to a table, his head rolled back in semi-sleep. He cleared his throat; his eyelids quivering, trying to open.

They popped open as his head fell silently onto a pile of dirty rags beside the chair. Blood squirted up soaking the ceiling beam. Metal rings screwed into the floor, secured five young women waiting for an end to their ordeal. One was biting her bottom lip, drawing blood, trying not to scream out.

In the dim light, she saw my forefinger pressed to my lips, indicating to be quiet. There are two guards asleep in bunk beds at the left wall. Empty rum bottles strewn across the floor presented obstacles to avoid.

I silently walked behind the other drunk at the table opposite the headless body. Turning my singing sword sideways, I swung heavily, breaking his neck. He slumped over the table. His leg jerked out and his foot struck the closest girl's leg. She broke her silence with a stifled, terrified scream.

The drunk in the bottom bunk stirred, his eyes opened as he raised his head to investigate the sound. Before I could take him out, his feet were swinging out to the floor, his eyes trying to focus on the scene.

He yelled an alarm while my still humming sword exposed his last meal to air. His arms reached out for me as he hit face down on the floor. His ruckus brought the other drunk to consciousness. All five girls screamed. The other drunk tried to jump from his bunk, slips and falls striking my shoulder as he continued head first to the floor.

He knocked himself out or broke his neck; I did not have the time to check. Quickly my blade cut the ropes tying the girls to the rings in the floor. I told them I was here to help. I could see in the dim light that they were terrified, and they continued to whimper as they struggled to their feet.

Dawn was near. Sun shafts warmed the canopy of the jungle. The birds sung their morning ritual songs. I heard a familiar voice. "I knew you could not resist my trap. I knew the sight of your slow painful death would be a pleasurable experience for me." I turned toward the voice. The girls gave up their efforts to escape, dropping back down to the floor.

"Get him," he ordered the two guards at his side. They were

pointing their rifles at me; big toothy smiles widened their pockmarked face. They were abreast of the table, one on each side, when one stumbled over the head on the floor, rolling it until it came to rest against a girl's leg. She screamed. The second guard stopped, looked at the hysterical girl.

Before the distracted guard fell, the top of his head was sliding down over his face, hitting the floor first. The first guard was trying to find me in the dimness not realizing I had jumped over the table and was standing behind him. No name yelled, "Behind you, behind you fool." Severed at the waist, he crumpled to the floor with a disbelieving look on his face.

The girls were cowering in the corner. No Name was no longer at the door, but outside loudly assembling his remaining troop of fools. His vision flashed through my mind ... Minkoto flashed to mind - my vow of revenge flashed to mind. I slammed the door shut, and helped the girls out the back window. I told them to hide under the floor, not to make a sound, and stay there until I came to get them.

No-name ordered me to come out. I followed the girls out the window, ran to the back of the yard, slid under the fence, and made my way around to the front gate. He was still ordering me to surrender, and had prepared a firing line, when I enter the unguarded gate. Searching the ground, I bent over, picked up a heavy fist size clump of semi-dried ox dung, and threw it against the back of no-name's head.

"Come. Come, to me, you pile of human waste. Your mother did not carry you in her womb. She was constipated. Come to me you bastard."

He turned to look, cursing me, ordering his lackeys of ten to bring me back alive. I ran down the west side of the fence, and partially crawled under the vine covered booby-trap, leaving my head and shoulders exposed.

No name followed his ten men out the gate, and pointed for them to follow me. I made sure they could see me, then rolled to the inside, and shook the fencing violently. As they approached my position, I moaned as if in the pain of death. They were amused and thought I had impaled myself on the bamboo.

They spread out at ease, coming to the fence to peer through the leaves when I released the draw-rope anchoring the axle springs. There were a few yells of pain before the fence stopped vibrating. No name was no longer at the gate, but had darted back inside the compound with his sword drawn. I approached him, circled around, and motioned for him to follow me out the gate. I was calm with the blood of a thousand before me pounding in my heart and head, knowing my moment of retribution was at hand. His eyes filled with rage, his face contorted by the evil in his heart, he followed me. He stalked me step for step.

I was twenty feet in front of him as I approached the outer circle's infrared light beams. I extended my sword blade over my shoulder, holding it in the beam, reflecting the light back to its source. I walked through the beams path, and swung the humming instrument of death over my head, as if to engage no name in battle.

I was ready to release my previously made triggering device as his body broke the beam, his expression, for an instant froze, knowing his fate. His eyes did not look to me for mercy, just hatred. His black heart had consumed his mind, and now his life. There was no pity in me for him. The twang of fifty crossbow strings sang in the early morning dawn, and then slowly fell silent.

His twitching body fell to the ground, his hand feebly tried to pull out one of the bolts that did not pass through, but found solid bone. His body stiffened and my sword was silent. The tears running down my cheeks released me from the trance where I was with Minkoto. I did not know how long I stood over my evil adversary, dreaming of what might have been. Wiping my eyes dry with the back of my hand, I went back to the building, in the middle of the field, told the girls to go, to follow the road, and find their way back to town. I slipped back into the jungle, to the trail of the pygmy, back to the base and my secret cave.

Chapter
THIRTEEN

My vow fulfilled. My sword became silent. I knew it belonged in its rightful place, in the room of knowledge, in the home of the Kikkawa. It took several weeks to arrange another R & R trip to Japan. The skipper was a little reluctant to let me go off so soon after the last time I went to Japan, but I assured him I only needed ten days, and my heaviest workload was not for another twenty, he agreed.

The return to Iwakuni took three days. I rushed to town, across the Kentai Bridge, and found a taxi to take me to the castle. Sitting on a boulder next to the road, I looked over the landscape, the castle, the faraway house built into the cliff, and my eyes focused on a young woman walking in the road, approaching me with a familiar graceful and poised stride. I called out "Minkoto" but before the name left my lips, my eyes cleared themselves of tears and I knew it is not her. The woman passed, looked down at me strangely, as I sat on the boulder with tears on my face. After she was out of sight, I stood with my concealed sword in hand, walked to the house in the cliff, through the sliding doors, and through the wall passage. One last time the sword was held high, but it remained silent.

Repeating the old man's words "With heart, mind, and body, I will protect, I am yours to command," while I returned the sword, knife, headband and white robe to their rightful place. I lit a torch and passed into the burial chamber. The reclined old man and Minkoto still encased in glass. Each looked as if they were still alive and sleeping. I studied them for a while before the question. *Who?* Broke my thoughts. I moved the torch around and switched on the lights. Everything was spotless and clean. *Who else knows the secrets?* I was puzzled. I went to the room of treasures. Everything was as before. I spent hours studying the books and manuscripts, returned to the reclining sentries at rest, and studied them, wondered about their lives and achievements, and how they died. Honorable, I was sure.

Coming to the glass-covered crypt containing Minkoto, I said a prayer, to whatever god was listening. I felt the prayer was more for me than her. I felt a little better, reassured, after saying a lengthy good-bye to Minkoto, knowing she was sharing a better place with her ancestors. After extinguishing the torch and turning off the lights, I returned to the cavern of knowledge, turned off the lights, walked through the wall passage, and watched the wall close behind me. I sat at the table until dark, dreaming of what might have been, had Minkoto not been killed. The older couple slid open the sliding front door and came in. I recognize them immediately. Minkoto's friends at the safe house. They expressed alarm until they recognized me. I told them, "Minkoto's death is avenged." They questioned me, and we talked through most of the night. From our conversation, I realized they had not acquired knowledge of the cavern rooms, nor of my Kikkawa blood. To them I was the man Minkoto loved, and the man her great grandfather trusted.

The old couple told me, "A trustee of the Kikkawa property came to us, and showed old documents verifying Kikkawa association and legal power to administer the estate." They said, "We could live in this home for as long as we want, but one full day and night, each month, we must leave while a group of trustees take temporary possession of the home, conducting estate business, maintaining Kikkawa traditions. We must leave before sunrise one day and return after sunrise the next day. However, we never see anyone come or go. It is a strange arrangement, but we enjoy the home. It is a comfort in our old age."

Since they could not acquire the property, they wished to return money I had previously sent them. I told them, "Use the money to fix up the home."

They declined, stating, "The trustee have made us caretakers, and pay for our work and materials needed. We are happy with the arrangement." They went on explaining how the elders said they come from a great distance to complete their work, and must leave before sunrise, that one-day a month. "There was never anything disturbed, it looked as though they are never really here. We never see food or drink and the hibachi is always cold when we return. It is very strange!" They insisted, that to keep their honor, they must return the money I sent them. Reluctantly I agreed. The next morning I left, telling them I would keep them informed of my address, as I moved around the world. I knew it would be too hard for me to return.

Gone for only four days, I gave the C.O. the excuse that "Japan was not what I thought it would be."

My normal night activities were non-existent now, as I enjoyed myself, watching nature, the interaction of other people, their shared companionship, and letting the world and time slip pass me. It was getting close to the time of my rotation back to the states. I did not know if I was looking forward to it or not. I knew that the rest of my life could be a continuous reaction to the challenges I encounter, but only if I allowed it.

Ten days before my transfer back to the states, a man approached me, refusing to identify himself. "You were referred to us as one who is competent, cool in a crisis, and capable to keep a plane in the air. We cannot tell you what you will be doing, or where you will be going. You will not receive any compensation. No acknowledgments, rewards, or recognition for what you will be doing. All I can promise you is a grateful nation."

His words intrigued me, as I was sure was his intent. Volunteering, and taking leave prior to my transfer becoming effective, were a pre-requisite to joining the mission. I would have to be in a non-accountable travel status.

My questions went unanswered. "We cannot tell you." He would not even tell me who the authority was over the operation. His proposal was too appealing for me to turn down. I had become lazy lately, as everything was calm and quiet. I needed something to get me going, to energize me, to clarify my senses. I agreed. I told him, "Yah! I'll volunteer." The next day I submitted my special request for leave, as instructed.

The skipper approved my request, only with my assurance to

train the reliefs to do the job. Two days later, I was at an old abandon World War II airstrip, isolated in the jungle, looking at an old decrepit DC-3. It had no markings to identify it, and it sure did not look air worthy to me. Introductions were by first or nicknames only. Red, was the pilot, and in charge of the mission. Around forty years old, he was tall, burly, with a bushy red beard and hair. He talked with an unfamiliar faint accent. Doc was a little older, five feet eight inches tall, slightly bald, and a little thick around the waist. Mac was tall and skinny. Dark hair grew over his body. *He must have a five o'clock shadow an hour after he shaves.* Mac was nervous, twitchy, and stuttered when he talked. The other man was very professional and only talked to Red, but never in front of us. His speech was clipped and concise. He did not greet us or acknowledge our presence. It was as though we were not there. He never looked us in the eye.

Red gathered us together, and we boarded the plane. There was hot coffee, cold beer, and cold sandwiches waiting for us inside. "Wait until we get airborne." cautioned Red. Red and the stranger kept talking to each other with whispers in the cockpit, constantly checking their watches, and listening to their headsets.

The stranger shouted back to us, "Strap yourselves in. This is it."

Mac appeared more nervous than ever. Doc and I told him everything was all right. "I know – I know, I'm always a little shaky before a mission." I figured from listening to Mac and Doc that they both had been on this type of mission before. Doc appeared to know what the mission was all about, but did not offer to tell Mac or myself.

After we were airborne, Red, called back, "Doc, break out the grub, and bring coffee and sandwiches up to the cockpit." Mac and I talked of neutral topics. Different ports-of-call we experienced, points of interest in the Far East, women, but nothing about where we were going.

We were in the air five hours, when Red started preparations to land. Doc told us. "Strap yourselves in." The old plane was still rolling out after touch down, when I notice the aircraft lined up on the tarmac had Taiwan insignia. We had landed at a Taiwan Air Force Base outside Taipei. We pulled up to a hangar that was remote from the main part of the airfield. A crew truck waited for us, took us to a ramshackle building.

Red told us. "Wait until I get back. This may take an hour or two. Just cool your feet." Red and the stranger left in the truck.

Again, cold beer and cold sandwiches waited for us. Mac was relaxed, and Doc quiet. We refreshed ourselves in silence. Two hours later Red returned alone. "It's time to go." Laughing, he told Doc. "Get the lock box and the flight suits from the truck." They all chuckled except me. I had no idea what was going on. It was as if they were all enjoying an inside joke. Everyone but me. Doc struggled back with some green suits draped over his shoulders, a box of tennis shoes, socks, and carried a large steel box, with a hasp on its lid. Everything dropped to the rotten wooden floor with a hollow dull crash. Red yelled. "Come on, take it easy Doc!"

Red looked at Mac and me, and said. "All right, shuck off those clothes, you know the drill, no I. D ..." He paused, looked at me – "I'm sorry Web; you've never done this before. Look, we cannot take anything with us. All your rings, I. D. Tags, wallets, pictures, religious medals, everything, also your skivvies go into these individual duffel bags, and it all gets put away in this lock box. You can also slip your ditty bag inside, if you want to, or else leave it loose. All we'll have on are these." Holding up a set of the greens, he adds. "It looks like we have old surgical outfits this time. Do you have any questions?"

"No" I replied. Red stopped talking, Mac and Doc were changed, and made me hustle to catch up. We were all changed, and I looked at this strange group of men dressed in tattered surgical suits, with mismatched shoes and socks. Looking down at myself, I started to laugh. It was a contagious laugh, as the rest join in.

"Come on in." Red said. The door opened, and a short Chinese man entered the room. Red leaned over, slipping a padlock through the closed hasp, locking the metal box. "Here, you'll have to watch this for us," said Red, as he tossed the key to the short man. Red and the newcomer spoke a few minutes, in Chinese (I think), and gave us the order to move out. "Crawl into that truck. We don't have time to spare."

It was dark; the back of the truck was dark, except from the headlights of passing vehicles. We had been riding in that truck for two hours, on a rough gravel road. Ever so often, the tire tread would pick up a rock and fling it against the underside of the wheel well, cracking like a shot. I was glad when we stopped. I heard the ocean surf, and smelled the salt air. I made out the silhouettes of PBY Catalina seaplanes. There were no lights, but Red escorted us, lighting the way with his flashlight, toward a wooden building. A dim light came from the windows facing us. I saw several people walking around inside.

Red stopped at the door, opened it, and motioned us in. It appeared to be a flight ready room. The stranger on our flight from the Philippines was with another tall slender man with sandy blonde hair. The new man was wearing glasses, a green suit and tennis shoes like us. The two stood up as we approached the table.

Charts, markers, navigational equipment, and round engineer/navigator calculators covered the table. Red introduced the new man to us as Paul. Mac leaned over and whispered. "That's not his real name, ya know." I nod my head.

Red asked the two men. "Is everything ready, everything O.K.?"

Paul looked over to him and answered. "Yep"

"We had better hit the sack," said Red. He motioned toward the far wall, "We'll use those bunks tonight. Get a good night sleep; we have a lot of work to do tomorrow. Breakfast will come at 6 p.m. Doc, you're in charge. You got that Mac?"

Mac nodded "yes" his head moving up and down. Red, Paul and the unnamed man from our flight left. I was tired. Taking the closer bunk, I took off my shoes, and slipped under the blanket. Mac and Doc were still over by the table arguing in a subdued voice. I closed my eyes and the sound of the surf drowned out the voices. Slipping into a dream, I welcomed Minkoto's visit.

Chapter
FOURTEEN

My sleep came to an abrupt halt when Doc yelled "Damn it Web, get up, chows coming." I raised myself up, and swung my feet over the bunk edge. Mac was watching out the window. "They're coming. They're here." Rushing over, he opened the door. Two beautiful Chinese girls came in, carrying platters of food, setting them down on the now empty chart table.

Mac was near slobbering, walked up to the shorter girl, rubbed his hands up and down her arm. Doc shouted angrily. "For Pete's sake Mac, knock it off. You know Red would have your ass if he caught you screwing around with his field operatives. They belong to him. Damn it, control yourself."

The girls look over to Doc and me, returned their eyes to each other, and giggled. Doc told the girls, "Bring that food over." He motioned toward a card table. The girls were still giggling as they moved the food over to the smaller table, bending over to set the platters down. Mac followed closely behind them, watching their every move, his eye revealed what was on his mind. Once again, Doc yelled out a warning to Mac. "Knock it off Mac."

Mac's eyes hardened as they shifted from the backside of

the girls over to Doc, and snarled. "Christ Doc, you're such a pain in the ass. What a dainty shit you are."

The girls turned around, walked past Mac, as Doc escorted them to the door. They looked back before leaving, taking in Mac and myself, and started giggling again. Doc walked outside with them, to their cart. Mac leaned over to me. "He's queer, ya know. Queer as a three dollar bill." Doc walked back in through the door. Mac quietly sat down to eat.

I took the mornings' activities in without a word, thinking to myself. *Getting involved with this was a big mistake.* I still had no idea what was going on.

We finished our food. I got up and walked toward the door when Doc stopped me. "Where do you think you're going?"

"Outside to look around. I'd like to take a look at the aircraft outside."

"Just wait, everyone will be here soon enough. You'll see enough of those lumbering birds later on." I returned and sat down. It was seven when Red and Paul arrived. Paul quizzed Doc. "How did everything go? Was there any problems?"

Doc shook his head no. "Nope, everything is fine." Red took a long look at Mac, and said. "Well, let's get going." Red and Paul led us outside.

We walked over to a PBY that was standing ready on a rocked seaplane ramp. I looked down and saw the huge wooden chocks that kept the craft's cradle from rolling down the incline into the water. A ladder hung on the port (left) side blister opening. Red went up first, followed by Paul, Doc, Mac and lastly, myself. The craft was bigger on the inside than it looked.

Red assigned our stations. "Doc, on the way over, you are at the navigator's table. Mac, you are the starboard gunner, and Web, you take the port station. Mac, I want you to check Web out on that piece of shit gun. He had better be able to tear it down and put it back together blindfolded. Show him how to sight it in and how to use the rangefinder. Don't forget to show him how to clear those damn misfires. Can you do that?"

Mac nodded his head "Yes," and as they walked away, whispered, "Dumb son of a bitch," took me over to his position, showed me the gun's operation. "We don't have tracers; you have to use this dumb rangefinder." He pointed to a glass sight bolted to the top of the breech. "These monsters are not very modern, but they'll knock down anything they hit."

"I've never used anything that looks like this before. Where's it from."

"Damned if I know," said Mac. "I think it's French. Shit, look at that." Pointing to the barrel. "Every time them locals get their grimy hands on these, they paint that crap on the barrels. They must think it's a type of bluing."

"What is it?" I ask.

"Hell, I don't know. It stinks like paint when the barrel burns it off. You get off fifty rounds, and this place will stink to high heaven. If it weren't for air vents, the fumes would kill you."

We spent all morning working on the two machine guns. Mac explained how the mount suspension attached to the bulkhead. He pointed to a kink in the horizontal bar at my station. "If we ground it down, it would lock up the slide bushing. It should work fine, even if it is a little sloppy. We have been using it like this for a long time, waiting for a new bar. You would think we could make one here."

Red motioned to me from the cockpit to come to him. "Web" he said. "You're going to have the critical position. Since your station will face the pier, you will be the first one out, to secure the plane, and provide cover as we exit through your bubble. Now here is the layout. Paul will stay in the cockpit, in case we encounter problems. Mac will provide cover from the starboard side in case a patrol craft tries to sneak up on us. You will be on the pier for support cover, keeping the pier secure, and rear cover when we come back. You understand you will be the last one back in the plane. You'll have an armalite, and in case of pursuit or a firefight, Mac will provide cover for your return to the craft with your mounted gun. We don't expect any trouble, but you never know."

"No one has told me what we're doing or where we're going. Can you tell me?" I asked Red.

"Yeah, I think it's O.K." His brow furrowed, as if reluctant to tell me, but felt coerced by my question. "We're going to the China Mainland to retrieve a compromised agent.

"Who am I doing this for? What agency."

"What you don't know you can't repeat." Red paused, frowned at Mac, who was reading a Playboy magazine, and continued. "We'll be landing near a fishing village, mainland friends of our man. It should take us thirty minutes to get in and out. We have a three-hour window in their sea and air patrol surveillance. We can't be late, and we cannot stay too long. Wouldn't be healthy. We have no I.D., and not in uniform. We would be shot on the spot as spies."

I must have given him an expression of disapproval. He paused, answering with a contorted frown that started at his chin, furrowed his face up through his hairline.

"You'll have to be all right with this," said Red, in a lowered voice and his words spaced a little further apart. "We don't have time to replace you. We leave before sunup tomorrow."

"This appears to be a team that worked together before. What happened to the person I'm replacing, and why me?"

"He got knifed in a brawl. Mac took him to some damn whorehouse, and got him killed. Stay away from Mac. His brains are in his pecker. He's good when the chips are down, you couldn't ask for a more reliable person to back you up, but when he gets back, he's like a dog in heat. Your selection was because you are diversified. You know planes inside and out. You are not overly specialized, work good under pressure with different kinds of people. We have a man at the flag, at the admiral's headquarters in Cubi Point. He tagged you for us when your orders came in. You're not accountable for the time. You can't be, not if you're with us." He paused, looked me in the eyes. "We have a permanent team member coming in, so this should be your only run with us, unless you're needed and available sometime in the future. If you come up with any other pressing concerns, get with me tonight, or first thing in the morning. Oh, one more thing, our chain of command is, me, Paul, Doc, and heaven forbid, Mac. Doc will be able to fill you in on most anything you want to know. Gotta go."

After lunch, Doc took me for instruction. Where to go if

we went down. What to say if we were caught and interrogated, and checked me out on the survival equipment on the plane. "Once we're past midpoint of the Formosa Strait, we on our own. We go south, and fly in low. Go south if we splash in. Hong Kong will be your best bet; its one hundred miles down the coastline from where we dock. You'll have to get to the embassy. Tell them who you are and what happened. They'll take care of you. Tell anyone else you are on leave, was mugged and lost everything. Tell them anything but the truth until you get to the embassy.

That evening, the two young girls came bringing supper, but Doc kept Mac busy, preventing contact with them. They giggled constantly. Watching them walk sent shivers through my body. I imagined it would make you like Mac, if they brought food to you daily.

I was the first one up. It was 4:00 a.m. I made a pot of coffee, and the smell woke everyone else. Red and Paul were sorting through charts when I served their coffee. Mac and Doc came wobbling into the kitchen area, looking for coffee. I showered and put that smelly green outfit on. I wondered how long it would take the odor to hit critical stage in that confined aircraft. This would be the third day, and not once did I see Mac clean up. Doc came in to use the toilet, and I mentioned Mac's lack of hygiene. Doc listened, finished his business, and left. I could hear him giving Mac the riot act. He told him to take a shower and clean up.

Red gathered us around the chart table, going over the details of our part in the mission, but did not give us a background, or the overall picture. Everyone was attentive, except

Mac, who was picking breakfast from his teeth.

Chapter
FIFTEEN

It was pre-dawn when we boarded the plane. Red and Paul completed their pre-flight check, and then eased down the ramp, out on the water. Red dropped the engines rpm when the craft was twenty feet out. Two Taiwan military personnel were manning ropes to retrieve the plane's carriage after we launched. Out on the bay, boats were sweeping the sea-lane for floating debris.

I could feel the old seaplane's sluggish response when we released from the carriage and lumbered out to the turn up area at the start of the sea-lane. Red advanced the throttles up, pushed the two engines to a high rpm pitch. We turned toward the open sea and picked up speed. The plane vibrated from the engines, and the hull slapped the waves. The frequency of the skipping and wave slapping motion increased to a smoother washboard ride, from wave crest to crest, finally broke water, and were airborne. The engines pulled hard. They sounded strained, as we climbed to a higher altitude.

My first flight in a seaplane, and I asked myself how I let this happen. I thought for sure the hull would spit open from the pounding water. Taking off from land is a lot easier than a wet lift off. This was the first time being in a situation where I had no control, having to be responsible to a group of men, did not know where I was going, or whom I was going for.

The sun came up over our starboard wing, peeking between the layered clouds hugging the horizon. After one hour and forty-five minutes, we approached the midway point of our flight. Red eased the plane down until we skimmed the water's surface. Mac came over to me "This is the part I hate." He said with a face strained with worry. "This bird wasn't made for this kind of flying." A shiver coursed through his body like a dog shedding water, and then he calmly returned to his station.

We flew for another two hours and I could see the coastline of the China mainland. Red called back. "Prepare for a wet landing," and eased back on the throttles, the sound of the engines changed from a loud high pitch, down to a quieter, gentler roar. The big plane slowly descended to the sea surface. The landing was like riding a high-speed boat on rough water. The pier came into view as Red eased the craft in. I slid my canopy bubble up, threw out a couple of bumpers, and tossed a line to a fisherman standing on the pier.

I had thought my training covered every possible aspect of the mission. The one thing I did not practice was getting in and out of that bubble canopy while carrying a weapon on a sling. The sling hung up on the hatch release, and I felt like an idiot trying to release it. I looked over to Mac's smiling face. He was shaking his head back and forth. Doc yelled out "Web, get it together, will ya."

I cleared the canopy; checked out the area and looked for anything out of the ordinary. I called out, "All Clear."

Red and Doc exited the plane, dragging two bicycles with them. After talking with the fisherman, Red turned to me. "Web, remember, you're our first line of security. If you see anything, anything at all that does not look right, inform Paul. He will decide what to do. And for heaven's sake, don't let Mac out of that craft. We should be back in thirty minutes. If we are later than forty-five minutes, get the hell out of here. Look for us to come over that hill behind the village. If it's not us, go. Got it?"

"Yes Sir. Get back as soon as you can." I watched them pedal down the dusty dirt path, through the middle of the fishermen's shacks, up the far hill, and disappear.

I became a little nervous, as more villagers came out on the pier, forming a small group around the first fisherman – the one Red and Doc were talking with. The first fisherman motioned for the villagers to return to their normal activities.

A little girl remained with the lone fisherman. She was young and cute. She hung onto the fisherman's leg, apparently her father, peeked at me from behind his legs, talking in that high-pitched voice that all younger children have.

She clutched a homemade stick doll, with carved arms and legs appended to a thicker piece of wood. The joints were wooden links, and rags wrapped thickly around the larger long stick formed the torso. She held her doll up for me to see, its arms and legs swinging back and forth from the momentum of her upward thrust. She asked me something, her face expressive, happy with a big smile.

I smiled back at her and asked her in English, "What's your dolls name?" fully knowing she could not understand me. She held her doll up toward me again, rocking the legs back and forth with her hand, to show me how the legs move in their wooden joints. Her father talked to her, in a voice soft and tender, reflecting his love for her, motioning her back toward the huts. She began walking back, her small bare feet made little puffs of dust clouds in the soft powdery road.

I watched her, as she made her way back to the second hut, sitting her doll in a small homemade chair, by the edge of the road, as if to let her watch the traffic go by, then went inside. The fisherman watched her short journey with a big smile, turned to me with a wave of acknowledgment, and walked back to the small gathering halfway between the first hut and where I stood, next to a fishing boat on skids for repair.

I spent too much time watching the little girl. I scanned the horizon. *How long has it been?* I asked myself. My watch showed they were only gone twenty minutes.

Paul has been keeping the rpm up on the starboard engine, just enough to keep the plane tight to the pier. I glanced back and saw Mac looking out to sea with binoculars, scanning the horizon. A far off noise drew my attention back to the road. I could see Red and Doc, on foot, pushing one of the bicycles. They came over the crest of the hill, a third person on the seat slumped over the handlebars. They were pushing and running as hard as they could. I recognized the sound that attracted my attention, gunfire. They were shouting.

I yelled back through the hatch opening, "Mac. Tell Paul

they're coming back. They're taking gunfire."

Seeing Mac talk over his headset mike, I return my attention to the trio coming down the hill, and advance to the spot where the group of fishermen had been talking, twenty-five feet down the road. They had scattered, the father of the girl to the second hut, some to the other huts, some to the boats, the others down the beach, toward a grove of trees.

Red motioned me back to the plane as they passed the last hut. An open topped carryall, with a man leaning on the windshield, was coming over the hillcrest, firing an automatic weapon. As the returning trio passed me, Red shouted. "Web get back to the plane."

"I'll be right there." I yelled back. Kneeling down on one knee, I returned fire, and the carryall swerved off the road, seeking cover behind a mound of earth. I jumped behind the fishing boat, five feet to my left. I could see the man on the bike bleeding from his wounds. Paul and Doc struggled to get him through the waist blister, into the plane.

The man was out of the carryall, on foot, fired short bursts at the plane. I eased out of my cover to return fire.

The little girl ran out of the hut's door, two arms reached out after her, trying to reach her, as she raced for her doll on the chair, at the edge of the road. As she stretched out her little arms to pick up her doll, the man from the carryall fired a long burst. Time went into slow motion. I could see every jerk, every painful expression, as the bullets ripped through the little body. She fell to the ground, continued jerking as the man kept firing. Anger clouded my reasoning. I stood up and shouted. "Stop you ass!

Can't you see what you're doing?" My words sounded hollow and slow, like they were echoing through a long tunnel, but he kept firing. I emptied my clip returning his fire. The barrel of my armelite was hot. Flipping the clip, I positioned a fresh supply of bullets. I saturated his position with another thirty rounds. My anger alone held the weapon on target. Everything was still in slow motion. I felt every round go down and out the barrel.

The little girl lay heaped in a pool of blood, no longer looking human, but rather like someone dumped out a bucket of slaughterhouse trimmings on the ground. A woman crawled out of the hut toward her, screaming, oblivious to the danger. A man followed to drag the woman back into the hut. That scene, that little girl, heaped on the ground, burned into my mind.

The man was no longer firing, and I stood in a daze. I saw the driver of the carryall running from his protective cover, behind the mound of earth, toward the man that was no longer firing. Mac yelled at me, but I did not recognize his words. He sounded far away, too far for me to understand. The driver was getting closer to the man lying on the ground, and leaned over to pick up his weapon.

The loud thunk–thunk–thunk of the plane's waist gun brought me back my senses. The driver dove for cover as the bullets made tracks down the road toward him. After untying the line that secured the plane to the pier, I dove through the blister opening rather than slow down to step in. My head and shoulder hit the tubular gun mounting. Mac was yelling at me, I could hear the engines rev up, and we eased out to open water.

I tried to find the driver of the carryall in my sights as his bullets smashed through the aircraft's skin, tracing holes from the tail, through the bubble Plexiglas, and forward toward the cockpit. I had that bastard in my sights, but could not return fire. He was standing in a direct line with the village huts. If I returned fire, I will surely kill those poor people that helped us. The plane turned to starboard, as I pulled in the bumpers. The thumping stopped as the aircraft skipped off the wave crests, and we were airborne.

Chapter
SIXTEEN

Red blood covered the front of that stinking green outfit I wore. I searched for wounds. A bump on my forehead, from diving into the aircraft had put a small gash in my scalp. I looked over to Mac. He was shaking his head at me, shouted above the strained drone of the engines in our climb out and the shrill whistling of the shattered canopy. "You'll never get the hang of this."

I reached down into a bag where we kept rags to clean our weapons. I retrieved a cleaner looking cloth and tied it around my head, covering the gash. Doc was tending to the wounded man, stretched out on the deck. He was bleeding from wounds in the shoulder and chest. He voiced his pain, and thrashed around. I jumped over a box of survival gear, to help Doc, when my foot slipped in the blood on the deck. Falling, my lower back struck the box edge. I thought the pain would cause me to pass out. My body froze in stiff convulsions.

Red was cussing at me to man my station. I heard Doc tell him I was hurt, and Mac said, "Like I said, he'll never get the hang of it."

The pain subsided and I pulled myself back to my station.

My back hurt like hell and started to stiffen, but I was mobile. Doc finished the dressings on the wounded man, and turned his attention to me. "Here, take these.", and handed me a couple of pills with a paper cup of water.

"What are they?"

"Pain killers. Take them, you'll feel better. Drink all the water."

I was drowsy and drifted into semi-sleep as Mac quietly told Doc. "I knew he wouldn't be any good at this."

Doc replied, "Shut up shit head."

The old man came toward me from the depths of the cavern, riding those misty clouds. "Aaah, my American warrior. Once again, you meet my original expectation of you. You are supposed to be like a ballerina, to be graceful, and light on your feet, not like a hippopotamus out of water. You were not prepared, thereby not in your element. You still have much to learn. Now sleep while I try to fill your feeble mind, Ha, Ha, Ha, Ha, with knowledge I doubt you can comprehend."

Doc woke me, and gave me an injection. I pulled myself to a sitting position. "Where are we?" I asked.

"We're refueling at an island. Take it easy, you'll be O.K. This was a rough first time for you, wasn't it?"

"Hell, I don't know." I said. "I feel like an ass, screwing up like that." Nodding toward the wounded man lying on the deck I inquire. "Is he going to make it, he's all right?"

"Sure, he's O.K. Now you should be going back to sleep, and the next thing you know we will be back at the base. We'll get you fixed up, and back to your unit. I don't think Red will have time to de-brief you, but he would say what he always says. "Remember, this never happened." Doc was right; I slipped back into sleep.

"Web, Web, wake up." Doc was lightly slapping my face. "Are you O.K.? Can you stand up?"

"Yeah, yeah - sure." I pulled myself up. My back was tight as hell, but there was no sharp pain. "Damn, my back must really be swollen. Look how tight these pants are Doc."

Doc pulled up my shirt and checked my back, painfully pushing in on the swollen flesh with his fingertips. "You'll be fine. We'll get you off this piece of shit, and into a bunk at the shack."

My gun swung aside, and the shattered blister Plexiglas slid up, opening the entire canopy. The plane was high and dry on the ramp, resting in its cradle. Mac was waiting at the bottom of the ladder hooked over the canopy rail. Raising my legs up and over that railing was the hardest part to get back on solid ground. Mac was gentler than I had expected. On the ground, he reached up to help guide me down the ladder, as Doc leaned out the blister hatch, holding me up with a strap around my chest, under my arms, and up the back of my shoulders.

Walking seemed comfortable, "I can make it to the shack. You don't have to hold me up" I told my two bearers.

"Sure you can, Sure." Said Doc, as my knees buckled, and he and Mac continued supporting me. Once inside, Doc put cushions at the head of a bunk, so I could lean back. Mac opened a girlie magazine. Doc asked, "What do you want to drink with your pills? Water or coffee?"

"Coffee. Your water taste like hell."

"Coffee is it, young man." Doc returned with a cup of coffee and another handful of pills. "Take these. Careful, that coffee is hot. We'll get you some food later, after you wake up."

I drifted off to sleep.

Chapter
SEVENTEEN

The morning sunlight warmed my face as I lay telling myself to open my eyelids. *No.* I thought; *that bright sunlight will hurt. No. First, I will face away from the sun, and then the light will not hurt - What is wrong with me,* having to think to myself like this, like some damn dumb fool. Those pills must still be in my system. I turned my face away from the sun, and when I opened my eyes, the light hurt. I covered my eyes with a hand, thinking that if someone could read my mind they would think me a loony. I slowly opened my eyes. A bright shaft of sunlight covered me, and looking into the darker part of the shack proved fruitless, but I smelled food.

"That sure smells good. What is it?" I said into the darkness, to whoever might be listening.

"Pork steak and eggs. If you want some, come and get it.

I pushed myself up while swinging my feet out over the edge of the bunk. A sharp pain stabbed me in the lower back. I heard myself yell out. "Shit. God Damn. Mmmmmm that hurt."

Doc yelled back at me. "Take is slow and easy. See if you can stand up."

I pushed myself up from the bunk rail. The best I could do was stand in a crouched position. I shuffled toward the table. Doc pulled a chair out for me. I found sitting much more comfortable than standing. Doc brought me a plate of fried pork and eggs, with a cup of coffee. One of the young giggling girls was standing at the hot plate on the counter, frying something, caught my attention, and then a voice. Mac was reading his magazine aloud from the corner of the room. He was sitting in his bunk and showed the other young girl the centerfold, asking her if she would like her picture taken like that. "Don't you wish you looked like this? If you did, you sure wouldn't have to stay here, in this line of work." She sat looking at him with a blank face, not saying a word.

The girl at the hot plate, moved to stand behind Doc, leaned over and rubbed her hands in a circular motion on his chest. I smiled, and continue eating.

Doc laughed and said. "We've known these two girls, Mei Ling and Michio, for some time. Mac has not scored once, and it's driving him nuts. If you think you can beat him out, remember, Red relies on them a lot. They always work as a team. The poor slobs they go after don't stand a chance. He does not want them all emotionally tied up inside, screwing up their work."

"That's O.K., who knows what kind of bugs jumped off you two anyway. I'll eat this and sit awhile."

"Well eat fast, Paul brought your stuff from the lock box, and your ride is coming soon. Hell, you're getting a first class trip back to the Philippines. You got a ride on a passenger transport with some diplomats going to the embassy in Manila. Yep, you're going first class. Hurry up, you've only an hour, and you can't travel grubby."

I finished my food and coffee, and shuffled my chair back away from the table. "Do you want Mei Ling to help you into the shower? Take your clothes in for you?" Asked Doc. He pushed the girl standing over him and pointed toward my ditty bag and clothes on the counter. "Go; go help him to the shower. Take his clothes with you. Go on."

"Walking over to the head (shower) can't be that hard. I think I can make it." I said.

Mei Ling came to my aid anyway. She helped me up from the chair, grabbed my bag of clothes and ditty bag as we passed the counter. I brushed my teeth while Mei Ling hung my clothes on a hanger next to the shower stall. Turning on the hot water produced clouds of steam that she swung my clothes through, to remove wrinkles. She took my clothes out the door, returned immediately with a chair for me. She pulled my pants down by the elastic, told me to sit, then squatted down, and slid them off by the bottom of the legs.

I was a little embarrassed, stripped down as though I was a total invalid. She did not seem bothered by what she was doing. After pulling my shirt off, she helped me stand up and walk to the shower. By the time I stepped in, and adjusted the water temperature, her dress was off and standing next to me under the running water. "Are you sure you're suppose to be doing this?" I asked. She did not answer, just smiled at me, while sliding a bar of soap across my body, producing a rich lather. She was very thorough, and attentive, in her task.

Stiffness and pain was slowly leaving from the soothing hot water, but my body could not stop responding to her presence. She enjoyed washing me, enjoyed my body's reaction to her, letting out that little giggle, whenever she saw me watch her work. When she finished, she shut off the water, stepped out, looked me over to examine her handiwork, and led me to sit in the chair again. Taking two towels from a shelf, she draped one over my head, giggled, and dried herself with the other.

It took me a long time to start using that towel. I felt like a voyeur, sitting there, watching her rub that towel softly over her body. Her movements were slow and deliberate, her body moved to music unheard by me, but she was dry before me. She was dressed, out the door, and returned with my briefs and pants before I was dry.

I was relieved someone had washed my underwear. It felt good to be back in clean clothes. Mei Ling watched as I eased myself to the sink and wiped the steam off the mirror with a towel. Tape, ointment and gauze patches sat on the shelf. I pulled off the tape and old gauze, applying the new ointment and a fresh bandage. The butterfly was still holding good. I splashed on some after-shave, and ran my hands through my hair with residual after-shave.

I was rechecking the bandage on my forehead, and Mei Ling helped me down in the chair, massaged my neck and back. Doc yelled to me. "Hey, what the hell is going on? If I have to come in there, there is going to be hell to pay? Web, remember your back." Loud boisterous laughter followed. Mei Ling stopped kneading my neck. I heard a soft "Ssshhhh" behind my ear, and felt a tender kiss on the side of my neck.

She left, but returned in seconds with my shirt. Floating the shirt around behind my back, she helped me slip my arms into the sleeves. Before I could reach the buttons, she slid her arms under my shirttail, around to my back, embraced me, pushed herself tight against me, slid her hands down, squeezed my buttocks, nibbled on my chest through the undershirt, giggled and walked out the room. She was teasing, letting me see, and know, what I was missing.

I took a deep breath before I tried to stand up, threw the old green outfit into the trashcan, and carefully walked back into the main room. Mac was still in bed reading aloud to the other young girl that was sitting across the room from him, while Doc was drinking a cup of coffee at the table. Mei Ling was back at the sink, washing dishes. She turned to face me, and saw no one was looking her way, wiggled her hips, and pursed her lips in a kiss with a silent smack. I blew a mock kiss back to her.

Doc, facing me, with his back to Mei Ling, had a devilish grin on his face. "If I didn't know your back was out of whack, you two would have had a chaperon in the shower."

I tried hard not to laugh. "I can't help it if you two characters have no self-will, discipline, and control over yourselves, like I do. Nothing gets to me unless I wanted it to." Loud stifled snorting and bursts of hyena like outcries, returned in reply.

The ring of the telephone startled me. I had not seen a phone in the shack. Doc jumped up, yanked open a cabinet door, and pulled out the receiver. "Yes, Yes, I got it. Yes Sir. He's fine, just a sore back. Just a little pain. Yes, he can travel tomorrow. Yes Sir, we'll be ready. Yes, they can stay here with him."

Doc hung up the phone, and turned to face me. "Shit, Damn the hell. Mac, get ready. We have to make a run to Kaohsiung. Get up, you dirty scuzz bucket. Get cleaned up. You are not spending time with me in the truck, down south and back, stinking like that. Two days smelling you would kill me."

Mac threw off his sheet, stepped up out of the bunk naked. The young girl, Michio sat in her chair, watched Mac with a bland expression on her face as he strutted over the floor like a horse, toward the showers, cussing the entire distance.

I turn to Doc, who was sitting down again, drinking coffee. "What's happening? What's going on, Doc?"

He looked up at me. "Well, things keep changing. First, you're not leaving today as planned, but tomorrow. They want to get you back tomorrow evening. Time enough for you to rest your back for the flight. Arrangements have been made on the diplomatic flight to Manila, make an overnight stop at Cubi Point, and transfer you to another flight for a straight shot back to the states, landing at Travis Air Force Base."

Doc paused to take a gulp of coffee. "The bad news is that they want Mac to drive down to Kaohsiumb, some shit hole down near the south end of Taiwan, to pick up a load. They want him to leave now, and it will take over a day on those gravel rural roads. I have to go with him to keep him out of trouble. Red and Paul do not have anyone to be with you, so the girls will have to be your company. They do not speak much, so you will have to entertain yourself. They're to make sure you're O.K., so you can rest your back and not hurt yourself. I will leave some pills for you to take, so you can sleep if you want to. They want you ready for that long flight. They'll have someone pick you up tomorrow morning. Red wants a doctor to see you for a checkup and to talk to you before you leave"

Doc turned toward the shower door, listening to the running water. "I hope shit head can get himself clean. I can't stand to be around him when he's stinking." Doc got up, walked over to Mei Ling, spoke to her in a tone too low for me to hear, and turned to me. "I'm going to pack a few things for the trip. Mei Ling will bring you some coffee, or whatever you want," Doc walked slowly to his locker.

Mei Ling looked at me with a smile; her dark eyes did not look so slanted to me now, as they slowly pan down my body. Her right hand rested on her cocked hip that was ever so slightly swaying to the music that her lips were silently keeping in beat to.

Pointing to Mac's coffee cup, then back to me, I said "Coffee."

Mei Ling picked up a freshly washed mug, filled it from the pot on the hot plate, and walked around behind me. Her breasts pushed my head forward as she leaned over my back, sliding them across and past my right ear, setting the mug on the table in front of me. "Coffee" she said softly, moving her body back and forth, slowly, and then hesitated, before brushing her lips over my cheek. She left a hint of a laugh in my ear before standing and walking back to the other side of the room.

Lifting the cup of coffee to my mouth, I thought of all the possibilities available to me after Doc and Mac left. I jerked the hot cup of coffee from my burning mouth, and sloshed the steamy hot stimulant down my clean shirt. "Shit." Multiple giggling swelled up from behind me. I slowly stood up, took off my recently cleaned shirt, hobble over to the sink, using the other chair back to support myself, and soaked it in cold water. Turning, I saw Michio next to Mei Ling, watching me, talking to Mei Ling in Chinese. The young girl giggled again, and Mei Ling pursed her lips in a kiss, smacking them again. Michio stood up, walked to the sink, and washed my soaking shirt. After rinsing my shirt, she took it outside.

Doc's words come back to me. *They want your back rested for that long flight back to the states.* Sitting in my chair, I smiled to myself, shaking my head. Picking up my cup, I cautiously sipped my coffee, sucking in more air than liquid to cool it. My mouth still tingled from my first attempt. The young girl returned from outside, went to Mei Ling, and continued talking to her in a low voice.

Mac came out of the shower, a towel wrapped around his waist. I guess modesty came with cleanliness. His skinny frame, his wild bushy hair, and slow gate struck me as funny, and I laugh. Mac stopped. "I hope you're not laughing at me."

"No." I said. "I'm laughing with you."

Mac cocked his mouth into half smile, half grimace. "Oh bull shit," and continued back to his locker.

Packing done, Doc ambled over and dropped his bag on the table. It hit with a crack. "Crap". He reached in and pulled out an issue .45 cal. Colt. He popped out the clip, cleared the chamber, reinserted the clip, and returned the gun to the bag.

"You never know when you'll need this," he said looking at me. "Mac, you had better get a move on."

"Yeah, Yeah." shouted back Mac, his head stuck inside his locker.

Doc sat down across from me. I tried to think of words to thank him for all he did for me. "I guess I'll be gone by the time Mac and you get back, won't I?"

"Yep, but at least you're going back to the states. Mac and I signed on for another five or six months. I don't know if Mac will be able to take it. He was suppose to go back a year ago, for R & R. He really needs that. He's been in this country over two years. His wife left him, and mailed him a copy of the divorce papers. He has been like this, ever since. That's why I have to keep an eye on him."

"Well," I said. "I want to let you two know my appreciation for everything you have done for me. I might not be alive and kicking, if it were not for you two. Hope we'll meet again, sometime, somewhere when I can return the favors."

Doc looked tired, "Maybe. For right now, Mac and I take one day at a time. When they're done with us, his brush with the law, smuggling, is suppose to disappear from his records, and me, I have problems that they are suppose to take care of." He stopped and stared into his cup for a moment. "Mac, are you ready?"

"Yeah, yeah," came from the other side of the room." Mac came walking toward us, carrying a bag. Looking down at me, and in a serious tone, he said. "You take care, don't let them screw you."

"The girls?"

"No, Red and his crew. I'm serious, watch your back," said Mac, as he and Doc started out the door, Mac shouted back. "Good luck. You might need it. Remember what I said about Red and his people." I heard the old truck start up, the gears grinding as Mac stripped first gear, and then the rumbling slowly grew fainter.

Mei Ling and Michio's conversation was in a low tone, punctuated every now and then with that little giggle. Not aware that they stopped talking, until Mei Ling walked past me heading for the bathroom while Michio was moving to the stove and made two cups of tea. She turned toward me, stirred the hot liquid in her hands, staring at me with a smile as if in a trance or daydreaming. Satisfied with the steeping of the tea, she picked up the cup and brought it on a saucer to the table, setting down across from me.

"How do you like my country?" She asked, speaking English without the singsong tongue, but rather like that learned and spoken in Hong Kong with an English accent. The clear articulated speech surprised me. This was the first time I heard Michio speak English.

"Fine. But it would be more enjoyable if I could see more of it. All I have seen so far has been the air base, and the inside of this shack."

"Do you like Mei Ling? Do you like Chinese women?" She lost a little of the British accent in her last two questions, but they had a more teasing quality to them.

"Yes, I think you two are great." I remembered Doc's warning how Red felt, and I started to feel a little uncomfortable about where this might be going.

Mei Ling came out of the bathroom, freshly showered, hair down and a little wet, wearing a colorful silk robe and slippers. Sitting down next to Michio, she said. "I think you must like Mei Ling more than me. You do not look at me like you look at her. Is it because she bathed you, or, is she more attractive than me?"

My body warmed up. Cautiously, carefully composing my words before speaking, I said. "No, I think Mei Ling has been in my sight, in front of me more than you. You are both beautiful women, to be looked at and appreciated." Michio smiled, got up and went to the bathroom. They were playing with me.

Mei Ling had a mischievous smile on her face. "I think you like me more than Michio. I think I am more beautiful than she is. Do you agree?"

The internal caution light starts flashing like a general quarter's alarm warning, *do not let them back you into a corner.* Smiling back with my best neutral face, my voice sounded a little weak. "I think you're both beautiful. Each one of you..." Mei Ling did not let me finish. "You have seen me. You have not seen Michio." She stood up and let her robe fall to the floor. "Now tell me that I am not more beautiful than Michio?" As I sat stammering, Mei Ling slowly came around the table toward me. "Well Mr. Web, how is your back? Rested I hope."

Still stammering, trying to appear in control of myself, Mei Ling pulls me to my feet, led me to a bunk, undressed me, and gently pushed me down onto the mattress. Later, thinking my education was complete, and in wonder of my back's new found resilience, a feeling of supreme satisfaction started to come over me - until I see Michio walking toward us, only wearing slippers. They were no longer teasing me, but have drained every spark of energy from my body. I discovered the true meaning of - *Hitting the wall - Getting your second wind - and Pulling up your inner strength.*

When I woke up, it was late in the morning, closer to noon. The girls were gone. Jerking up to the edge of the bunk produced a sudden *yip* of pain to come from my mouth. My back was telling me that over-exertion did not help. The struggle to my feet produced pure agony. The shower was a long way off. I found the pills Doc left me, and downed them with a cup of tepid coffee.

The hot shower was soothing, lulling me into a daydream of the earlier morning activities, interrupted by a ringing phone. Walking to the cabinet, I answered "Hello."

"Web, is that you?" Red asked.

"Yes." I grunted.

"Have Doc and Mac left?"

"Yes they did. Right after you called earlier."

"Are the girls there?"

"No, they were, but left a few minutes ago."

"Damn, they are supposed to stay with you. How do you feel?"

"Fine." I lied.

"Good. Get ready, Paul is on his way to pick you up. Your travel arrangements have been made, and as soon as the Doctor checks you out, you'll be on your way."

"I'll be ready." I hung up the phone. I made my way back to

the shower, but walked stiff and sore, from overuse and abuse. My thoughts kept wandering back to Mei Ling and Michio, knowing now, why someone would spill their guts, after falling to their charms. Paul and a short stocky man, with a medical bag, walked in as I laced my last shoe.

"Web. You here?"

I answered, "Sure," and walked out of the shadows to the table, resting my rear on the back of the chair.

"I brought along a doctor to check you out before your flight," said Paul, motioning the short oriental man to me. The doctor was not introduced, nor did he introduce himself to me, but motioned me toward the bunks. Walking to the bunk Paul had used, rather than use my torn up bunk, I sat down. The doctor, speaking in Chinese, and Paul interpreting, told me to take off my clothes and roll on my stomach.

The examination took fifteen minutes, after which the doctor apparently pronounced me fit to travel. "He said you'll be like new in a day or two. No permanent injury, but you should change the bandage on your head twice a day, and use this ointment." said Paul, tossing a small tube over to the bed. "Get dressed and we'll get going."

Paul was driving a small foreign car that kept bottoming out from our weight, jarring my body in every pothole, and shaking over every washboard in the dirt road.

Chapter
EIGHTEEN

As promised, a U.S. DC-7 transport plane was waiting for me at the airport. The flight returning to the Philippines was faster than the flight coming. The flight was comfortable, and a tall, leggy, brunette flight attendant was nice too. Every time I looked at the attendant, I visualized her in a silk robe and wet hair, and my thoughts returned to my morning's workout. As the flight progressed, I felt a little alienated. The only person that talked to me was the attendant. Everyone apparently knew each other, but they would not acknowledge my presence. Silent nods and turned backs return all my attempts to converse.

I asked the attendant for a cup of coffee, and followed her back to the galley. She said a fresh pot was on. "You must be a very important person?" She asked filling my cup. "We had to wait for you over two hours, and there are some really high VIPs up front." Her eyes and face came closer to me as she held the coffee pot off to her side.

I raised the cup to my mouth, remembering not to burn my mouth, sucked in a lot of air with that first sip, and replied, "No, just a guy hung up in the back country."

Setting the pot down in its cradle, she turned to me, coming close enough to drink from my cup. "I bet. You are not at all like those stiff shirts up front, who think their position gives them the right to paw, to grab whatever and whenever they want. You are different. You're quiet, but there is something about you – something I can't put my finger on." She had a big smile, flaunting her near perfect white teeth. "You're someone special, right?"

"Thanks for the compliment, I think. You're talking to a nobody, someone who just needed a lift." She had her hand on my forearm, holding my arm and cup of coffee down, pulled it off to the side. Leaning in and lifting her face, she kissed me on the cheek. "Too bad... Too bad this flight is so short. We're going to Manila, then Cubi Point for a lay over, and then up to Japan." She noticed my eye jerk. "What, what did I say?"

"How long will you be laying over at Cubi Point?"

"Overnight. Why?"

Nodding forward, "Are those bozos getting off in the Philippines, or staying on to Japan."

"Their getting off at Manila. I would never be able to take their crap all the way up to Japan."

"Well." I said. "Maybe we can spend some time together. I might be able to swing up to Japan with you. Where are you landing?"

She was smiling, snuggled closer. "We're going to refuel at Atsugi, then continue on to Iwakuni. Is that O.K.?"

"You damn right. That's perfect." I was on a mental high, anticipating a return to Iwakuni and Kentai.

"You won't have to find a place to stay. Another girl and I

share an apartment, off the base, down from the RTO at Iwakuni. You can stay with me. I'm off for a whole week."

The rigors of the early morning returned to mind. "She won't be there will she?"

"Betty? No, she is going on a stateside flight. I was stuck on this government charter circuit, and it bores me out of my mind. Too many government officials stuck on themselves. Not many like you."

A light on the call panel above the galley hatch came on. "Damn, someone in the cockpit is calling for me. We'll get back together a little later." She leaned over to me, kissed me. Her breath was hot on my face. "Here's something to hold you over." She said.

I heard and felt something hit my shoes. Looking down I saw my shaky hands sloshed coffee from the cup. *I have to get a grip on myself.* Not daring to refill the cup, I put it in a plastic tub, and return to my seat.

Her attendant's nametag spelled "Sha'Rie." Speaking her name, as she came near me in the aisle, gave me goose bumps of anticipation. Sha'Rie returned my shiver with a promising smile.

Sha'Rie paused to touch me every time she walked past me. I was thankful for having a back seat, not up front with that noisy lot.

The plane touched down on that familiar strip in the bay, NAS Cubi Pt., and pulled up to the terminal. Sha'Rie held me back to depart last, and whispered to me, "Wait for me in the snack bar. I won't be long."

I only waited a few minutes when she entered the

terminal with the aircraft crew, talking to them until they left in a base cab. She smiled as I approached. "I have a room at the BOQ. Room 209. Can you find it Web?"

"In my sleep. What time?"

"It's four now. How would nine be? Would that be too late?"

"Perfect. I have a little business to take care of first." Headlights flashed from across the ramp, followed a few minutes later by a base cab coming around the curve behind the terminal. Sha'Rie came closer, "My cab is here," we kissed, and my arms gently squeezed her in a warm embrace. "Later." I spoke softly, "I'll see you later."

I watched her cab drive off and headed in the same direction toward the hangar, and the squadron offices. I heard those familiar steel steps ring under my feet. It brought the realization that this would be my last time here. A flood of memories came to me, good and bad. I walked past the duty room, and knocked on the skipper's door. "Come in." The barrel chested commander sat behind his desk, talking to someone on the telephone. Motioning me to a chair, he finished his conversation, and cradled the receiver. "Web, you look fit, except for the stiff walk of yours. Does that have anything to do with that flight attendant you were with?" His deep laugh was followed with. "I just got here myself, and saw you standing over at the terminal with her. She really looks good."

"Yes. She could be a keeper." Pausing to change the subject. "I need a last favor. Her flight is leaving tomorrow morning, headed for Japan, and a little leave there would be nice. I'll make my own travel arrangements getting back to the states."

The skipper thought a few seconds, "Sure, that won't be a problem. I will have the personnel office endorse your orders, to modify them for open travel. They will be ready in a few minutes. Why don't you have a cup of coffee with the men relieving you? I think they have a lot of questions for you concerning the logs and reports."

"Sure, I could use a little coffee and a bull session."

"If I don't see you again before you leave, I want you to know that your work here made my job a lot easier. If we're lucky, we might get stationed together again. Maybe I could request your assignment to a future command. Anyway, good luck." With a smile and a knowing wink, "And, have a good time. If anyone deserves one, you do."

"Thanks." We shook hands; I headed for the coffee mess, and my old office. Thirty minutes later, my orders modified, and the last few personal items from my old desk, I headed for the barracks. Earlier, I had shipped most of my gear back home. I packed my remaining gear in a duffel bag but kept out a change of clothes.

That last night before leaving the Philippines, I went out to town to drink a San Miguel beer at a sidewalk cafe when a boisterous local, a known troublemaker, was bragging to a woman sitting at his table that he was the "Protector of the night." Standing up, he looked around until he spotted me. "I am going to throw all you Americans out of the Philippines and you will be the first to go." He stated.

I got up off my chair and stood away from the table. His

right open hand was inches from my face when my left hand shot up, grabbed his index finger, and bend it backwards until I heard it snap. He went down to his knees, cried out in pain; his left hand came up to pull my hand away. I shot my right hand up, grabbed his forefinger; I broke it too, leaving him a pile of sobbing wimp, heaped on the floor. Placing a five-peso bill on the table, I left. *I am only twenty years old, what will the rest of my life be like.*

I stopped at the cave one last time. There are more woodcarvings left inside the entrance to the cave. I pulled extra vines to cover the large opening. Maybe the vines will grow thick enough where no one will ever find the entrance. Maybe.

It was eight-thirty when I made it back to the barracks. A quick shower, a change of clothes, and off to BOQ. It was a restricted area for me, but what the hell. No one was in sight when I looked through the glass main door. I silently made my way to the stairwell, up to the second floor, to room 209. A soft knock on the door was answered. "Yes, who is it?"

"Web. Hurry up, open the door."

Sha'Rie stood in the open door wearing a silk kimono. "I bought this in Japan, for a special event." She was untying the front as I closed the door behind me.

"Yes," I spoke softly, "This is very special. You are very special." That night was very special.

A knock on the door woke me. "Wake up call. Time to get up." said a voice outside. The clock on the wall showed five o'clock. Sha'Rie was up, answering "Thank you." to the voice outside the door, and said. "Web, you should hurry up. The flight leaves at six. Did you check your luggage last night?"

"No, not yet, but it won't take me long."

Sha'Rie stepped into the shower. "Do you want to take a shower with me?" She asked through the open door.

"No. I will never make the plane. We can meet at the terminal." My hand pulled the shower curtain back, produced a laughing squeal, a wet shirt, and a warm kiss. "See you in a little bit." My gaze covered her body, from head to foot. "You're gorgeous." A pat on her buttocks, I pulled the curtain shut, dried my hands and face, and left.

Someone called to me while leaving through the main entrance. "Web, what the hell are you doing here?" It was Beset, "Your not allowed in BOQ. You can get into a lot of trouble. What do you think you're doing?"

Laughing, "It's O.K. I dropped off some papers and stuff with a crewmember, to go to Japan. A flight is leaving this morning."

"Oh, then I guess that's all right. When are you transferring out?"

"Today, this morning in fact. I have to finish packing."

"Well, the best of luck. I hope we see each other again sometime." Beset said over his shoulder, as he flagged down a ride.

It took me several minutes to get back to the barracks, another twenty minutes to clean up, and grab my duffel bag. I saw Nick, the squadron driver walk past the door. I called out for him to wait. "I need a lift down to the terminal."

I made it to the terminal with time to spare, but Sha'Rie looked worried, looking at her watch, waiting at the counter with the crew. She was turning away from the group when she spotted me. She turned to the pilot. "Here's the passenger that needs a lift to Iwakuni."

The pilot turned to me. "We're flying empty. You got orders?"

"Sure do." I said, handing a copy over to him.

He read the orders, and handed them to the sailor behind the counter. "Add him to the flight sheet. He'll be traveling with us." Turning back to me. "Take your baggage with you boarding the plane. You can strap it in an empty seat."

Sha'Rie leaned down and picked up my smaller bag. "I'll help him board the plane, and secure everything for take off." As we walked across the tarmac, she said. "I was starting to get a little worried about you. The pilot wanted to take off early, since there were no scheduled passengers or baggage."

As we walked close to the plane, I looked back and saw a group of Igorots, standing in a clearing on the side of the hill overlooking the tarmac, silently watching. Stopping, I acknowledged their presence with a nod of my head and a fast snappy salute. We boarded the plane, and Sha'Rie seated me next to the galley.

In a few minutes, we were airborne. Later, high over the Pacific, I looked down on the clouds, reflecting on my past three years, and it all seemed a dream. I remembered the group of Igorots, standing stiffly erect, clustered together on a knoll overlooking the terminal, watching as I walked across the tarmac. They stood motionless, their long spears at their sides, as if in a silent salute. Leaning back in my seat, thinking what my future may hold for me, I fell asleep, and enjoyed a visit from the past.

Minkoto came to me through a mist, like the puffy cottony clouds that enveloped the aircraft. She told me how her great-grandfather knew from that first night, that I was destined to be his successor. He told me "Even his name, Web Drache, revealed what he will be. Weiss Drache is a direct translation of *White Dragon*, in his ancestral guttural language, German."

She related how proud he was of me. "But he would never tell you himself. He would never reveal his inner self to anyone. To him, that would be a sign of weakness, and a true Jonin, never shows weakness."

A tickling sensation on my neck woke me. "Wake up sleepyhead. What were you saying in your sleep? It sounded Japanese, but I could not understand it. You don't have a girl friend up there do you?"

"No. No I don't," I said groggily.

"Here," She handed me a paper cup. "Maybe some coffee will wake you. We'll be eating soon, and after the crew is taken care of, we can have some time to ourselves."

The coffee cleared my head, pushing back the memory of Minkoto's dream. Later, after Sha'Rie served lunch to the crew, we sat together eating, *enjoying a get to know each other* conversation.

"In a few minutes, half the crew will be napping. Two fly while two sleep. We will have hours to ourselves. A small bunk is behind the galley, for the flight attendants, but we can fit on it."

My back was feeling better. I think the heavy exercise I had been experiencing lately, is loosening it up. While Sha'Rie was finishing up with the flight crew, I helped straighten the

159

galley. I was back in my seat, waiting, when Sha'Rie came out the cockpit door, walked down the aisle, and unbuttoned her jacket. She was in a hurry. I followed her back to the bunk.

The flight could have been longer. The gentle wafting of the aircraft lent an erotic overtone to our doubled up passage. The plane landed at Atsugi Naval Air Station, staying on the ground long enough to refuel. Sha'Rie did not have time to spend with me while on the ground. She was preparing for the next leg of the flight. After boarding the passengers and baggage, we took off, touching down on Iwakuni's runway at dusk.

Chapter
NINETEEN

While I waited for Sha'Rie to come into the terminal, my thoughts were a year earlier. The last time I was at Iwakuni.

I heard, "A penny for your thoughts." I looked up to watch Sha'Rie walk toward me. Walking on solid ground accentuated her sensual walk. The heavy flight bag pulled her shoulder back with its wide strap. Her jacket gaped open, her breast jiggled under the blouse from her crisp stride – her smile warmed me from head to toe.

I took the bag from her, and escorted her out of the terminal to a waiting taxi, where our gear was stored in the trunk. We got into the cab, Sha'Rie gave the driver her address, and we settled back for the ride. "Web." She asked. "What's the matter with your back? You're not walking straight."

"Just look at that." I said. "We have known each other for only two days, and already you've ruined me. Lady, you are going to have to be gentler with me. You should be building up my strength, not sapping my energy dry. I should have a lot more years in me."

"Oh, you men. Is that all you think about?"

"Men." I exclaimed. "Men – you're the one that brought it up – and in more ways than one. I am a poor naive sailor, trying to lead an honest life, and then you took my mind hostage, corrupting it with your wiles and body. What is a poor defenseless guy like me supposed to do, under your bewitching spell? Now you tell me!"

Sha'Rie answered with a swipe to my shoulder, and we snuggled until the cab stopped in front of her apartment building.

The driver helped me carry the luggage, following Sha'Rie into the entrance, up the stairs to her apartment. Setting down the luggage, I paid the driver. She had the door open, stepped inside holding her right arm up in the air with a ballerina twirl, and showed off the interior décor. I put the luggage down; she had her jacket, skirt off, and pulled me through an opening between large screens that separated the main room from the sleeping area. We stripped off the rest of our clothes and laid down on the tatami (a straw mat).

She was insatiable. Later, lying still and resting, I started moaning. She was concerned. "What's wrong? What's the matter?"

Trying to keep a serious look on my face, without laughing, "Now you have really ruined me. I think you broke my back. Standing will be impossible. We may have to lie here forever."

She screamed with laughter, "I'll fix your damn back, just you wait." She jumped on top of me, her hair hung down across my face. Her flowing hair added another dimension to our entangled efforts.

Noises from the street and the light coming in through the

window woke me. Sha'Rie was lying with her head propped up on her hand, staring into my face. She leaned over, kissed my eyes, causing me to close them. "That's better. You look sexier when you sleep." I opened my eyes. "No, keep them shut." She commanded. I like looking at you like this. When you are awake, I look into your eyes, and it is as if you are two people. One is outside. The one you want people to see. But in your eyes, down deep, there is someone, or something else. Something dangerous. I think that is what drew me to you. You are not like other people. You are kind, not demanding, gentle, and yet dangerous. Like a stick of dynamite nestled in a bed of soft cotton, waiting for a spark to ignite you. Are you like that? Is there something else inside? Something waiting to explode?"

Opening my eyes again, I saw a very serious face, not the playful vision of a few minutes before. She was suddenly concerned. "What brought this on? You look worried?"

"I don't know." Said Sha'Rie. "I was watching you sleep, and remembered the feeling I got when staring into your eyes yesterday. It was not a cold feeling, not scary or anything like that, but.... Oh, I do not know, like it is dangerous being around you. You are so calm sleeping, but underneath, something is waiting to happen. Is there a hidden trigger inside you, waiting to set you off? Am I in danger being with you? And could I ever be part of you? I was thinking that I might just be a fling for you, something to play with until the newness wears off, and thrown away to be replaced with another new toy."

I tried to soothe her, tried to interrupt her, she shushed me. "Don't try to stop me from talking." She said. "Let me finish while the words are fresh in my mind. Watching you sleep, thinking that I could transfer to another airline, so we could be together, close to each other. I am not saying we should get married, or anything like that, but be together once in while, to see if we can grow on each other, you know – really fall in love. I think I could really fall in love with you, but that deep feeling I have, a warning I see deep inside you, is holding me off, not allowing me to come too close. Tell me, is this true? Is something there, something that should be holding me off?"

I was surprised at Sha'Rie perceptiveness. It was somewhat scary for me, to have someone analyze me with such accuracy. I was temporarily lost for words, stuttered and stammered.

Taking a deep breath, I told Sha'Rie a little about myself. "Yes, there was once a love of my life. It was not a sexual love, but a young, deeply committed love nevertheless, that was destined never to be, by her murder. I am still recovering from her death. The fact that I avenged her death, killed the men who murdered her and the man who ordered it, helped my healing process. Yes, there are times when it is dangerous to be associated with me, but I hope that is all past me. I am now at peace with myself."

I rolled over, covered Sha'Rie's lips with mine, in a deep, long kiss. Pulling away, I looked into her eyes. "Yes, I do have a deep feeling for you. I would love to develop what we have into something meaningful, seriously." We laid in each other's arms for a long time, not saying a word.

"Web, are you hungry? I know this fabulous little sidewalk cafe not far from here. We could walk to it in no time."

I answered with "Last one dressed, is a rotten egg," as I got up and raced to get my clothes on. Sha'Rie did not move. "I'm not going anywhere, until I shower. And you better not leave without me."

"You have a shower?" I said in mocked surprise. "Pray tell, where?" Turning around in a circle, I repeated myself. "Pray tell, where?"

"Get away from the window. People from the street will see you prancing around with no clothes on. I'll be too embarrassed to go outside." She got up from the bedding, walked to the end of the room, pulled back two sections of panels, and exposed a small bathroom, with a small triangular shower in the corner. There was not enough room to squeeze both of us into the shower, so I sat, watched Sha'Rie's silhouette through the curtain, told her how erotic it was seeing her shower. "Damn it, stop watching, you're making me self conscious. I'll never to able to get done knowing you're watching."

Later, when I showered, Sha'Rie gave me direction. How to bend over, to wash my legs. How to stretch. In what direction to stand. How close to the curtain to stand. When to push up against the curtain. My shower took longer, but she said. "Web, you needed more direction than I did."

The restaurant she took me to was near the approach to the Kentai Bridge. "Have you ever been here before?" Asked Sha'Rie.

"Yes. When stationed here in 1956 and 57. Have you been out to the castle?"

"What castle?"

"The Kentai Castle. Damyo Kikkawa, the feudal lord of

Iwakuni, Hiroyoski Kikkawa built it. There is not a lot left of it, but the countryside is beautiful. Do you want to see it?" I asked.

"When? Now?"

"Yes. We can walk across the bridge, catch a taxi, and drive out to it in no time."

Sha'Rie thought walking over the serpentine ripple of the Kentai Bridge was wonderful. We hailed a cab on the other side. In no time, we were at the castle, viewing the ruins. We walked over the courtyard, through the corridors, and down the steps to the outside door. I was walking slowly, my thoughts several years past.

I noticed a short man in brown dressing, following us. Not telling Sha'Rie, I led her around broken stonewalls to the outside. Putting my finger to my lips, I cautioned her to be quiet. The short man turned to come through the break in the wall when I grabbed him. Putting pressure on his shoulder nerves, I immobilized his arms. "Who are you and why are you following us?" I asked. A quick look at Sha'Rie, I saw her eyes wide open in fear. "Answer me."

He looked straight into my eyes. "Excuse me; I am but a poor man. I thought the lady would have some money in her purse. You are American. You can afford to let me have something of value." His articulated speech too polished to be a common thief. He did not cower, did not bow his head in shame as a common thief would. Instead, he held his head high, proud and defiant.

I spun him around to face the wall, pulled his feet out with my foot, and searched him, finding a long knife hidden in his sash behind him. Ripping his clothes caused Sha'Rie to catch her breath. Pulling the ripped clothing apart revealed a large tattoo on his back. The tattoo of the black hearts. A black star above two facing serpents. I kicked his feet out from under him. He landed on the ground hard, striking the wall with a loud crack, and his head snapped back.

"Who is your master, and what do you want with me? I will not ask again." Sha'Rie's face was ashen. "Sha'Rie, go over and sit on that bench. This will be over soon." She slowly complied with my request. I knelt beside the man on the ground, held his knife to his throat. I said, "I will not ask again. Are you willing to meet your ancestors today?"

"I am to watch the house across the field. The old ones have come together for their annual gathering. I am to identify them, and report to my chunin, (an intermediary), what I have learned. All in the organization know your face. You are our enemy. Anyone who kills you will receive riches and power. You are Ryu Hakujin. You must die."

Luckily, Sha'Rie was too far away to hear the interrogation, but I heard her footsteps in the grass, coming back to us. I pulled the short man back up to his feet, not knowing what to do with him, with Sha'Rie present. She screamed. The short man had a shuriken, a knife normally used for throwing, cleverly hidden in his sleeve by his wrist. I jumped back just in time, from her cry of warning. The razor sharp blade sliced my shirt. My left hand pushed the thrust of his right hand around to his left side, sticking it into his left rib cage, while my right hand, still holding the knife I took from his sash, disemboweled him. He collapsed to the ground, gasping and grunting, his body jerking, convulsing to a stilled state.

Sha'Rie became hysterical, "What did you do? Why did he want to hurt you?" She sat on the ground, covered her face with her hands.

I wiped the blood off my hands with the man's torn clothes, walked over to the nearby stream, and finished washing them. I came back to get Sha'Rie, "Come, we must go. Don't cry you are safe." But her earlier observations of my inner person, the dangerous one, came to mind. I began to question myself, asking if I was an asset, or a liability to society.

Sha'Rie was reluctant to come with me, until I told her we were going to the nearest house. I did not tell her that it was the Kikkawa house, where the old ones were meeting. No one cried out discovery of the body before we reached the house.

I knocked on the door. An elderly man in a white robe, the robe of Izumo, the White Dragon, answered. He recognized me immediately, bowing to me, speaking in Japanese. He called out, and another white robed man approached. He spoke English. He asked us to come in. I could tell Sha'Rie understood they knew me. She kept pulling on my hand, wanting to talk. Seated at the table, he offered fresh fruit and tea.

The man who greeted us in English spoke. "My name is Onon. We did not know you would visit us, or bring a friend. We are honored by your presence, but we are not prepared." Sha'Rie still trembled, but sipped her tea, refused the fruit when offered again.

"Sha'Rie, I must wash myself. I will only be gone a few

minutes. You are safe here. This is my sanctuary." The great stone door opened in the wall. Sha'Rie's eyes were fixed, wide open with pupils dilated, as she stared at the opening. "Don't leave me, please. Web, not by myself. Please Web." She begged.

"This guard is an honored man. You are the first outside the gathering to have seen such as him. You are safer here, now, than anywhere else in the world. I won't be long." I could hear her soft pleading cry as I went through the door, into the first chamber, the door closed behind me.

As soon as the door closed, the lights came on. There were twenty people, all dressed in white, who stopped their activities to bow to me as I entered. Motioning toward the room of knowledge, the doors opened. Stopping to view Minkoto and the old man, still looking as though they were asleep, I said a short prayer for them, and their ancestors. Entering the last chamber was something to behold. Everyone was in the midst of cleaning and polishing. Onon motioned me to sit at a table.

"We have been praying and waiting for your return for a long time. The black hearts have been whittling away at our numbers until we are only half of what we were. They have spies everywhere, identifying us for later execution. All the murders appear to be suicides." A novice ninja brought water and soap for me. A young girl stands by with a towel. I finished washing, and dried myself. A senior ninja approached with an old friend, the singing sword, and handed me a fresh white robe. As I sat down, I laid the sword and robe on the table.

"I am aware of the danger you are encountering. Just minutes ago, the taking of my life was attempted by an evil one.

He failed, and paid with his life. My waiting friend, who would not and does not understand the ways of old, witnessed this thwarted attack. Can she be made to forget all that she has seen?"

"Yes, this will be done as we speak." Onon barked out a few more commands, and people scurried out the door. "We must speak of your protection. We must arrange for a security guard."

I held up my hand to stop him. "No. This would be too obvious. I must meet this challenge alone. My old friend, the Sword of Izumo, will protect me. I must go, but will return when all is done, to return the singing sword to its rightful place."

Onon pauses as if posing a question. "It is written, that the sword only sings when held by the White Dragon and danger is imminent. We have never heard its music. Will you allow us to listen, to allow the followers to hear its music, to more understand the magic it holds, and to reflect the danger at hand?"

I could not think of any reason not to comply with his request. I drew the sword from its white scabbard, held it high, and turned the blade from side to side. Everyone knelt as the humming swelled through the caverns. Their monotone chanting intensified until I sheathed the blade. "I need something to carry the sword in, a rug, or a tube." A long tubular container made to hold a fishing rod was handed to me. It was obviously old, made centuries earlier for this purpose.

Onon escorted me back to the kitchen, where Sha'Rie appeared to be dozing. There was an empty green cup with a golden dragon inlaid on it, sitting on the table in front of her. "She is in a dream state, but can hear and obey you. Take her back to a place that is more familiar to her. When she awakes, she will remember nothing of the violence she saw, or this house of the living and the spirits of the dead."

Sha'Rie was like a zombie. Slow to react to my directions to stand up and walk with me. All she wanted to do was sleep. I managed to get her out to the road, where a taxi driver, who was suspicious of her condition, agreed to take us to the Kentai Bridge.

We stopped at the sidewalk restaurant and the still suspicious driver offered to help get Sha'Rie seated at a nearby table. He leaned over to look closer at Sha'Rie sitting calmly. He was suspicious and concerned, checking her for some dastardly deed I may have done. Laughing, I offered to buy him a cup of tea, and when the waiter came, ordered three, one for each of us.

She was wakening, and focused her eyes on me. "Where are we? I thought we were going to walk around the castle grounds." She saw the bridge. "How did we get here?"

The driver was smiling and nodding his head, as if to say; "Yes, she was O.K."

"Sha'Rie, how do you feel?" I asked. "You scared me the hell out of me back at the castle. All of a sudden, you turned pale, and weak in the knees. I thought it best if I brought you back here. I hailed a cab." I pushed a cup toward her. "Here, this will help clear your head."

The driver, assured that she recovered, thanked me for the tea, and left, looking for new fares.

"Web, something is not right. I don't faint. What really happened back at the castle?" "

"What is the last thing you remember?"

"Going down the steps, and through the door, then

nothing."

"Well, that's where you passed out. Some people helped me get you back up where I could hail a cab. Finish your tea, and I will order us a light lunch. That should help."

As the waiter returned with our order, winding around and through the tables, he passed a man who was watching us. Throughout the lunch, my eye caught his surveillance. Sha'Rie felt better after we ate. "We better go back to your apartment. You could use a nap." Reluctant, she agreed.

"What's that? When did you get it?" She said, noticing the tube in my hand.

"Why it's a souvenir I picked up back by the castle, and you can't see it."

She smiled. "Is it a present for me?"

"Maybe." I said.

The man watching us got up when we left, walked at a fast pace, and positioned himself to follow us. We hailed a taxi, and went down-river to a bridge that carries vehicular traffic to the other side of the river, then to the apartment. The man followed in another taxi, staying two hundred feet behind us.

We stopped at Sha'Rie's apartment, and I thought we had lost him, but on the upper steps, I could look over the crowd of people. He was down the street, watching, writing on a notepad.

I convinced Sha'Rie to take a nap; she finally stretched out and fell into a light sleep. At the window, I saw our stalker across the street, waiting. I found a loose board in the back of her closet, I pried it open, remove the sword and white robe from its tube, ease them into the opening, and push the board back into place.

Now, I will have to find something, a gift, to put in the tube. I was fascinated to watch her, and comforted to watch over her. I looked out the window again. The intrusive man was still waiting. A dark cloud descended on me.

Sha'Rie had been sleeping for over two hours. It was time she woke up. Getting down next to her, I leaned over, and gently kissed her soft lips. Her eyes cracked open and arms came up around my neck, held me tight. Her breath was musky and sweet. Her arms locked my lips to an eager mouth. "Come on. Get up you lazy thing. We have the whole evening ahead of us." I said as she pulled me down to her.

She rolled over on top of me, her legs straddled my hips, and her hands pinned my wrists down to the bedding in mock play. "We're not getting up. You are my prisoner, my sex-slave, and you will do what ever I say. Do you understand? Do you acknowledge your subservient position?" She commanded. I acknowledged, obeyed, and enjoyed.

Preparing her favorite meal, Sha'Rie refused to tell me what it was. She was wearing a robe, standing over a hot plate, stir-frying in a wok when I ask. "When is your room mate flying in?"

"Sometime tonight, or tomorrow morning. Why?"

"Well, it might get a little crowded, especially if she brings a friend. Why don't I get a room for us on base, or at least somewhere else, then you could call her tonight, or tomorrow morning, and tell her where you are. You could just pack an overnighter until everyone decides what they want to do."

"I think she will be expecting me. She's the worrying type,

and would be concerned if she found the room empty."

"Leave her a note. Once we've made arrangements, we can come back, pack what we need, and you can write another note, telling her where you are." I countered.

"Well – all right, but we have to be sure and come back to leave a note." Sha'Rie finished preparing the meal, and served it Japanese style. It was good, and she took delight at my compliments and being unable to identify the meal. Later, we went on base, rented a room, came back to pack and left her roommate, Betty, a note. We left the apartment building by a back door, walked down an alley to get to the main street. It was easier to flag down a cab in the heavier traffic. We dropped our bags off at the base hotel, and then went to a USO show featuring Rita Moreno at the base club. We were tired, and fell asleep as soon as we return to our room.

Chapter
TWENTY

The hotel desk had no phone calls or messages for us in the morning, and a call to the apartment went unanswered. We had breakfast at the base restaurant. Of all the foods in the world, one keeps coming back to the American cuisine for day in and day out breakfast. Pancakes and sausage, butter, syrup, with orange juice and coffee, is hard to beat. Sha'Rie ordered toast, juice and coffee. "I would be fat as a pig if I ate like you. You're a bad influence on me." She said, watching me mop up syrup with the last morsel of pancake.

After breakfast, a phone call to the air terminal verified that Betty's flight came in late last night. A second call to the apartment went unanswered. "We better go out and check. This is not like Betty, not at all." Sha'Rie's face furrowed in frown as she spoke. I too was worried, thinking of the man who trailed us back to the apartment.

We arrived at the apartment and found nothing out of place, but Sha'Rie found Betty's empty flight bag, and her clothes hung neatly in the closet. A man's flight bag sat on the chair, and his suits were hanging with Betty's. Their worn clothes tossed in two piles, the man's pockets turned inside out. Her purse was empty, the contents scattered across the dresser top. Her bed rumpled, slept in, but not made. Sha'Rie commented. "She is extremely meticulous, and would never leave without making the bed, or putting everything away. This is not her. Something is not right."

The showerhead drip caught my attention. I opened the screen and pulled back the curtain, I saw two bodies crammed onto the shower base. Imbedded in the soft flesh of their necks was the wires used to garrote them. Both had been severely tortured. The man and I had the same facial features and body build. Betty had the same build, hair coloring and styling as Sha'Rie, standard stewardess fare.

Sha'Rie started walking toward me. "What did you find Web? What is it?" I held out my hand to stop her. "No, don't come any closer. Go back and call the police." Before I could stop her, she came closer, looked around me, and saw the two in the shower. She fell to her knees, screaming "No, Oh no," and cried out Betty's name. I pulled her to her feet; and guided her over to a chair, where she sat crying. I called the police, told them what we had found, our names, and our location, telling them, "I will stay until you arrive". I hung up the receiver. I returned to the murder scene, and examined them more closely. Their wounds are gruesome. A cursory examination, made without touching them, showed that they suffered burns, cuts, broken bones, fingernails pulled out, and mutilation before they died. Her gag was still in place, but he had partially swallowed his. They had suffered dearly. Tears come as I thought of their suffering.

The police arrived to question in depth. They requested we come to the station to give our statements. I turned to pick up Sha'Rie's purse as they were turning over Betty's body. She had a fresh brand on her shoulder, done before she died. A black star over two facing dragons. I was the reason for their death. Their assailants thought they had killed Sha'Rie and I.

The statements and questions took three hours, going over details of our activities for the past three days, since leaving the Philippines. Standing up to leave, I asked the police lieutenant if he would inform the military authorities, and request security for Sha'Rie. He assured me he would, before ordering us a ride back to the base hotel.

Twenty minutes after we arrived at the hotel, two Marine guards knocked on our door. One stood guard at our door and the other took me to see the base security officer. I went over the same details given to the local police lieutenant. He told me we were not to leave the base, and the guards would escort us wherever we had to go. I requested that a medical doctor see her, and possibly prescribe something to help her sleep, after her traumatic experience. Later that day, a doctor arrived, checked Sha'Rie's vitals, and left a small bottle of sleeping pills. "These are potent. Do not take more than two of them and not for more than two days straight." He warned as he was leaving.

That night, after a little encouraging, Sha'Rie took two of the pills. I checked on the guard at the door. He looked a little startled when the door opened. "Just checking to make sure a guard is posted." I said. Later, laying at Sha'Rie's side, listening to her breathing, and waiting for her deep sleep, I planned how to draw out my adversaries.

Putting on the darkest clothing in my baggage, I opened the rear window, dropped to the ground then made my way to a dimly lit section of the fencing. I climbed to the top of a small tree, swung out, forced it to bow down landing with my feet on the ground, and pushed up letting the recoil of the tree boost me to clear the top of the fence. *It will be another matter to get back on the base.* I thought. It took five minutes to walk a short distance up the road from the main gate before hailing a cab.

A police car was still in front of the apartment as the cab rolled to a stop at the corner. I paid the driver, got out and walked down a back alley, stayed in the shadows, let my sight, hearing and smell take the forefront of my senses, led by my most important detector, my instinct.

All sources of light were avoided; my eyes quickly acquired their maximum night acuity, and focused in on a dark outline, standing in a black entrance, watching the police going back and forth in the brightly lit apartment. I shielded my eyes from the apartment window, and watched him looking up into the bright light.

The lights went out, and I heard the police car drive off. It was late. No one was walking in the street. The man walked slowly toward the front of the building. I scaled the electric pole, jumped over to a low roof jutting out below the apartment window. I silently eased up the unlocked window, entered, and went to the closet. Completely suited with sword in hand I was by the front door when a voice called out. The guard asked who was there, followed by a deep grunt, and a body fell to the floor. The door opened and a shadowy figure entered the darken room.

I switched on the light with my elbow, my sword humming as I held it at ready. The man spun around, reaching toward his left armpit with his right hand. The severed hand still gripped a pistol, as it fell to the floor, dying nerves sent spasms throughout the flesh. He stood in mental shock, looking at his nubbed wrist, his blood running on the floor.

"Go; Go tell your master, ancestors await his arrival and judgment. I am the White Dragon and their doorway to hell." I pushed the light switch off with my elbow, leapt out the window, my body rolled off the low roof, silently landed on the roadway below.

I rushed around the building, toward the front. The man stumbled out the front door, his lower right arm wrapped in his suit coat. Following him through the empty dark streets was easy as he led me to a more fashionable part of town, with larger, more grandeur homes. He was yelling as he entered a walled estate through a gate under an overlooking guardhouse. The lights of the house came on, back lighting the man as he made his way to the front entrance. The guard was watching the man, staggering toward the house, listening to his shouts, as I rushed up the stairwell, slipping behind him. His neck cracked, followed by a dead thud as he fell to the floor.

There was a crowd of armed men that filled cars and drove out the gate under me, followed by darkly dressed men that spilled out into the shadows – Black Ninja. A rope noose dropped from above, down around my head and tightened on my neck. Yanking down with all my strength, I gained enough slack to throw a couple of hitches around a post, allowing me to enlarge the noose in the rope and slip it off. My sword had fallen to the floor, and the second guard a Black Ninja, was flying across the floor with sword in hand. Assurance of an easy kill made him over-confident. I sidestepped, going down to my left, cushioned my fall with my right hand across my chest, and left forearm extended. As my body contacted the floor, my cocked right foot kicked out, against the hurtling guard's knee, breaking it. His hand had twisted up, his face slid along the length of the exposed blade's sharp edge. He was making a whining - moaning sound, as I pulled his sword out from underneath him, the blade made a light scratching sound, as it sliced across the front of his neck bone. The barely audible gurgling stopped after a few moments. I left his blade on the floor, retrieved my own, the white handle glowing in the moon light.

Hearing padded feet of the mercenary guard running up the steps; I stepped out the window, and ran along the top of the wall to a section of trees. I jumped into a clump of bushes on the ground, stretching myself out; I covered myself with leaves and watched my pursuers continue down the wall, followed by another group, hugging the bottom of the wall, searching the ground.

Even under the cover layer of leaves, my white robe was hard to hide in the moonlight. None of the passing searchers detected me, except for the last man, who was thirty feet behind the main group. He was headed straight for the bushes that concealed me. Waiting until his raised foot was poised to step on me, I thrust my sword up, through his stomach, to his neck, severing his vocal cords. He stood rigid for an instant, and then silently and slowly slid down on the blade. There was not enough room to withdraw the blade before he settled down over it. The leaves rustled as I rolled his body over, to pull out the sword.

I followed the searchers looking for me, using their noise to cover my own. Eventually, they reported to the house that I had escaped. The voice inside was furious, calling them incompetent fools. "Go out into the streets. Do not stop searching, and do not return, until you can bring me his head on a spiked display board. Go and bring me his head."

To watch them leave through the main gate was a relief. Two remained in the gatehouse, taking up positions of the two guards dispatched earlier. The man in the house was alone. There are no other voices, shadows, or footsteps. The numerous lights turned off as he leaves each room. Finally, only two rooms remained with light.

Cautiously I made my way up the post under the back roof, toward the brightly lit rooms. Peering through an open window, under a painted shade, I saw a tall, lean man, with an athletic build, muscular – no fat. He walked smoothly across the floor, with balance and grace. His fighting ability should not be taken lightly. His face was drawn, his eyes black as coal. His body stiffened. His head turned to look in my direction.

I stepped through the window, "Yes, I am here." And pushed the shade aside. "I am here to avenge all those that went before me by your evil hand. Nodding to a wall displaying weaponry, "Arm yourself." I commanded.

He kept his eyes on me, his long arm reached out to take

the first weapon available. A long spear. His cold face became more demonic as he smiled. "I have waited many years for this. I have prepared all my life, for this one encounter. A White Dragon has killed many brothers, uncles, and ancestors. I will make you suffer the pain of many deaths before relieving you of your head. I will...."

Interrupting him, I said. "You dumb shit. Your head will be used for a public footstool after you are dead. I did not come here to hear an idiot brag. Prepare to die."

His spear shortened to uselessness after his many lunges. He expended another weapon of chains, and threw several star shaped blades, shurikens, with one striking my left upper arm. As I hesitated to pull it out, he lunged with a sword that was in arm's reach. Barely deflecting the strike away, I lost my firm footing. He saw my unbalanced state, and prepared for a fatal strike.

He was drawing his blade back over his right shoulder, preparing for a massive fatal swing. I threw myself toward him, my body rolling, my singing sword held by both hands, my elbows locked to my side, my blade swung around me like a circular power saw blade, sliced through his head, split him open down into his upper chest. My body rested across his opened chest, my white robe soaked with his blood. It was over.

I took off my robe, pinned it to the wall with the many displayed weapons, so the emblazoned golden dragon looked down on the slain evil one. Going into the next room, I ripped his bedding to bandage my wounds, taking some of his clothing to dress myself. I selected darker clothing. They were not a good fit, to large for my small frame, but I will not be wearing them long.

Tired and weary from combat, I forced myself back to the apartment; changed into my own clothing, taking his clothing and my sword as I leave. I threw his rags into the river as I crossed over the bridge.

It was over and the sword could return to its proper place. It took a while to find a taxi to take me to the Kikkawa home. The driver was hard to convince that it would be worth his while to wait for me. "It will only take me thirty or forty minutes, and I will pay you double for your time." He agreed.

The elderly couple was sleeping sound, their lamp turned down to a night light luminance. My stealth allowed for my entrance to the house and through the secret passage to the cave behind undetected. I held the sword high above my head and it remained silent. Our mission was done. I visited Minkoto; she still looked as though she were sleeping. I told her all of what happened, knowing that she was already aware of the events. It felt good to be able to speak of what happened. I knew she was listening, in Tokoyo-No-Koni (The eternal land of the gods) with her ancestors, with Izumo, Chinju-Same (The god of peace and protection), and all the other deities.

I said good-bye to Minkoto and the old man, swearing to them that I would honor them, to carry on as best I could. Going back to the great room, I returned with a cup of sake, toasted them, relayed the honor I felt in knowing them and able to follow their traditional teachings. Looking around to ensure everything is in its proper place, I left, taking new uniforms, one white - emblazoned with gold thread, and one black - for stealth and invisibility. I silently left the way I came - undetected.

The taxi was still waiting for me. The trip to the base was with anxiety as night was waning. I managed to get onto the base, after finding a tree limb jutting out across the top of the fence; I pulled myself up a pole, that someone was refinishing, and into our room. Reaching back through the window, I lifted the pole off the ground, and dropped it back onto the yard.

Chapter
TWENTY
ONE

It was dawn when I stepped out of the shower and bandaged my wounds, taping them with Band-Aids found in the medicine cabinet. I just slipped into bed when a knock on the door roused me. Looking over, Sha'Rie still looks zonked, pulled on a pair of pants, and a shirt, and answered the door. Two marine guards, the security lieutenant, and the local Iwakuni police lieutenant, were waiting.

The base security officer said. "Drache, it seems that your friend's threat is over. The head of the local Japanese Mafia has been killed at his home, and according to Lieutenant Yomatido, it was at his direction that the couple was murdered in your friends apartment."

"So you think she is out of danger?" I asked.

Lieutenant Yomatido picked up the conversation. "Yes. There is evidence that he was killed by another element. A legendary secret society, headed by a man called the White Dragon. Their history goes back over two thousand years, and their presence is rarely visible. They appear to be a last resort involvement, flexing their muscle, when others have gone too far. We would have not known of their current involvement, except the killer bragged, hanging a distinctive robe on the wall over the dead body." The base security officer added. "We will be pulling the guard detail back in."

Lieutenant Yomatido continued. "You two can return to your apartment, if you want too. We are done with it."

"Thank you for letting us know. I know Sha'Rie will also appreciate knowing, but I doubt she will ever want to sleep in that apartment again." I said.

They let me know they would be available for any additional information, if needed, and Sha'Rie could come to the police station to pick up any personal effects that may have been picked up for evidence. The closing door woke Sha'Rie. The sheets rustled from her movement.

"Sha'Rie, Good morning. It's all over. The killers are dead." I said, walking over to the bed.

Sitting up in bed, the sheet slipped down to her waist. Pursing my lips to blow a soft wolf whistle produced a modest upward glance, and a big smile. "Does this?" She said, gesturing to herself with both hands, "Deserve a compliment like that."

"That and more." I said, sitting down on the bed beside her.

"Web, what happened to you? You're hurt." Her hand went to my wounds, making me visibly wince.

"I went down for a cup of coffee last night, after you fell asleep, tripped on the stairs, and busted myself up a little. The little sleep I had last night left me with a drowsy head. It is full of cobwebs. How are you feeling? Are you rested?"

"Yes, and feeling a lot better than you look. I had a lot of weird dreams last night. I dreamt you were a martial arts master, there were killer Ninja's, and garbage like that. I do not normally dream trash like that. None of it made any sense. I'm hungry. I will eat anything within reach. If I do not get breakfast soon..., Gggrrrrr." She nibbled playfully at my ears, neck, shoulder, chest, pulled me down flat on the bed, and worked her way down to my toes.

"O.K., leave some for the undertaker. We'll get breakfast. On or off base?"

"Surprise me."

"Off base. I'll order something for you that is out of this world." Sha'Rie showered; we dressed, and went out to a restaurant in town by the RTO.

I pushed aside the menu handed me, looked Sha'Rie in the eyes, I said. "This will be a breakfast from the imperial kitchens. Do not ask what it is until after we eat, and only if you like it. I hope you are really hungry." Looking up at the waiter, I ordered. "Aka-Shiro Miso-shitate Kyokoimo Shiitake (Soup of red and white beans, sliced shiitake mushrooms, and spices); Udo Karashizuke (an asparagus like vegetable in a mustard sauce); Tai-kazaboshi Hanasansho (sea bream fillet, broiled and peppered); Imadegawa-tofu Uchi-saya Nori-an (prepared fish between tofu, covered with white sauce,). Can your kitchen prepare my order?"

"Hai (Yes)" replied the waiter, a large toothy smile acknowledged his approval.

It took a while, but when the first course came, Sha'Rie concentrated on the presentation, then the aroma, and then tasted the soup, accented with the side vegetable, softened the furrows in her forehead with an appreciative smile. "What's next?" She asked.

"Amah" (wait) I said." A nod toward the waiter brought the second course, the sea bream.

Laughing, Sha'Rie had a surprised look on her face. "Fish, fish for breakfast. I have never had fish for breakfast."

"Hey, I said no comments until you have finished the meal. Remember? Try it."

Again, the food produced a smile on her face. "Hhhhmmmm. That is good." Shaking my head no, she responded. "O.K., O.K."

My nod brought the last course, the fish and tofu under a Japanese style white sauce, served with a green tea flavored with freshly squeezed mandarin juice.

"More fish," exclaimed Sha'Rie. "I know, keep my comments to myself." After tasting the food, she said" You are a devil. You must like fat women. Where did you learn all this?"

"From reading and from trying different foods. I thought you would like this."

"I ate like a lumberjack. I'm stuffed. I won't be able to eat another thing for the rest of the day. You are a horrible man Web. Only a devious mind would concoct a breakfast like this. We'll have to do this again, but in another year or so. It will take me that long to work all this off."

"Would you be surprised, if I told you there is no fat, very low in calories, and everything in the meal is good for you?" Trying to put on my best lecherous look, I whispered. "This is really an aphrodisiac meal, meant to be totally worked off, in an absolutely most natural way, before the next day's dawning."

Trying to stifle a laugh, choking, she sputtered. "Web Drache, you impossible. I'll never know what it is in you that attract me."

"Well." I said. "You admit you're attracted to me. Is there anything else about me you like?" Feeling a shoeless foot lock behind my leg, sliding up and down, from knee to ankle, almost made me drop my tea.

"Yes, there is something else I like, something I like very much, something only you can do best." Her look made me put my teacup down, reach out and pickup her outstretched hand, lift it to my lowering head, gently kissed her palm, and massaged it with the tip of my tongue.

"I do what I can. I try." My mind flashed back to an earlier view of Sha'Rie, one that provoked a wolf whistle. "We should go back, and lie down for a while, rest a while before we check out of the hotel. Don't you think?"

A husky "Yes" floated back from across the table.

That afternoon we checked out of the hotel and looked for a new apartment for Sha'Rie. Instead, we found an older, more traditional house. The rent also paid an elderly couple, to maintain the house and grounds. They lived on the grounds, in a small gatehouse.

Going to the old apartment, Sha'Rie became very melancholy, softly crying. "What's wrong?" I asked.

"I was thinking about Betty, and her friend. I do not think I can go back into that place. I cannot believe I will never see her again. We were best friends. We would tell each other our secrets, trade flights, and share what we liked about each other's latest heartthrob. We were like sisters."

We arrived at the apartment. It took a lot of urging to get her through the door. "You have to move your clothes to the house. You cannot buy all new clothes. Come on now."

She opened the door, and we step in. The room was spotless. All her clothes were in the right place and Betty's things were gone. Shipped back to her parents, I guess. There was a note from the charter airline, asking Sha'Rie to give them a call, when she felt up to it. The police lieutenant indicated on the slip, that he took the message while he was here.

"I might as well get it over with," She said. "I'll call them." I heard her say "Yes." a lot during the conversation. Her voice became lower, and slower. "Yes, I understand. I'll be there."

Turning to face me, she had tears running down her cheeks. "They want me to take a flight out tonight. There is a spot on a chartered Frisco to Tokyo flight they want me to fill. Staying busy will help me, they said. They did not give me a choice."

We held each other in a tight embrace, comforting each other for a long time. I called the house, telling them Sha'Rie transferred to a different position, and could not complete the lease. We stayed in the apartment; I told her my home address and telephone number, my new address at Newport, RI. She gave me the address and telephone number of the airline headquarters, where I could always get a message to her.

"We will not forget each other. We will find each other later." All our promises were sincere, but sounded hollow. We both knew what the chances are of establishing a common place to meet, to rewarm a heart allowed to cool, but we promised to try. That night I kissed Sha'Rie good-bye, a painful separation, and my heart was heavy as I watched her plane take off, disappearing into the darkness of the night. I did not tell her that I tried to get on her flight, but failed. It was overbooked. Purposely not attempting to visit the old Kikkawa home, I left Iwakuni the next morning, getting a military flight to Travis AFB, Calif.

Chapter
TWENTY
TWO

The plane touched down at Travis SFB, California on June 11, 1960, and two days before I turned twenty-one. Everywhere I looked appeared strange and foreign. The women wore outlandish make-up, with green or bright red hair. Their language was a gibberish of slang. I felt estranged from my own culture, or rather; the people I thought were from my culture.

I bought an American Airline ticket to St. Louis, and then a bus home. Getting off at the bus stop in Highland, Illinois was like waking in another time, a period of peace, void of turmoil and pain of loss. As I waited by the steps of the local drug store for my duffel bags to be unloaded, I looked up and down Broadway, the main thoroughfare through town, looking for a familiar face.

There were smiles of recognition, but I could not piece names and faces together. I felt that so much had happened to me in the past four years, that my mind overflowed, and that part of my memory just evaporated, dissipated into a place unreachable by me. It was an anxious moment, trying to get a grip to the door of my past, and not knowing if I wanted to know what was on the other side.

Two young, well-mannered children, a boy and girl were sitting on the steps of the drugstore. "Who are you?" I asked.

The young boy replied. "I'm Travis William, and this is my cousin."

The girl cut in. "My name is Dyllan Adele. We're cousins, and we are waiting for our mommy's to come out."

Travis William continued. "Yeah, we're spending the day together, and later, if we are good and don't fight, will get a big ice cream sundae, or a milkshake, or what ever we want."

"Well, I bet you'll get what you want. What flavor do you like?"

With enthusiasm, the boy said. "I like Chocolate."

The girl, not to be outdone said. "I want strawberry and marshmallow." Two lovely young mothers came out of the drugstore, and down the steps. "Mommy, mommy." the two children shouted in unison. The young women smiled at me, as mothers do when strangers are complimentary of their children.

"Come on kids, we have a lot to do yet before your daddy comes home." Said the darker haired, first woman.

"Yes, we have to get done early, so you have time to eat your ice cream." Said the lighter haired second woman. With little hands held safely in their mother's hands, they skipped down the sidewalk, talking to each other about subjects that excite young minds.

Doug, an old friend, and past schoolmate approached and offered to take my baggage home. "I'll drop it off later. I have a couple of things to take care of uptown." We talked for a few minutes, threw my gear onto his back seat, and agreed to meet later for a few beers.

Walking home from uptown took fifteen minutes; Highland is not a large community. The walk felt good after being crammed in the bus from St. Louis. June's early summer sun warmed my face, as I turned south off Broadway, onto Olive Street.

I felt strangely detached, out of tune with the hum of activity around me. It was like visiting a place after reading all the information available on it. You know all about it, but you are not part of it, no matter how hard to try to enmesh yourself. I forced these alien thoughts out of my mind as I approached my family home, and my pace quickened in anticipation of rejoining my family's protective embrace.

My warm reception removed any anticipated awkwardness. Some were trying to update me on people, places and things, while others questioned me about life in the Navy and foreign lands. We talked all afternoon, until Doug brought my duffel bags.

He waited while I opened the bags, passing out presents and souvenirs that I brought from the Far East. Doug drove me to his favorite restaurant, where the current love of his life waitressed. I ordered a hamburger, fries and milk. Fresh food was still a novelty to me, after years of frozen and/or reconstituted food and drink. Doug smiled, as he watched me gulp down the food and shook his head as I washed it down with the glass of milk. "I thought we were going to have a few beers, not milk. I bet that hamburger went down before you could taste it. There was no way you could have." He said between his chuckles. We had made plans to go out on the town that evening, but ended up staying in the restaurant, and talking until it closed. Doug drove me home and before getting out, we agreed to paint the town red, at our first opportunity.

It was midnight, and I still felt like walking around town, to enjoy the good feeling of returning to my roots, and reclaiming the memories tied to this town. It was three in the morning before I found myself ascending the steps to the front door. The bed made for me, I showered off the dried sweat and grime from the trip home. I got into bed and immediately fell asleep. The okina (old man) and Minkoto must have realized that my need for rest was greater now, than a nurtured love, and guidance from a dream's visit.

I slept in late the next morning. The smell of fresh coffee and hot pancakes was enough to rouse the dead. Fresh clothes and filling my belly with home cooked food, made me feel more vigorous and alive than I had felt in a long time. After eating, my Mom and I sat talking for hours. She could sense my detached state from home life; I began to project a more confident outlook.

Later, I went to the park, to the tree where I, on an earlier military leave, pondered my differences from others who did not change, but maintained continuity, a thread of contact, an attachment to their brood nest. I let my mind drift, and it carried to where it always went, back to Iwakuni, back to where my life's abrupt change began.

When I returned home, Mom told me that Doug called.

"He said to be ready at six." She said. "And it's almost six now." Smiling, I thanked Mom, showered and changed clothes for the evening. Doug was right on time, out front in his old Oldsmobile, a two door hardtop, radio blaring, and chomping at the bit, waiting.

I was ready for a little diversion. Getting into his car I asked, "Where we going?"

"Well, what do you want to do? Drinking or women?" he countered, laughing.

"Both." We left with tires screeching in billowing smoke, leaving the telltale mark of young men in a hurry - black peel marks on the pavement.

Doug was still updating me on who did what; who married whom, who had whose children, and whose dreams were shattered by the mistake of bad choices and chance. We turned into a parking lot of a nightclub, below the Collinsville bluffs. I could tell by the music vibrating through the car windows, that this was not a laid-back, lemonade social.

Doug shouted, "This place will blow your socks off." above the blasting music and the overpowering volume of people trying to talk. My first instinct was to find the quietest corner, and hide from the crowd, but Doug yelled, "Hey, I know those two girls," and led me to a table near the dance floor, occupied by two young women. I felt nervous and out of place. The writhing masses on the dance floor, caught up in rhythms and contortions, reminded me more of pygmy fertility rites, than dance steps of a modern Western culture.

Facial expressions communication was easier than trying

to talk. I spent the next twenty minutes, smiling and nodding my head yes. I had no idea what the questions were. The girl near me, Patsy, stood up and held her hands out to me, gesturing toward the dance floor. I returned a questioning shrug and joined her on the floor. Her smooth movements, in rhythm with the music, made me feel like I had two left feet, tone deaf, and trying to walk a straight line through a forest of stumps. Looking over at Doug, I saw him enjoying himself, at ease in his own environment. Seeing my distress, Patsy nodded to the side of the dance floor, took my hand, and pulled me toward an exit sign above a hallway, and through a door into the fresh evening air. We were in a different parking lot, off the side of the building. "Thanks" I said, coughing from my smoke filled lungs.

"I could tell you were uncomfortable. You're not from around here are you?" asked Patsy.

"No."

"Well, where are you from?" Before I could answer, she said." You sure don't talk much do you?"

"Well, actually – Yes I do" I stammered "But, I'm still trying to catch my breath from that workout. That's not what I'm use to." A crowd of people pushed through the door, almost knocking us down. "Let's move over there, out of the way." I said, taking her hand and walk to a more isolated area of the parking lot.

We sat on a ledge of a planter wall and talked. I told her I was away, in the Navy for the past four years, places stationed, and that I was on my way to Newport, RI. She told me about herself. She was from Collinsville and worked as a secretary at a law firm. She found life very boring, and that she would like to travel as I have. We discussed likes and dislikes. A group of couples walked toward us. The men were tough looking, strutted with beers in hand, pushed people aside, out of their way. The girls were dressed as if advertising themselves for rent.

"Get out of my way," the tall man at the front of the group growled. He was five feet away, when Patsy, sounding alarmed, asked me to take her inside. I was trying to accommodate her, but not fast enough. "Damn it, I said move." the tall man said.

"Come on." Patsy begged. I turned toward Patsy, and took her by the hand.

A two handed push, knocked me to the ground. "Punk! Move when I say move." The mocking voice said. I looked up and saw Patsy was scared. The group surrounded us, looked down at me with superior grins, taunting me with "Do you want to make something of it, Punk!" I picked up my glasses, and started to pick myself up when he shoved me over again. "Well, answer me Punk!" Looking up to Patsy, I saw she was frightened.

"No." I said, attempting to stand again.

"Don't get smart, Punk!" The tall man left saying "Dumb-shit Punk." walking over to a group of cars in a far corner of the lot. The entourage followed, leaving comments as they pass - "Dumb-shit, Punk."

"Come on, let's go back in." begged Patsy. I followed her, brushing the dust off my clothes, back into the club. When we got back to the table, the musicians were taking a break, while quieter canned music came through the speakers.

"Where have you two been." Said a grinning Doug. "I had no idea you would get along, sooo good, sooo soooon."

"No." Snapped Patsy, irritated by the tone of Doug's voice. "We damn near got killed. That wild Cheops gang was trying to pick a fight with Web. We're lucky he didn't talk back to them."

"The Cheops', boy they're bad news, Web. What the hell did you say to them?"

"Nothing, just nothing, I didn't want to make anything out of them pushing me around. I guess I did not give them an excuse to get physical with me. Nothing happened," I sighed. Patsy did not pay much attention to me after our encounter with the *gang* outside.

Doug and I sat at the table with his new acquaintance and Patsy for the next hour. I excused myself, to go the men's room. When I was done, I went out through the side door, to vent my lungs of all that smoke. I needed fresh air again. Outside, I looked around. The Cheops gang and their cars were gone. I was by myself in the lot; looked at the clouds in the sky threatening rain. A car tore into the lot, slid sideways with locked brakes, gravel flying in all directions. I tried to wave the dust away from my face with my hands. That damn tall guy and two of his sidekicks came pouring out of the car, laughing and yelling. They stopped when they saw me sitting.

"Well, if it ain't the Punk. Didn't learn his lesson before." He said, looking down at me. "What do you think guys, should we teach him a lesson." "Yeh, Yeh" came from his two cronies. I sized him up. He was a solid five feet, ten inches tall, muscular with a slender build, black curly hair, heavily tanned, and a mean snarling twisted mouth.

I told them. "Now I don't want any trouble," which

provoked boisterous laughter.

"Get him up and over there," grunted the tall guy, nodding over to where their cars had been parked earlier. The two yanked me to my feet, and pulled me over in the dark. I was reluctant to go with them, but did not resist. Reaching the corner of the lot, they turned me around to face the tall guy, and again held me by the arms. "Now we're going to teach you to respect your betters, Punk!" The tall guy, their leader, backlit from the parking lot lights, his silhouette sharply detailed, as he pulled his right arm back to throw a punch at me. The two restraining men tightened their grip on my arms in anticipation of the swing. My relaxed stance turned rigid. I pulled the man on my left, over and in front of me. Their leader cried out in pain, as his fist crunched into the hard skull of the man I pulled. The hard skulled man that was holding my left arm went down to his knees. Hands on his head, suggested he was suffering from a massive, chronic migraine. I brought my left hand up, with thumb extended upright, into the soft-fleshed area between the jaw and throat of the man still holding my right arm. His grip locked tight, until the message of pain reached his Neanderthal brain. His hands went to his throat, tried to alleviate the painful cramping that locked up his muscles.

I slowly turned to their leader who was standing at half crouch, cradling his right hand in his left. "What lesson were you going to teach me?" I said, mocking his earlier condescending words.

"You son-of-a-bitch" he replied. "I'll show ..." And attempted to connect with a feeble swing of his left hand.

I grabbed his arm with my left hand, pulled him off

balance, and as he fell over my extended foot, accelerated his fall to the dirt by pushing down on his back with my right hand between his shoulder blades. His perfect three-point landing in the dirt stirred up a cloud of dust that gently blew away in the mild June breeze. He lay, gasping for breath. His snore-like labor for air, accompanied by the groaning from a headache, and the rattle of restricted air from throat muscles clenched up, sounded like an animalistic attempt to keep time to a musical rendition.

I brushed the dust off myself, returned to the building and sat down with Doug. "Where are the girls?"

Doug looked a little put out. "Man, where the hell you been? Susan wanted to leave with me and you were nowhere around. Patsy was completely bummed out, and talked Susan into leaving with her."

"I'm sorry Doug. I was talking to some guys out in the parking lot."

Doug looked down and saw my glass was empty, threw down the last few swallows of his beer. "Let's get out of here."

Doug was quiet on the drive to my house. He pulled up to the curb, and looked at me, "I think Susan likes me. She gave me her phone number when I asked her to go out with me. I like talking to her. She is nice, but that Patsy, she is a cold fish. Do you two have anything in common?"

"She's nice, but she doesn't know what she's looking for, yet. She knows I will be leaving soon, and is looking for someone who will be around. I don't think she is looking for someone like me. Not Macho enough."

Doug looked at me. "Hell. Isn't anything wrong with you."

Laughing I said "Stay away from me; I don't go in for that kinky stuff."

Doug started laughing – "You know what I mean."

We did not make any definite plans, just assumed we would go out again in the next few nights. The rest of the week was uneventful. I spent my time browsing around town, talking to old friends, gradually feeling, once again, that I had a place to call home. A real hometown. Friday afternoon, I walked into the drugstore for a soda, and saw Patsy.

Her eyes lit up when I walked in. Getting off her stool, she rushed over to me, excited. "What did you do? The Cheops gang is looking for you, they're dangerous. They're out for blood. You must have done, or said something to them." Patsy kept talking, cautioning me of their persistent and vengeful history. She finished with a look of bewilderment, as my look did not reflect a level of concern desired of her warning.

Smiling, I said. "I'm not too worried. People can only bully you if you let them." She looked at me with tight lips. "You're a fool not to take them seriously, they'll hunt you down. They have done it before." She turned and returned to her stool, while I followed and sat next to her. "Do you mind if I join you?" "No, sit down, it's a free country." She said.

It was a little clumsy. She did not make it easy to talk with her, not making eye contact, and giving short replies to my attempts to engage her in conversation. "I really enjoyed your company the other night at the club, and appreciate you trying to teach me those dance steps."

"That's O.K. Anytime." Came her monotone reply. I finished

my drink, stood up, and said, "See you around".

As I walked off, I hear a faint reply behind me. "Yes, see you around." I let the whole incident leave my mind as I got outside, under the warm balmy June sun.

I started to avoid groups of people, not wanting conversation with questions of my time overseas. It was too cumbersome trying to gauge my answers. They could not visualize the Kentai Bridge and Castle, or the everyday customs of the Japanese culture. They did not believe me when I told them of my visit with the pygmy tribes and their head chief, or my visits with the headhunters, the gold and silver mines of Baguio, or how the people there were good human beings – not savages.

Of course, I did not reveal to them my activities of the night, or my acquired responsibilities, but casual observations that a tourist, or visitor might make. "You did not really stay at a pygmy camp. You were never in a headhunters hut. You never saw..." was their comments to my stories of travel. Someone calling me a liar was not comfortable for me. It was easier to maintain a quiet profile, stating that I had spent the last four years in the Navy, nothing more, just a dull pencil pusher killing time.

My days were more and more sitting under that huge oak tree at Lindendale Park, thinking of Minkoto and times past. I knew that this was not mentally healthy, dwelling in the past so much, but I could not force myself into any other activity.

One afternoon, walking back home from the park, a carload of the Cheops gang came screeching to a halt, sliding off the road onto the shoulder, next to where I was walking. Five young men piled out, yelling and hollering. They were as rowdy in the daylight, as they were that evening I last saw them. They were pumping themselves up with self-importance. I did not want to contribute toward their self-imposed upward spiral, and did not show any emotion, or cause for alarm.

They surrounded me. "Hey Punk. You're coming with us Punk. You better give your soul to God, because your ass is mine, Punk." They were spouting all the quips they could remember from the rebel-rousing movies they watched. I went along with their pulling me over and into the back seat of their car. They were whooping and hollering as they drove me down the hill and around the backside of the park, where it was secluded. They drove off the road, under a tree canopy cover, and piled out of the car, taking me with them.

They encircled me, taunting me they thought, with words of what they were going to do to me. "Beat the hell out of you, and hang you out to dry." "Strip you naked, and throw me out on the town square." "Tear you limb from limb, and take me back into the woods so far you won't be able to hear the hounds howl," All the old clichés.

I stood in their midst, relaxed, looking at their eyes. The tall one, their leader, was tired of their words having no effect on me. "Come on guys, he's no fun." They come in closer, shoving me from one side of the circle to the other. I knew the time had come to put a end to this. They were overgrown kids and I should not hurt them. They need guidance, and guidance they would get. As the next one was cocking his arms to shove me back through the circle, I kicked him in the groin, and as he bent over in pain, I took his outstretched arm and spun him off his feet, over into the group on the other side of the ever-tightening circle. They went down like bowling pins.

Two were still standing, facing each other. I motioned for them to come to me. "Come, come closer," I said. Their tall leader came at me with vengeance. His foot struck out in a kick. Stepping aside, I grabbed the heel of his shoe and pushed it up, continuing the arc into a half-circle. He screamed in pain, (I remembered that scream from a couple of weeks earlier), as his legs were spread far beyond their limit. He lay on the ground crying, holding his groin. I turned to the last one, and looked into his eyes. "Sit, or would you like a lesson on self defense."

He was on the ground before I finished the sentence. I pulled three of the men over to the fifth, leaving their leader's pain to ease before aggravating his muscle spasms with movement.

"Look guys. I told you before; I do not want any trouble. You should never mess around with anyone until you know who, and what your adversaries are. I'm a patient person, and I don't like violence." The moans became quieter behind me. I turned and saw the tall one trying to pull his feet under him, squatting. "Drag yourself over here with the others, so I can see you." I said, pointing to his group. With a couple of yips of pain when he overstretched his muscles, he slowly made his way to the rest of his group.

"You people need a purpose in life. Do any of you have jobs?" They all shook their heads no. "Well get one."

The last kid that I stared down asked. "Where did you learn to do that?"

I laughed, "Overseas. Join the military, you'll learn."

"Are you a Marine?"

"No" I said, "I'm a sailor, just a pencil pusher. In fact, the service is where you should be. You better go down and test for enlistment. Give one of the recruiters a call, they'll be more than happy to accommodate you." They were all a little more attentive, and the tall one is obviously no longer in pain. "Guys, I don't want to go through this again with you. Do you understand?"

One of them mumbled back "Yes."

"I said, do you understand?" shouting a little for emphasis. I heard a resounding "Yes" reply. "Now, get up and drive me back to where you found me."

The short trip back to the field treats me with a new respect, or for my abilities. I had found new friends that did not voice disbelief. After this encounter, it seemed they were always around, less boisterous, more attentive, and more polite to others.

If I was walking, they would slow and ask if I wanted a lift. If I was sitting on a bench in the park, they stopped and talked. If I was at a store or a tavern, they offered to buy my drink.

One day, while talking with the group in the park, Patsy walked by with a look of disbelief on her face, but did not stop to talk or to greet me.

Doug and I went out together a few more times, but he wanted me to get a date so I can double with him and Susan. I was getting a little eager to go on, and made plans to continue to Newport, Rhode Island. My next duty station.

Chapter
TWENTY
THREE

My transfer was to the Officer Candidate Schools staff, Naval Schools Command, Newport, Rhode Island. We staffed the pre-commissioning training of the OCS (Officer Candidate School), NROTC (Naval Reserve Officer Training Corps), LDO (Limited Duty Officer), and Navy Nurses. It was boring work, very repetitious and had little challenge. I met Paul Nethrum at a party. He was the curator of the local university museum. Learning of my military service in the Far East, he told me of a strange and rare sword his museum recently acquired. "It is a long, slightly curved, and slender weapon, very old, and made before the technology to manufacturer it was known. There are only two known swords like this in the world. The university has one, found in an ancient armory, entombed in a cave on the border of Tibet. The other is incomplete; its blade never finished. The Tokyo museum found it while excavating near a castle, called Kentai, in Japan. There is a dragon engraved on the blade, with ..."

I surprised myself having involuntarily interrupted his

sentence, blurting out "with a sun over his head." Instantly, I realized the mistake. "Oh, I'm sorry for interrupting you." With a look of shock on his face, Paul asked, "What do you know about these swords?"

I tried to divert the subject by casually and with an air of disinterested in my response. "Oh, just some legends I heard from the elders of a fishing village, on the coast near Iwakuni."

"I would like to hear more of these legends." said Paul, and asked Jim, our host, if he had a recorder so he could tape me. Trying to remove the foot from my mouth, I tried to excuse myself due to the late hour, and my long drive back to the base.

Paul was insistent, asking me if I could visit him at the university. He said he had to hear the legends, and he would arrange for me to see the sword, something very few people had seen. "Would Sunday at 2:00 p.m. be convenient for you Web?"

"Yes, I replied."

"Do you need directions?"

Picking up my jacket while walking toward the door, I said, "I'll find it."

Sunday morning, and I still could not decide what I was going to say, or how to get out of going to the university. I started to call Paul several times, but not being able to piece together a credible excuse, always ended hanging up. I had to go.

It was late August and the foliage at the university had not started turning to their fall colors. The campus was very peaceful and quiet, but it was Sunday. The map on the directory board at the entrance accurately led me to the museum.

Entering the main doors, the guard stopped me and said

that the building was not open on Sundays. "I'm here to see Mr. Nethrum. My name is Drache, Web Drache."

"Mr. Nethrum said to direct you to his office. Go down the left corridor and to the fifth door on the left, Mr. Drache."

The building was overly warm; I took off my jacket and draped it over my arm, and followed the guard's directions.

Knocking on the fifth door, Paul responded, "Come on in." The room looked more like an artifact warehousing area than an office. Paul sat behind an old abused oak desk. "Glad you could make it. Come in and pull up a chair." I walked in and put my coat across the back of the chair.

On the desk, in a long lacquered box lined with white cloth emblazoned with the golden Dragon Izumo, was the sword. I was mesmerized. My eyes and mind thousands of miles away, back to the Kikkawa home, visions of Minkoto and the old man. I felt my eyes tear up and my throat tightened. I would use the chill in the air to explain my appearance, if asked. I was weak with emotion. I struggled to maintain my composure and balance, grabbed the chair and sat down.

Paul's words were coming through my mind's curtain. "Web, what do you think of it?"

He did not notice my emotional state. I stood up and leaned over close to the sword mumbling, "It's beautiful, can I hold it?"

Paul was a little apprehensive, "Well I don't ..." The telephone rang and Paul answered. "Excuse me Web, the guard called. Someone is at the front security desk, asking for me. Put on these gloves to examine the sword and try to remember everything you can about those legends. I'll be right back."

Reaching down, I carefully opened the ties with both hands, remove the sword from the box, and raise it to my forehead. The old man's words were coming out of my mouth "with heart, mind, and body, I will protect. I am yours to command."

The sword was glistening in the light. There were no nicks, scratches or wear. The engraving was bright and sharp. This was not a used weapon. I grasped the handle in my right hand. The white sharkskin handle molded in my hand was reliving an old memory. "We meet again, old friend." I held it high over my head. The vibration and humming from the sword brought tears to my eyes.

Energy pulsed through my body, completing the connection between my mental and physical being. Paul's shouts and the sounds of a scuffle alerted my attention. A shot echoed through the corridor. With the sword still in hand, I jumped to the door, opened it, and leaned out, to look down the long corridor. Two dark figures turned into the passage. I carefully eased the door shut and stood at the wall, waiting.

Two dark silhouettes appeared through the frosted glass pane. The door slowly opened. A revolver, followed by two Japanese men, cautiously and deliberately entered the room. The broad side of the sword came down on the hand holding the revolver. The gun dropped to the floor. "Kimi wa dare desu ka?" (Who are you?) I said. The two figures jumped to the other side of the room.

Humming filled the air. "Watashi ne, sono himitsur shitte

iru no" (Listen, I know the secret behind that) said the second man. The first man eased up from a crouched position and asked, "Who are you?"

"Ninjutsu Hakujin, Ryu Hakujin Watakushi Wa. (White Ninja, I am the White Dragon,)" I growled. They looked at each other, and drew long curved knives and encircle me. "Come to me, your ancestors await you," I said, looking into their eyes.

The sound of a police car siren drowned out the hum filling the air. One man ran past me to the door. I swung the sword to my left, dropping to a stooped posture, when a knife thrust from the other man, sliced through my shirt and the flesh on top of my left shoulder. The wound was not deep, a flesh wound, but bleeding heavy. My hesitation from the wound was enough for both to escape. I ran out the door and looked up and down the corridor. It was empty. Quickly I returned the sword to the lacquered box, and knotted the ties. I tore off my shirtsleeve to tie around the wound and slipped on my jacket.

Going to the front entrance, I saw Paul and the guard on the floor unconscious. They had some nasty looking bumps on their heads. Two policemen come in with guns drawn. "What's happening? Who tripped the alarm?"

I told them, "I don't know", and asked that they call for an ambulance. Paul was coming around, mumbling about the two men wanting to see the sword. The tall policeman said "What sword?"

Paul looked at me and asked if the sword is O.K. and I said "yes." The tall police officer again asked what was going on. I told him what I knew, describing the two Orientals, that they rushed past the door and down the corridor. Paul was getting up off the floor, then sat in the guard's chair.

He stated that when he arrived at the front entrance, the two Orientals were arguing with the guard, wanting to enter the museum, wanting to see the sword. It was then that the guard pushed the silent alarm button. When the Orientals saw what he did, a struggle started. They pulled out two pieced clubs connected with a short chain. He heard the gunshot when hit on the head and lost consciousness.

The shorter police officer checking the guard said, "He's not wounded, but his gun is missing".

I told him "Oh yes, one of the intruders dropped it as he ran past Paul's office. It's on the floor, inside his office door."

The ambulance pulled up behind the police car. The attendants took the guard after checking Paul. He refused going to the hospital. The shorter police officer helped get the guard out to the ambulance. The taller officer, Paul and I went back to the office.

I was hoping that nothing showed of the struggle that took place in the office. We walked into the room; I pointed to the revolver on the floor, and noticed a small puddle of blood from my shoulder on the floor. While their attention was on the gun, I slid a small throw rug over the puddle with my shoe. Paul checked the sword. "It's O.K.," he said, and turning to the window, opened it. "It's hot in here."

The officer bagged the gun, and called his station, telling them what happened. Hanging up he turned his attention to Paul and me, asking all the standard and expected questions.

Paul related how the two Orientals apparently thought the museum was completely empty, displayed forged credentials telling the guard they were new professors on the campus and were supposed to be examining some Japanese artifacts for the museum. When the guard refused them entry, they became very vocal and threatening. Paul's sudden appearance intensified their aggressiveness. As Paul said what happened, the second officer called in through the open window saying he searched around the building but did not find anything.

I was shifting my attention from Paul talking, to the open window, and noticed a sharkskin handle from a sword sticking out of a rolled up cloth positioned halfway under a shelving unit. I got up; walked over to the bundle, slowly slid it completely under the bottom shelf with my toe. I returned to the table, picked up the sword from its case, and examined the handle and blade engraving. Paul noticed my scrutiny "Is something wrong Web?"

"I don't know. With all the confusion of the dating process, how did you authenticate this piece?"

Paul looked at me, looked at the sword and said, "The museum staff initially verified the results of our first outside laboratory, and a second lab was used to certify the first dating."

The first cop stated he had everything he needed, but would contact us if more questions come up during the investigation. Excusing himself, he left. Paul asked me if I would be O.K. by myself for a while, told me where the staff lounge was located for coffee or soft drinks, and that he had to inform the dean of the security breech. "I'll only be gone for fifteen to twenty minutes." He said as he went through the door. When the sound of Paul's footsteps diminished down the corridor, I rushed over to the shelving, picked up the sword, went to the table, and compared the two. At first, they appeared identical, but the sword from the enameled box had better artisanship.

The sword from the floor did not have a balanced feel and the engraving was a little rough. I picked up the second sword from the bundle, by the handle – nothing. I picked up the first sword from the ornate box and immediately felt the vibration from the humming. Without hesitation, I switched swords and wrapped the real sword with the cloth from the bundle, packed it in a shipping box from off the floor and filled the box with crumpled old newspapers. After sealing the box with some wrapping tape, I went to the open window and dropped the box behind the hedge next to the outside wall. Looking around to cover my deed, I remembered the blood on the floor. Most of the blood was soaked up in the rug. *Damn.* Taking the rug over to a large trash drum, I dumped out half of the waste, threw in the rug, and replaced the trash. Sweat was running down my face, and my left shoulder throbbed.

Is the blood soaking through my coat? No. Thanks for that break. I checked the room over again. Everything looked fine. I went to the lounge. The coffee pot was empty, but putting some coins into the soda machine produced a 7-Up. Opening the soda, I poured half the contents down the sink, set the drink on the table, and quickly wiped off my face with a dampened, cool, paper towel. I was taking my first sip when Paul walked in.

"Web, I think we will have to get together some other time to go over those legends. This business today has me going around in circles. Is that O.K. with you?"

Acting disappointed, I told Paul that my availability was at his convenience. I finished my soda, and Paul walked me to the front entrance.

I stepped off the bottom steps, turned to wave and check if Paul was still at the entrance doors – he was gone. Good. I walked to the side of the building to retrieve the sword. Approaching the open window of Paul's office, I heard him talking on the telephone, assuring someone that the sword was still in the museum's possession and not harmed in any way. Quietly I stooped down, picked up the cardboard box and walked back to my car in the parking lot. No one had seen me. I only drove two miles away from the campus when anxiety got the best of me. I pulled off the road and tore open the box. I sat, looking at my prize, knowing that at some time in the future, it would have to return to its proper place, wherever that place may be. The need to find a secure yet accessible place was taxing my mind, as I drove off.

That night, after locking the door to my room and lowering the window shade, I let my eyes wander around my small room in the barracks. I had previously achieved a promotional level entitling me to a private room. I had furnished it with four lockers, a refrigerator, and a bunk with two mattresses. The floor was made of different kinds of wood, then looking up to the ceiling; I noticed loose boards above a counter on the wall. Putting a chair on the counter to stand on, I could easily reach the loose boards. Dust had built up around the board edges and fell to the floor as when I pushed them up. I found an old ammo box. In the box were a few sheets of notebook paper covered with numbers, nautical terms and navigational formulas. Ha, I had found some old crib sheets for Officer Candidate Classes from years ago. I had found a good hiding place. I picked up the box with sword, placed it on the counter, and carefully cut the strapping tape. Digging through the crumpled paper, I pulled out the bundled sword and laid it down. I slowly removed the cloth wrapping the blade.

My hands were trembling as my finger lightly slid down the smooth blade, feeling every line of inlay, the sun, the dragon, then, first then, discovered the other symbols struck into the metal, not inlaid. I remembered part of the symbols, the hands under the sun and rays, as those on the far wall of the chamber of knowledge, but under that are embossed two crossed swords. Only the samurai from long ago could carry two swords, and those were larger, clumsy weapons compared to this more delicate work of art. Again, I could not detect a nick, or the smallest scratch or abrasion on the finish, not like its twin I knew so well in Iwakuni.

Removing a new white cotton undershirt from a locker, I carefully wiped the weapon while wondering why there is no scabbard to protect the blade. *This was not a weapon used in battle. What was its use?* I carefully located the wooden pin that locked the handle to the steel blade shank. Pushing out the pin released the wooden handle. I was expecting the signature, a mark of the sword's maker, but the shank was smooth and gilded with a layer of gold. Closer examination with a magnifying glass revealed a textured border around the edge of the shank. The two sides appeared to be different from each other. This sword was different from the sword I left deep in the bowels of the Kikkawa home. In one of the old man's visits, he showed me the mark on the sword and how it corresponded with the same script symbol engrave on the dungeon walls.

I know there was a connection to the old man and his ancestry that I did not understand. When I reached out to lay the blade down, I noticed I must have nicked my finger while handling the blade accidentally smearing blood on the shank. I was mortified. *How could I let this happen?* Quickly I picked up a clean white tee shirt, twisting a portion around my finger and wet it in the water of my drinking glass. As I wiped the blood from the shank, a script symbol showed itself in the gold gild. Slowly the image emerged, changing from a dark gold to a lighter yellow, turned pink to a white silvery luster with a darker silver outline. I remembered the old man talking in his monotone voice, saying that each master's sword was not complete until tempered with blood. Only then will the sword and master be one onto the other. I continued staring at the uncovered shank, and I knew that the symbol was mine. Entranced in my thoughts, I replaced the handle; pushed the wooden pin back into the hole, locking the handle to the blade shank. I grabbed the handle in my hand and lifted it above my head. It felt different from before. The vibrating hum was part of me. It felt like I found myself. The sword and I shared the same blood. We are one.

I memorized every detail before rewrapping the sword, placed the bundle back into the box, resealing the flaps and placed it up in the crawl space. I checked again. Not finding any wires, ducts or removable panels, I pulled the boards back into place. *Everything looks normal and undisturbed.* I felt good. The old balance of mind and body rekindled.

Chapter
TWENTY
FOUR

It was late and as I prepared for bed, memories of past challenges returned, and as I drifted off to sleep, Minkoto came to me. The visions of the dream-unlocked events long blocked from consciousness mingle with the symbols on the sword. It was a night of enlightenment, riddles and cryptic messages. During Minkoto's visit, she forecasted danger for me, especially from a black star. "You must use all your knowledge and resources to defeat the black star. You are the last blood of Izumo and Kikkawa. In you, lives all that was original Nippon. You are the last."

The old man also returned to me in his normal fuzzy state, riding on a cloud of smoke, telling me of Izumo, and spoke in a language that I could never remember or consciously understand, to prepare me, subliminally, for events to come.

The symbolism (shochoteki imi) and the Dragon engraving from the sword became animated and alive in my visions. The dragon was holding the sword high with his right arm, in battle with a huge ninja dressed in black with a black star on his forehead. The dragon was moving in slow motion, revealing the movements of engagement, while a large sparkling green jewel danced from a golden necklace around his long armored neck, and a golden mirror that appeared to have extreme depth, held in his left hand. Positioned above his craned head was a large bright sun, over his right up-stretched arm holding the sword. A ray of light came from the sun, reflected off the sword's sparkling edge, and off the mirror onto the face of the opponent.

The jewel suspended from the dragon's neck glowed and pulsated, with an unknown power. After seemingly hours of battle, the man in black was defeated, cut into eight pieces laid out in the pattern of the eight main islands of Japan, floating on a red sea, pointing out a path to the distant horizon. The dragon turned to stare; he was staring at me. I was more than a spectator in this vision, and as the dragon approached me, he extended the sword out to my right hand and said "Kuzanagi katana." a term unknown to me.

He removed his jeweled necklace and placed it around my neck; extended the mirror to my left hand and spoke "Susanowo.", another term I did not know. The dragon became an outlined mist and with the sun moved to a new location above my head and over my right shoulder. I look back while walking down the path, and saw the cloud that looked like a dragon's head following ten feet back and to my right side.

The next morning I woke drenched with sweat, tired and stiff as though I had finished an Olympian marathon. I remembered every detail of the dream. The details were sharp and clear, but the meanings were as fuzzy as the old man's misty cloud. *Why would I have to worry about some guy with a black star?* I knew my archenemy as *no name*. I killed him long ago in the Philippines; and the second adversary killed in Iwakuni. They were the only enemy I could associate with a *black star.* The other symbolic parts of the dream also confused me. I need to find a key to decode the dream, and the more I studied, the more confused I became. I knew I could not forget the dream; each detail etched into my mind. I pondered over the dream for days, during every moment of spare time, and every theory hit a dead end. I knew I would keep at it, I knew I had to keep at it, until I unraveled every nuance.

Friday and I had not heard from Paul all week. The base library did not contain reference books on ancient Japanese history, mythology or legends. I knew that a trip to a large library would be in order to satisfy my questions. Tomorrow, Saturday, I will go to the library in Providence for researching my visions of the night and their meaning.

I woke early on Saturday. The trip to Providence was not long and the comfortable drive in my trusty black and white 1955 Ford Victoria allowed my mind to wander through my dreams and the methodology of my research. Using a city map, I located the library. A large, gray limestone building that was both cold and intimidating. The librarian at the information desk was very helpful. In no time, I accumulated a large pile of reference books. After five hours of scanning page after page, I exhausted my material. I was replacing the books in their proper place when I noticed an old, leather bound book that had slipped behind the neat row of reading material. It had dropped down between the shelving and the wall. Only a couple of inches was protruding up from a cross brace. I reached back, stretched my arm to pull the dusty book out to the light, to read the title. Printed in an odd font was - *Nippon Sun*. The cover made cracking sounds, resisting the pressure needed to open the aged binding. The parchment pages inside revealed old Japanese script written on odd numbered paged with a hand-written translation on even numbered pages.

As I read this account of early Japan, a flood of visions and information from the old man's visits came to mind and meshed with the ancient myths and history that lay before my eyes. The more I read the more information surged up from my mind's hidden recesses. I was reading and re-reading the pages, revealing historical data, when my attention focused on a drawing of the sun with rays over the cupped hands and crossed swords under which was the title *The Legend of the White Ninja*. My body trembled and my hands shook as I turned the yellowed pages to read. I was fighting to control my emotions of joy. Maybe I could learn what I am, to see where I am going.

My concentration was broken when the librarian asked if I was feeling O.K. "Yes. Yes. I'm fine." I replied.

Looking down at the old book in my hand, she said she did not remember seeing that book before, "Are you interested in that book?"

I answered through a choked throat. "Yes, yes I am."

She asked me to wait a few minutes while she looked it up in their new inventory system. After five minutes she returned and told me, "The library is running out of room and any nonreference book over fifteen years old that has not been checked out during the past ten years would be sold." She smiled. "I think we could let you have this book for, Oh I don't know, maybe a dollar if you're interested in acquiring it now, instead of waiting until next month for the sale."

Laughing at my fumbling, trying to take a dollar bill out of my wallet, she said. "Wait – wait until I can write out a receipt. I'll be right back." I could not believe my luck and the timing. That wonderful woman returned with my receipt and asked, "Is there anything else you want to look for?"

I could have kissed and hugged her, but instead said. "Thanks, this will be enough for me today." On the drive back to Newport, I stopped at a secluded area, on a cliff, off the road outside Bristol, to read more of the book. It was a sunny spot overlooking the bay. I did not have a bookmark to mark my page; I used a new crisp dollar bill instead.

The warm evening sun shined through the windshield. The excitement of the day with the adrenal that pumped all afternoon now ended. Exhausted, with a vortex of memories spinning in my mind, my brain, and body shut down, and I fell into a deep sleep. By the time I awoke, it was dark, nearly 10:00 p.m. I started my Ford and continued the drive back to base.

I was still exhausted when I arrived at the barracks and carefully placed my newfound treasure on the shelf of my locker, lock the door and crawl into bed. My sleep was consumed with visions of the past, dreams of the future, flashing pictures and feelings of exquisite pleasure intermingled with emotional pain, a pain that my subconscious state of mind realized was a love that could never be, the love of Minkoto.

I woke early Sunday morning; the bright late autumn sun flooding my room with a warm light. Not bothering to cleanup or eat breakfast, I went straight to my locker. I fumbled with the key, unlocked the door, and carefully retrieved the book. Drawings and descriptive phrases vividly returned from the night before, tossed together, and all trying to come to the forefront of my mind at the same time. I opened the book to the dollar bill thinking that I would wait until I completely read the book before starting over again.

The book reinforced what the old man told me in my dreams. The White Ninja was an ultra-secret organization of a select few from all social strata. The lineage leaders, the White Dragons of Izumo held mystical powers. Knowledge accumulated and compounded from generation to generation; enabled conjuring, from ancient to current Jonins, the High-Man Masters, through a process of visions and dream visits. This passage of knowledge, as described, was like programming a futuristic computer, or hypnotic implanting, with events and/or other stimulus triggering recall of specific information and/or visions while one slept. The pages did not specify the actual sequential process.

The book revealed answers for most my questions poised during the past three years, but did not address the meanings of my past-encrypted dream. Why did the dragon give me the sword, mirror and jewel? I was aware of the historical meaning of another sword, mirror and jewel to the Japanese people, their crown jewels or regalia, but I could not tie the two together in how it should affect the sun and me with the mist following to my side and slightly behind me. *What could that mean?* I must put these searching thoughts behind me in order to continue my life in a more rational vein. This could all be just a dream I told myself, but down deep, down in my subconscious, I knew better. I knew this was the basis of a forewarning. A forewarning tied to the Black Star. I always wondered about the statement, *the human mind only utilizes ten percent of its capacity* and wondered why we evolved with, but did not use the other ninety percent. I knew the use for some of that percentage, and that thought would only open the door to unimaginable possibilities.

Chapter
TWENTY
FIVE

A week passed before Paul called and apologized for not getting back to me earlier. "Web, can you come up to the university this afternoon. I want to hear more of the legends you mentioned."

"Yes, I can. You can expect me around Three O'clock."

"Fine and we'll eat at a local restaurant when we're done, my treat."

I shifted my brain into high gear, trying to put together a story that flowed, sounded interesting, but still credible. My newly acquired book was a godsend. I pieced together parts of the book, supplemented with information from the old man's visits and my vivid imagination; I had enough material for an intriguing story, but did not sound like I was an authority on the sword's origins and its legends.

As on my prior visit, the guard expected me and directed me down to Paul's crammed office. The office door was half-open when I knocked, while calling out, "Paul, its Web."

A muffled "Come on in", came through the opening. I

found Paul's barely visible form hunched over an open rounded steamer trunk top, in the far corner, behind shelves overloaded with sundry items.

I called out, "Hey! What are you up too?"

Another muffled reply, "I can never find what I'm looking for. What a helluva mess. Damn! I have a broken sword handle that I wanted to get your opinion on, and now it's nowhere to be found."

Laughing, "I guess this place is too well organized." and in a more serious tone I added, "What you should do, is get a student worker to put everything in order, or if nothing else try to inventory what's here."

An open magazine was on Paul's desk, an article headline caught my eye. *Aborigine woodcarvings found in hidden cave, in Luzon, Philippines.* Printed on the second page was a photograph of the carvings. Some of the carvings looked like me. Memories of the Protector of the Night flashed. A thunderous silence in the room returned me to the present.

Paul stopped his rooting in the trunk, stood and walked toward me. "It's funny you should say that. I did request a student worker; in fact, there is a graduate assistant from this department assigned to help. And, if I'm not mistaken, he is supposed to come by sometime this afternoon for an interview."

As Paul finished talking, a light tapping knock came from the door behind me, and a quiet, sweet melodic voice wafted across the room – "Professor Nethrum, Professor Nethrum, are you here?"

Paul and I looked at each other quizzically. "Yes. Yes. Come in."

Turning, I saw this beautiful, delicate and enchanting girl pass through the door opening and into the light of the ceiling fixture. I felt faint - lightheaded, my heart and head pounded. My mouth was dry, and I stuttered and stammered trying to talk. After giving a perfect performance of a drooling, delirious, and tongue-tied idiot, I blurted out a shout "Minkoto." The outburst was agonizing in its contrast with the silence that followed. The young woman was indeed frightened by my sudden outburst, visibly shaken. Paul's mouth was open and he was staring at me in surprise. I was weak, knees trembled, stomach tight, and head apparently empty.

I was taking my first step toward her as I gave my apologies for startling her while she responded by staggering backwards toward the door she just entered, leaving a trail of papers and folders on the floor. Paul did not respond to the rapidly escalating situation-taking place. By the time I became coherent, the young woman had backed out into the hallway with her right arm raised in defense, her other arm across her chest and her hand clutched a few sheets of notebook paper. Her face was pale and drawn; turning a light pink as she apparently came to the realization to what happened. A blubbering idiot made a fool of himself. I tried to communicate in an understandable manner, and she must have concluded that I meant her no harm.

"I'm extremely sorry; I did not mean to frighten you. It's that you reminded me of someone I knew long ago, and you look just like ..." and I started babbling again.

Paul injected himself into the scene just in time. "I'm

Professor Paul Nethrum, what can I do for you?"

My mouth hung open, and I checked to make sure drool was not running down to my shoes. I forced myself to project a more normalized state, calmly listened as she replied.

"Hi Professor Nethrum, I'm Myoko Omasati. Professor Blandett referred me to you for a graduate student assistant position." Her voice slowly regained confidence and returned to the earlier heard musical quality, but she warily kept her eyes on me while she spoke. Paul and I both tried to answer at the same time. I started to apologize again, while Paul stammered that he was expecting a male student to report.

I interrupted with an apologetic "Excuse me.", retreated to a chair by Paul's desk, and listened while Paul finish explaining that it was a misunderstanding on his part. I now had control of my faculties and mentally coerced my hands and focus to inane activity on Paul's desk. I picked up the magazine, and read the article about the woodcarvings found in the Philippines.

I heard Paul invite Myoko back in to his desk. As she came near, she pulled an empty chair to the opposite side of the desk, took off her coat, laid it across the chair back, and sat down facing me. I could tell she still regarded me with suspicion. I started to apologize again, but Paul interrupted explaining I was a person highly interested in, and knowledgeable of, the myths and legends of Japan. Paul asked "Miss Omasati is it all right with you if Mr. Drache sits in on the job overview?" Myoko answered by nodding her head yes, as she gave me another sideways glance.

As I listened to Paul ask questions and Myoko's answers, I saw Minkoto. Myoko's gestures, the tilt of her head, her habit of looking at one with a playful sideways glance; her head down a little; looking upward, into the eyes of who she is speaking to, the slight upward angle of her head while contemplating an answer. She was a twin of Minkoto in every physical and visual way. I realized that my constant staring, and apparent total absorption in study, was making her uneasy again. I turned my attention back to the magazine. I was still completely attentive to the conversation as Myoko replied to Paul's questions.

"Where is your home?"

"Tokyo, Japan."

"Where did you complete your undergraduate studies?"

"University of Illinois."

"What is your major?"

"Anthropology – especially Far Eastern Anthropology."

She paused to glance my way again, and continued. "That is why Professor Blandett asked me to come see you. Obviously you are involved with a project that I have some expertise in." The interview continued for another fifteen minutes, and I while acted not interested, I soaked up every tid bit of information, mentally repeating the words and memorized each word, each detail.

Paul again referred to me as having an interest in his project and I gave a physically alert posture, engaged in a normal conversation about the well-known stories of old Japan.

After a period of light talk, Paul excused himself saying, "Myoko, I have a rare, little known artifact, and I would like your opinion of it. Give me a second to get it."

Paul's absence gave me an opportunity to reassure Myoko of my presence of mind and demeanor. I address my original outburst stating how she could be an identical twin of Minkoto, and how I knew her, but made no mention of my deep involvement with her, or how and why she died.

Paul returned with the wooden case containing the fake sword. Damn, I thought he was getting the broken sword handle he had previously referred to. Gently setting the sword down on his desktop, he lifted the lid, and exposed the cloth covering the sword. Myoko stood, clearly interested, and as Paul unwrapped the sword she softly spoke. "That's beautiful." Paul had a huge broad smile on his face as he picked up the sword and extended it to Myoko. She frowned slightly, reached down and slid her hands under the cloth, lifting the cloth closer to her face. She meticulously examined the golden crest, reached over with a lifting movement and cradled the sword and cloth in her hands. Again, she lifted her hands and their contents up closer for examination. I could see her focus go back and forth between the cloth, the blade finish, to the cloth and back to the etchings on the blade. Myoko softly muttered something under her breath that I could not understand, and from Paul's facial expression, neither could he.

She again uttered something that neither Paul nor I could understand, and laid both the cloth and sword down. With her bare hands, she reached for the sword handle. I had a feeling she was going to check the sword makers mark. All she had to do was to push out one wooden pin, to disassemble the handle, to reveal the maker's mark. I should have done this check when I first switched the swords, but I did not have time to take it apart. Myoko murmured, this time understandably. "This is the first samurai sword with this style of sharkskin handle that I have ever seen. I had heard of it in stories, but never seen one."

She asked Paul for a punch, or a piece of tapered doweling. Taking the wooden peg Paul handed her, she deftly pushed the wooden pin out of the handle. The handle grips slipped off the sword and fell. There was the maker's mark stamped into the metal. "This is a forgery! However, it is a good replica. Someone tried to achieve an original quality, but vainness clouded his reasoning."

Paul was beside himself "What do you mean, it's a forgery. We had this checked out. All the staff experts and the two outside labs verified the age of the sword."

"The age was verified, but did they authenticate the sword historically?" asked Myoko.

"No" replied Paul, "They were not aware on any possible historical attachment or provenance."

Myoko commented, "What you have here is an old sword that was redone in recent years to imitate a sword of legend. The sword of Izumo Kikkawa Bungei Shuto Ke Suru. The sword of the God Izumo, The First Martial Arts Master of the Kikkawa family lineage.

Knowledge of the secret ancient society that followed is minimal. In Japan's folklore, it is basis of stories and myths concerning the White Ninja, and their leader Jonin, the White Dragon.

The legends are like the European stories of the white knights, and you know there is a connecting thread. Did you know that the original inhabitants of Japan were Caucasoid? They were the Ainu, and some of them still live in northern Japan, but none is full blooded. There are no full blooded Ainu living anymore."

"How can you be sure?" I said.

Myoko raised her eyes to my eyes and locked on them for at least a full minute. She had a deep penetrating gaze. I studied her facial features. Standing next to her was like standing next to Minkoto. After the minute pause, I broke the silence by adding "What you are describing is a Ryu Hakujin, the White Dragon who rides the mists, and winds, and was not spoken of aloud in ancient Japan. The entity that became the Divine Wind, the Kamikaze, in Japan's old war with Korea, and more recently became the Kamikaze in current history. Is that not right?"

Myoko appeared startled, and again gazed into my eyes, but this time her gaze was markedly colder. Paul noticed the chill and was getting apprehensive. Myoko blurted out "What do you know of Japanese history, and the true nature of the people? You Americans and your atomic weapons. What do you know of the spirit of Japan?" I immediately knew I overstepped good caution.

Chapter
TWENTY
SIX

Trying to defuse the situation, I commented, "I'm sorry if I said anything to offend you, I read a lot and must be repeating something I read. I do not have opinions in the area; I find the history of Japan and its legends interesting. I'm ..."

Paul interrupted with "Hey guys, lighten up. Myoko, I am a little hungry and I owe Web a meal to settle a debt. I would like to have you come along with us. I would like to discuss your working with me. I think we could set up a good display with this sword, even if it is a phony, and the history it portrays. I think we could do a thorough job with your help. What do you say? Are you hungry?"

"Yes, Yes I will accompany you. I am sorry for being so defensive of my history. Mr. Drache, please forgive my rudeness. I am sorry for being so curt while talking to you. Please do not think of me personally attacking you."

I smiled as I looked into her eyes. I knew in my heart, that she was blood with Minkoto and the old man. "Don't think anything of it; you have nothing to be sorry for." I could tell from her expression she was satisfied by my reply to her apology.

Paul said, "All right, let's go get some Italian. Myoko, you do like Italian food?"

"Yes. I love it. I could eat Italian until I burst." Paul went to the clothes rack to get his coat while I picked up Myoko's jacket from her chair, helped her get in it, and then slipped on my jacket from off the floor where it had fallen.

We left Paul's office, and stopped at the main door while Paul gave the guard phone numbers where he could be reached. Looking at Myoko and me, he said that leaving numbers was a standard precaution since the trouble with intruders. Myoko gave Paul an expressionless look and did not say anything. Paul declared aloud "Since I'm buying and know where the restaurant is at, I'll drive."

Once at the parking lot we got into Paul's old Dodge station wagon. I held the passenger side door open for Myoko, and started to close it, commenting I would sit in the back seat. Myoko quickly said. "Nonsense, come and sit in the front, I can slide over to the middle." She shifted herself over to the middle of the bench seat as I duck in.

Once seated beside her, she eased back next to me, close but not touching. Turning her head to look at me, she said, "What was that name you called me? Minkoto? I remember a sister, and my adopted parents telling me I had a twin, a girl named Minkoto, but they said she died with the rest of my family at Hiroshima. I do not remember what she looked like, but was told, that we are identical twins. I am the only one left." She dropped her head. "All the rest died from the bomb. This is why I am so sensitive about my history. I hope you understand."

"Yes, I understand, but there is no way I can feel the loss you feel. I am sorry you had to endure all you did." *Yes, Yes* I told myself. *Myoko is blood to the old man and Minkoto.* I was trying to control myself, not to let my elated state show. I must remain cool. I must find out all the information I can. I put my arm on top of the seat lean behind Myoko's head. I could feel her moving a little closer to me. Did I find my heaven again? And if I did, what must I do to keep it.

All through our meal, Myoko's and my eyes locked onto each other. I kept telling myself not to see something that was not there, not to let my imagination run away. I cautioned myself not to rush. I told myself how lucky I was for this second opportunity for happiness when Myoko questioned me. "How long were you in Japan? And where were you stationed?"

Her questions took me by surprise, as I was deep in thought – "Oh not long, maybe six months at Iwakuni."

"Oh, did you ever visit the Kentai castle? That is my ancestral home. That is why I know of the History of the Kikkawa."

Smiling, I slowly said, "Yes, I was at Kentai" I hesitated, looked down at the hairline scar in my palm left by the old man. "I too know a little of the Kikkawa history." I could not keep out the visions of Minkoto, and our moments of happiness, from flashing through my mind.

Myoko must have sensed something – she reached over the table and placed her hand over mine. My eyes moist, I hoped my face did not reveal my feelings. Looking into her eyes, I felt release and relief from the years of pent-up pains. It dawned on me; I had forgotten that Paul was sitting with us. A glance over to him, showed an expression on his face I never saw before, a Cheshire grin. I collected myself, and returned to my food, whatever it was. I ate without tasting, looking up in between small talk to look into Myoko's eyes.

From the first sight of her, all I could see was Minkoto, but then gradually saw Myoko, more and more. But what of Minkoto's visits? I knew that I would have to deal with my many emotions before any involvement with Myoko was possible. I muddled through the meal and the coffee afterwards. Paul kept talking about an exhibit featuring the sword and the history it represented. He was trying to stir up enthusiasm in Myoko and myself but he was not making headway. During the drive back to the museum parking lot, Myoko and I kept looking at each other, neither saying a word. Paul was also quiet. In fact, he was almost patronizing us by not initiating conversation. He stopped by my car. As I was getting out, Paul asked if I would be free to come back to the museum again the following Sunday, or some evening during the week. I said "Sure, either way."

Paul replies, "Great, Sunday it is, same time, same place. Myoko, do you need a ride home?"

"No, Web will take me." She gently squeezed my hand. "Won't you?"

"Yes" I whispered. I felt like a teenager. I did not remember closing the door, forcing me to look back to Paul's car to reassure myself. I opened the door to my old Ford for Myoko. Not a word said until I was behind the steering wheel.

Myoko broke the silence "I feel a bond between us, but I do not know how or why. An inner force is drawing me to you. Who are you and how do you know of my family?" She was trembling. She was sitting next to me and I could feel the energy from her body pulsate out to engulf me.

I could not tell her my story. It was too soon. Her reaction would be disastrous to any future we might have. "I'm just another sailor, we'll have plenty time to talk about me. You are the one with an interesting past and I feel I must know more of you." Laughing I said, "Now where do you live?"

Chapter
TWENTY
SEVEN

Myoko stared at me for a few moments. The silence was heart wrenching. "I live a few miles away from the university. I will give you directions as we go along. First, drive down to the main road at the university's main entrance, and then take a right into the woods." My male ego, stronger than common sense, made me think she was directing me to a secluded spot, but the directions were just a short cut.

Mentally kicking myself, I ordered myself to shape up, and blamed my relegated presence of mind to the events of the day, and the excitement that overcame me, as they unfolded. After driving under Myoko's direction for 20 minutes, we drove up to a small white house, with a yard light that revealed a manicured yard surrounded with a white picket fence, bordered with flowers. Stopping the car ended the small talk that consumed our short trip. I shut off the engine and looked over.

Myoko asked me in for a cup of coffee. "It's not late and I would like to talk."

I smiled broadly and asked how she knew good coffee was the way to my heart. "I would love to come in to learn everything about you." She blushed and replied that she did not think she made good coffee and there was not much to learn.

It took me little time to get out, race around the car and open the door. I took her delicate hand, escorted her through the fence gate, up to the front door. After asking for the key, I opened the front door. She turned on a light that flooded a foyer with a soft glow. Myoko had her coat off before I had a chance to offer assistance, and she was helping me with my coat before I had time to react. As she was placing the coats across a slender hall table, I looked over the Japanese decor that reflected a meticulous attention to detail, that would look good in either Japanese or an American environment.

There were slippers by the door. I took off my shoes, and discovered my feet were too large for the slippers. Myoko smiled. I chuckled. "My socks are O.K. I don't need slippers." There appeared to be four main rooms in the house. Myoko guided me to the living room where a brightly enameled tea table sat in the center, on a luxurious oriental rug. I walked over to the table, sat down and said, "You don't have to make a pot of coffee for me; Oolong tea will do fine, if you have it."

"Oolong – you know Oolong?"

"Yes" I replied, "or Mandarin flavored green tea, whatever you have."

As she sailed out of the room, she threw over her shoulder "Make yourself comfortable while I make the tea, it will not take but a minute." Myoko reappeared in an ornately decorated kimono carrying a tray holding a small bottle of sake, a kettle of steaming water, a teapot, two small porcelain teacups, and some rice cakes.

She placed a cup in front of me, and, after placing the second cup on the opposite side of the table, poured the hot water into the teapot. The aroma took me back to the times that replayed in my dreams. I returned to the present when Myoko asks, "Web, what are your thoughts of? You have a different look on your face."

"Oh, just of the past, my mind was wandering through the years to the last time I enjoyed oolong laced with sake" and laughingly said, "What made you think of this, preparing oolong tea with sake?"

"A voice inside me," Myoko said, "a small distant voice, told me you would enjoy tea made this way. It is not customarily prepared in this manner." Myoko poured tea with a little sake into my cup, and then looked up into my eyes.

I picked up the cup and tasted the tea, "This is very good. Are you going to join me?"

She poured herself a cup and took a few sips, giggling, said "I should not drink too much sake; it will make me forget herself."

We finished the tea and rice cakes. I asked, "Are your adopted parents still in Tokyo?"

"No. They are both dead, and I have no other family. I had always wanted to come to America, to see how they live and what their customs are like. So, when I received my inheritance, I came to study at the University of Illinois. My teacher Omasati was a family friend in Tokyo, and had a relative on the faculty that arranged my attendance. I was always apprehensive and guarded, even here, where I came for my graduate studies.

When I first met you, I felt confused. I thought that you were not to be trusted, but you are different and I feel a calm in myself when near you. My mind and rationale were fighting each other. However, it was when I first touched you, touched you hand when you helped me with my coat in Professor Nethrum's office, I knew you have a friendly aura, and I feel right being near you. I will have to pray to my parents, and ask for their guidance. Oh, Please forgive me, I did not mean to bore you with my prattling."

"No. No." I interrupt. "I enjoy listening to you. I would like to learn everything about you, and your family. I am sorry, I do not want to bring back sad memories to you, but earlier you said that your whole family died in Hiroshima during the war. That must have been a terrible time for you. How is it that you came to be with your adopted parents? What was the family name of your true parents?"

Myoko paused as if trying to remember, answered, "My true parent's family name is Kikkawa. They were at Hiroshima when the atomic bomb dropped. I was not feeling well, and staying at a distant relative's home in Yamaguchi. They sent me there, so my twin sister would not acquire my illness. The family was meeting at Hiroshima for a *tsudoi*, a family reunion, when I took ill. Two days after I left to go to the Omasati residence in Yamaguchi, the Americans dropped the bomb. I was too young to remember. Later I went to the family home at Yokoyama-Iwakuni, to learn of my family history. I spent a whole year exploring the Kintai Castle, and the home of Kikkawa Hiroyoshi, an old daimyo, the feudal lord of Iwakuni. Now, how do you know of the Kikkawa family?"

"Yes, I do know of the Kikkawa. In 1956 I was honored to meet and get to know a venerable old man who lived in the original family home of Kikkawa, built after the castle, but before the newer house, now called the Kikkawa residence. He mentioned the White Ninja, a connection to something called the White Dragon. He lived with his great-granddaughter Minkoto. I spoke her name when you came through the door of Paul's office.

They told me that they were the only family survivors of the bomb. Myoko was silent and tears ran down her cheeks. "My sister lives?" Minkoto's memory brought tears to my eyes also, as I told how the old man and Minkoto died at the hands of the black hearted Yakusa. I was careful not to reveal everything. I knew the full story would defy explanation. "Yes"–said Myoko, "I have heard the stories and legends of a secret society, somewhere back in the Kikkawa ancestry. The complete facts and details of my family's role in the organization have always eluded me. No one knows. All I can find out is bits and pieces, most of which is unreliable."

I reached out and held Myoko's hand. "I know of the Kikkawa enemies of old. They are still active in their pursuits, and worst, they are here. They want the sword in the museum's vault, and if they knew you are Kikkawa, they would want you too. The sword and you would clench their claim to a long hidden fortune and a power waited for, for over a thousand years. Neither of which is their birthright, but the birthright of Kikkawa blood."

"Oh Web, stop it. I do not know where you found all that

nonsense, but I have heard those old fairy tales since I was first able to talk. Mama Omasati told of the old legends, and that is what they were, old legends. And that old man and the girl you call Minkoto must have been impostors. The real Minkoto died in Hiroshima. Her grandfather was also Mama Omasati's grandfather, Kikkawa Ryozo, who was like ... like a keeper of those old legends.

My family spoke of him with great respect and said that he led a very reclusive life. However, he also died in Hiroshima. I was at the Omasati's, and on August 6, 1945, Minkoto and our family were to visit with the other family members, but they never came. That was when the great bomb dropped on the city. That is why I know they are all dead."

I knew further talk on the subject would be fruitless, so I said how sorry I was to dredge up all those old memories. Looking at a wall clock, I mentioned how late it was. "Maybe I could see you again? Maybe I could take you out to dinner sometime this week. I saw Myoko's eyes light up a little.

"Yes, but not early this week, I have midterm exams Friday morning. Would Friday evening be good for you?"

Without hesitation, I said "Yes, Friday evening at 6 o'clock, yes that will be great." We both got up and I stretched. "Wow, I'm not use to sitting like this," and ask if she can write down her telephone number and address for me – in case I got lost. She complied, and then walked me to the door. We stopped and I turned to her, leaned over and gave her a tender kiss. It was not a passionate kiss, but a kiss. She neither encouraged nor discouraged the kiss nor the embrace that lingered afterwards. I studied her eyes that darted back and forth between my eyes and mouth. I pulled away releasing my hold on her. "Thank you for a wonderful evening. I am looking forward to Friday evening Myoko."

"Web, yes I also enjoyed myself. Yes, I'll be waiting for you Friday evening," Replied Myoko.

I opened the door and stepped out. Myoko stood in the doorway and waved as I made my way down the sidewalk, through the gate and to my car. Waving back to her, I called out, "Goodnight, goodnight Myoko." I got into the car and drove away. I went over all the information from the day while driving back to the base. It was a long day, a long drive and it would take a long time to process it all.

I did not sleep sound that night. I dreamed constantly. It was like a family reunion. The old man visited with warnings of danger and caution. Minkoto came to me saying Myoko was her twin sister and separated at birth to ensure the bloodline continued if one or the other were to meet misfortune. Minkoto told me she could rest, knowing that Myoko and I would soon find happiness together. The old man appeared cautioning me to be protective and keep Myoko safe, to guide her to a suitor worthy of her station, to silence my heart because I am blood Kikkawa. He reminded me that his blood mingles with mine. It did not matter that I was an unwilling participant in that family-blood mingling ceremony conducted so many years before, while I lay asleep. He stressed that it was my obligation to protect Myoko, and the pure bloodline, at all cost. Their visits went back and forth all night. I woke the next morning, dead to the world.

I called the office and told them I was not feeling well and would be going to sick call, then lay down to collect my thoughts. It dawned on me that last night's visits could not have been a reaction to a post-hypnotic suggestion, or a mental programming. Anticipation to this sequence of events could have never happen. Last night's visits canceled out all the reasoning I had built up over the years to protect my sanity. It made most of the theories and explanations in my old book, *Nippon Sun*, worthless. I spent the whole morning trying to explain away my present dilemma. I searched fruitlessly through the old book looking for possible answers or clues.

At one o'clock, I reported to the office, but after one look at my face, the lieutenant sent me back to the barracks. He said I look terrible, and asked if I needed to go back to sick call. I said "No, not now, but if I start to feel worse, I would drive myself." The next morning I felt good enough to go back to work. The visits from Minkoto and her great grandfather consumed my sleep every night that week. By Friday morning, I knew what I must do.

Chapter
TWENTY
EIGHT

I got off work at noon Friday and returned to my room without eating. Taking down the sword, I carefully cleaned it, and then sheathed it in the cheap cover that came with an imitation samurai sword recently purchased. The imitation sword replaced the real one in the overhead. I showered, rested, and prepared myself for the evening.

At six o'clock sharp, I lightly tapped on Myoko's door. There was no response. Concerned, I knocked louder and still no response. I heard a muffled crash, and a voice called out. My body quivered, and my throat became tight with a restraining growl. I quickly shucked off my heavy outer garments, freed my sword, and hurried around to the back door in a crouch. The sword was singing and I knew Myoko was in trouble. I raised my sword over my left shoulder and quietly pushed through the remnants of the destroyed door hanging in its frame.

The kitchen was in shambles, all the drawers' contents thrown to the middle of the floor. The door to the pantry was open and I could see everything strewn about. I heard voices in the next room. I eased my way to the door, being careful not to make any noise while threading my way through a barricade of the kitchen's contents. They were in the bedroom. Tied to a chair at the foot of the bed, Myoto's skirt hiked to her waist, and her blouse ripped open. Her head hung back and I could hear her crying. "Please take anything you want. I have nothing of value."

Three scruffy looking young men were around the chair. One was sitting on the bed with a knife, cutting strands of hair off Myoko's head, verbally threatening to shave off all her hair. Another was still rifling through a chest of drawers. The third? He tempted all reasoning. He was pawing her chest and thighs saying that he had never had an oriental girl before. He had a dirty sounding laugh that stopped when the sword's singing turned to a ring as its razor edge cut through the vertebrae of his neck. His spurting blood did not go far, just to the ceiling. The second villain tried standing erect on the soft unstable mattress until his torso became two halves. The end of the last maneuver positioned me facing the third man who was going through the chest of drawers. His eyes were open with horror and his mouth gaped open. His quivering jaw started to move, trying to talk. "Who are you?" I asked. His eyes focused on the raised humming blade covered with blood. He mumbled something that I could not understand. His jaw was not working.

I made a lunge that made him jump backward, almost falling. "Who are you and what are you doing here?" His body was shaking from fright and his teeth rattled when he tried to talk. I understood from his incoherent babbling that an oriental man hired them to search the house at this address for any oriental swords, and to look for any maps, charts or old books that might be hidden, and if Myoko was in her house, they were to question her where the items were. They were to take Myoko with them, and stash away anything they found until they met with him at a restaurant bar, a Manny's Ringside in Bristol, Rhode Island at 10 o'clock that evening.

His crying and wailing turned into a screech that stopped short when the flat of my blade struck his head, knocking him out. Turning my attention to Myoko, I moved to free her from her bindings. She was sobbing and crying, her eyes tightly shut. She screamed as I touched her trying to untie the rope. She opened her eyes and screamed again as I raised the sword to cut the ropes. I cut the ropes and the sword became silent as I laid it down on the floor.

I pulled Myoko stiffly to her feet. She tried to pull away from me. I pulled her to me. Looking up at me, she stuttered, "Who are you?" I answered softly "Ryu Hakujin - Bungei Shuto Ku Suru - Ninjitsu Hakujin (White Dragon, The Master of Martial Arts - White Ninja)." She became calm and clutched me in a strong embrace. Her eyes dropped to the sword on the floor. She pushed me away, bent down to reach for the sword. I quickly put my foot on the blade, "Don't, I will clean it first."

Holding her aside, I reached down and wiped the blood from the blade off onto the shirt of the first man to die, then with both hands extended the blade to her.

She looked the blade over carefully, looked to me and asked me "Where did you get this?"

I did not address her question but stated, "There is another, an exact match, in a cavern, a room of knowledge, at the old Kikkawa home in Iwakuni Konagowa Ken. It was there that my trials of experience first began. It was there that an old man, the previous White Dragon, became my mentor. It was there that my eyes and heart opened to see the world. But we do not have time for this discussion."

Taking the sword from Myoko, and gently laying it on the dresser, I notice my image in the mirror. My face and clothing covered with spattered blood. I stood for a minute examining the image scrutinizing me. I wiped the blood from my face; I asked the image "Yes. Who are you? What are you, and where are you going?" I turned toward Myoko. "Where are we going?" Myoko gave me a strange worried look.

Quickly tying the arms and legs of the third intruder, and taping his mouth, we started cleaning up the mess as best we could. I stopped when the trussed up garbage of humanity became conscious. I asked Myoko if she was able to finish cleaning up the blood. Her composure had returned. She nodded yes.

Knowing that there was no time to clean myself, I dragged the stuttering idiot into the kitchen, righted a chair, and set him on it. He was fully conscious, but his eyes reflected terror and panic. He had a large welt across his head. His cherry red ear stuck out like a pruned tree limb.

Putting my face close to his, I told him "You don't want to die, do you?" He nodded - no. "Then you will do my bidding. If you screw up..." I nodded my head toward the bedroom and his dead companions.

"You are going to make your appointment tonight. You will tell your boss that you had found many items of interest and that you have Myoko, but they are worth much more than your agreed price, at least triple. You will haggle over the price at length, but agree to whatever price he offers."

I gave him directions to that secluded spot outside Bristol where I had stopped to read my book *Nippon Sun.* "Tell him that is where your two partners are holding Myoko and the loot from her house. Tell him that the girl is safe and untouched. Tell him to be there at midnight with the rest of the money. Do you think you can do this?" He nodded his head yes. "Do you know what will happen if you mess this up?" He nodded his head again, but more vigorously. "Do this and I will let you live. Do you have any questions?" He solemnly shook his head, no. "I am going to remove the tape and untie you. Do not disappoint me. I will be watching you."

I ripped off the tape, causing him to screech again. He was whining as I finished removing the ropes and thanked me for sparing his life as I pushed him out the front door. I stooped over and picked up my overcoat, jacket and shoes, stepped back and closed the door. Checking if Myoko was all right, and she was, I finished cleaning myself up. Myoko had a kimono waiting for me when I stepped out of the shower. As I entered the clean kitchen, she told me my clothes were still slightly damp. "I could not finish cleaning the bedroom, not with those dead things lying there."

I told her not to worry; "I'll take care of them. Pack what you need for the weekend." Luckily, the house was the only one on the street. I carried the body's one at a time in the blood soaked bedspread, taking them out to my car trunk. When I was done, Myoko had finished packing. We locked up the house and left.

I knew a Navy Chief, Red, that recently retired, and managed a motel on the opposite end of Bristol. Driving up to the office, I saw his car out front. I told Myoko to wait in the car while I checked her in. Opening the door, she grabbed my hand that was still on the steering wheel. "No, I can't be alone with those things in the trunk. I am too scared to be alone anywhere. Please do not leave me." She had a frightened look in her eyes, wet and misty, on the verge of tears. I silently cussed myself for not realizing how traumatic this was on her, for not consoling her.

Her grip on my hand told me she was drowning in fear and I was the straw she was clutching. "Come along with me." I opened the door and got out with Myoko following, her hand still locked in mine.

Standing outside the car, under the motel's vacancy light, I took my handkerchief, dried the wetness from her eyes, and lightly embraced her. She tightened the embrace as if to plead for me not to ever leave her, but time was getting short. I pushed the slender body away from me, and gently said, "We must finish our work tonight, or it will be too late." I turned toward the office with her hand in mine.

Entering the office door, I saw big Red, a six feet six inch gorilla of a man, with a thick stand of carrot red hair, sculpted into a flat top, standing behind his counter. "Chief, you old sand crab, how are you?" I yelled.

"Well, I'll be damned, if it isn't that young pencil pusher

Drache. What the hell ya doin in my neck of the woods?" Red looked at Myoko with a roguish eye, his facial features softened as he noticed the anguish in her face. "Are you two having problems? ... What ..."

"No, No" I blurted out. "This is my friend. She is experiencing some family problems. She will not tell me who, and what they are. I need a favor. Would you have a room, a quiet room that she could have for the weekend? She needs some time by herself to sort through things, to resolve some of the problems that have been dropped on her."

"Sure, anything for an old shipmate. We'll get her signed in and..."

I interrupted again, "Chief we don't want anyone to find out where she is, could you log her in under an assumed name? Could you do me that favor?"

"Drache, I'm insulted that you thought you would have to ask. I'll take care of it." Reaching back into a key locker, laughing, Red tossed a key over the counter to me. "Here, drive around to the left. The road curves back into a grove of trees. That's our honeymoon suite. No one will bother the young lady, and it's more comfortable, more room for her to move around."

The expression on Red's face became serious. "What the hell, where are my manners," as he picked up an empty cup, "hows-about a cup of coffee?"

Shaking my head sideways, I said. "Thanks a lot, but I'll take a rain check on that. I have a lot to do tonight, but I promise I will have time to sit and talk over old times later this weekend. I'm going to get her settled in, and I'll drop back in as I leave."

Putting the coffee cup back down, Red shot back "Well I'll be here."

Myoko and I returned to the car. She was a little hesitant to get in, sending a quick look back to the trunk. However, a little nudge started her through the open door. We drove back to the isolated cabin. After bringing in the luggage, we surveyed Myoko's temporary residence. It was clean, neat and comfortable. Myoko was visibly exhausted. I helped her unpack one bag, and told her I had to leave, but that she should expect me back sometime from one to three in the morning.

"Do not open the door for anyone but Red or me. The office phone number is right next to the telephone. Call Red if you hear any noise. You'll be safe. Now I have to go."

"No. No. Please don't leave me." Her arms gripped tight around my neck tenaciously. As I pulled one off, the other arm wrapped around me. I had a wrist in each hand, and prying off her arms, pulling them down and around to the back of her tiny waist, I kissed her gently on the mouth and softly told her "You know I must go, not for me, or for you, but for the Kikkawa. Your family must continue Myoko Omasati, Myoko Kikkawa."

She relaxed as I released my grip on her wrists. She again had tears welling up in her eyes. Looking up into my face, she said, "I don't understand all this. I am scared. I don't know what's happening."

I embraced her again, "Everything will be O.K. Trust me. I will return to you." I pulled away, walked out to the car, got in, and drove back to the office. Red was waiting for me inside the door. As I entered, he stepped over out of my way and asked,

"What's the matter? Is there anything I can do? That little lady has something heavy hanging over her."

"You bet you can help Chief." I told Red how important it is that no one knows where we are. "I believe the problem is that her family, following old Japanese traditions, has arranged a marriage for political family maneuvering, to someone she doesn't know, so she ran away. What is worse, they know that we are close friends, and that she left with me. You will have to be alert Chief; they will have people looking for her all over the place.

That is why I do not want you to know her name. You cannot repeat what you do not know. Chief, I'll never forget this favor."

"What," exclaimed Red, "with all the favors you did for me in the past; I owe you this one and a lot more to come."

"Red, I'll be back sometime between one to three in the morning. Unscrew one of those two bulbs in your counter lamp if there are any problems, and if I see you in the office, I will flash my headlights to let you know I am O.K. If you are not around when I come in, I will see you later tomorrow morning. Bye."

Chapter
TWENTY
NINE

I left the chief's office and hopped into my car. The bodies in the trunk were giving off an odor. Once you have smelled a lot of human blood, you never forget the coppery scent. I opened all the windows, and hoped no police would notice me, and drove to the cliff by the sea. Arriving, I was relieved, no parkers. I backed up to the edge, got out and opened the trunk. Those damn scumbags were already stiff.

I had a hard time getting them out of my trunk. Sprawled out, they did not roll very well. They slid down the cliff's face until they bumped up against some shrubs. Come first light, some tourist will make a grisly discovery. The wind was behind me, blowing out to sea. I threw the blood soaked bedspread out from the cliff edge, up into the rising air-stream, and watched it sail out over the surf below. Checking my trunk liner, I was surprised that no blood soaked through onto the upholstered bottom panel. But it still smelled of death.

Leaving the overlook, I checked the time. There were few

minutes to spare. I pulled into a gas station and filled up. There was a card display of small aerosol spray tubes of car air freshener. I selected the *New Auto Leather* scent, and paid my bill. Pausing long enough to spray down my trunk and car interior, I was on my way.

Arriving at Manny's Ringside early, I deposited my dragging rear onto a chair in the far dark corner. A young waitress, walked up with a menu. Her nametag spelled *Helen.* She looked like a typical high school student.

I knew what I wanted without looking, steamed sea-clams and a cup of coffee. She gave me a big tip-fetching smile, bounced around flipping her ponytail up in the air toward me, and fairly skipped away with the order. It was not as busy as I had hoped. Newspapers were stacked on a table next to an elderly man drinking a beer. I got up and walked over to the stack, picking up several sections. Stopping by the old man, I complimented him on his hat. It was large, worn, wide brimmed, with a leather band. I commented that I had always wanted a hat like that and offered him five dollars for it.

He smiled big, revealing a toothless mouth, removed his hat from his baldhead, and handed it up to me. I return a toothy smile, put the hat on my fully haired head and handed him a five-dollar bill. We both said "Thanks" simultaneously, and he burst out laughing.

Turning toward my table I saw my redheaded server, Helen, waiting for me with a tray of steaming sea clams, a bowl of hot water to wash them; a bowl of steaming hot butter to dip them in; and a mug of coffee. I ate a good number of clams, and washed them down with the strong hot coffee. This was my first food since breakfast. I felt a lot better, and wondered if Myoko ate before I arrived at her house. I saw a gulp of coffee left in my cup. I threw it down as the waitress returned.

She picked up the dishes and asked if I wanted a refill as she jauntily turned away. "Yes." My reply followed her back toward the kitchen. She was returning with a fresh pot of coffee, rolling up on her toes as she walked, and I noticed her young breasts quivered like rubberized springs beneath her uniform. I could not help myself, from watching with a smile. As she refilled my cup, I looked up and said "Thank you Helen. You do very nice work."

She said something back to me, but I did not pay any attention to her words. A short stocky oriental man, dressed in a black suit had stepped in. I pulled my paper up in front of my face, reaching around it to pick up my coffee. With my hat brim pulled down to my eyebrows, and the paper held below my eyes, I could safely observe the whole room from my dark hole in the corner.

He turned into the light of the bar. It was one of the men who broke into the museum, trying to switch swords. He did not appear nervous, but casually, and with the ease of experience surveyed the whole room, including me with a quick sweep. He did not I. D. me, or if he did, did not reveal it with his deadpan expressionless face.

Sitting down at a table near the front door, he ordered a glass of draft. The barkeep walked it over, wiping the table off in front of him before sitting down the glass. The dark intruder did not look up, but dropped a crumpled bill on the table for payment. He picked up the glass and studied it for a while, took a few sips and set it back down.

He started to turn his head, as if to look around the room again, when my babbling idiot fell through the door. Not looking to see if I was watching, he went straight to the black suit's table, leaning on it with his stretched out arms. He was excited, his body making jerking motions. I could not hear what he was saying, but black suit motioned him to sit down. He was reluctant and it took another hand gesture to get him down in the chair.

They were looking at each other, totally absorbed in their conversation, as I stood and walked to the kitchen. I was glad that the idiot did not see me in my topcoat, and satisfied that my hurried disguise was so effective. Money was in my extended hand as I approached Helen. "Thank you Helen; can I leave through that side door?" I said, pointing to the door at the far side of the kitchen. "Sure thing honey, the walkway goes right around to the parking lot." She was smiling big time, mentally figuring up her tip, while I made my way through the kitchen clutter, to the exit.

Once outside I raced to the parking lot and found it near empty. A big fancy Lincoln parked with two men sitting in it, and mine. Bingo! I casually walked over to my car, got in and started it, trying not to rev up the engine, trying not to attract attention to myself. I saw the two men in the car were watching the entrance as I snuck my Ford around behind them.

I took a short cut to the overlook and backed my car into a maintenance lane, off the parking area. I had brought along my shinobi shozoku (invisible warrior's clothing) and a kami-shimo (black samurai formal dress) clothing with my sword. Congratulating myself on my coincidental good fortune, I attired myself in the shinobi shozoku cloaking. I rubbed my face with mud from the ground, and armed myself with my scabbard encased sword, and my Tanta dagger. Stepping out in the open, I felt as though the black clothing really did make me invisible to my adversaries. Pausing to view the moon over the surf, I made a mental note to return to this same spot, later, with Myoko, so she too could view this grandeur, and then quickly moved to the entrance to seal off any possible escape.

During my earlier visit of the evening, I noticed a barricade thrown down between some trees to the side of the entrance. I partially reassembled the boards and waited. I started to worry that my trap would not work, when the black Lincoln turned off the main highway, onto the access road. As it passed my position, I placed the barricade across the road, wedged between the branches of a forked trunk, and followed the Lincoln up the road. I could feel the rough gravel through my tabis (split toed slippers).

The side of the road would be more comfortable, but the hard surface of the road was quieter. They did not hear, nor see me, as I approach. My idiot was with them. He did not follow my instructions. He had maintained a loyalty to them. He was stupid. The dark suit from the tavern was cursing him that he would pay with his life if that fool who dabbles in the martial arts did not show. He panicked, and ran in my direction when a shuriken (a multi-pointed throwing blade) struck him in the neck. He saw me as he fell to the ground, reaching out to me. I fell to the ground with him to prevent detection. He lay; his eyes bulged out, making nasal noises, then became quiet.

The three men were looking out, searching in different areas, each one's view overlapping the other. I rolled off the road to secure myself in the tree shadows and moved toward the center of the trio. I was proud of my prowess and stealth. I was unsheathing my sword, shouting "Ryu Hakujin Kuru" (The White Dragon Comes) as I went into a counter clockwise sweep with my singing blade.

Only two rings rang out and felt, as the blade passed through two necks, followed by the thuds as their heads hit the ground. My momentum carried me back to my starting position and posture. Where was the third bastard?

I dropped to a crouch as a shuriken whistled over my head. I did a fast side step and threw myself over into the shadows again. I waited. There was no noise and no motion, another shuriken whistle through the air, cracking into a tree somewhere off to my right, behind me. It was a blade thrown wild. I heard a rustle in front of me and to my left. I removed my Tanta and waited.

I was in a shallow run-off ditch at the edge of the parking area where I was out of sight. I strained my eyes, trying to see into the darkness. A black movement was moving across the graveled lot. I shouted teishi (stop/halt). A gunshot replied to my order. My tanta sparkled in the moonlight as it flew to its target. The black blob fell to the ground with a painful scream followed by a softer moan.

I rose to a short crouch and worked my way to a position above his head, approaching him slowly. His stainless steel pistol lay five feet away from his head, glistening in the moonlight. I approached him cautiously, as you would a wounded wild tiger. I reached out and pulled my tanta out of his neck. Blood from his wound, spurted onto the ground as I rolled him over. He tried to move his fist toward me in a boshi-ken (a fist configuration utilizing the thumb, only used by the ninja) manner, but he was too weak to follow through. He wheezed and weakly asked, "You are not the White Dragon?"

He died as I told him "Yes, White Ninja, Kikkawa is blood of my blood."

I pulled the three limber bodies, and the two heads, to the edge of the cliff, and rolled them down to the surf. They rolled fast, carrying the previously snagged bodies down with them, to the surf below. I went to the Lincoln, searching for any information, but it was clean. The idiot was still lying between the barricade and the Lincoln. I walked over to him, knelt down and felt his pulse. There was none. I picked him up and put him in the driver's seat, leaned over and started the engine. Putting the dead weight of his foot on the accelerator raced the engine. The rear tires spun when I slipped the shift lever into drive, and as I stood there, watched it race over the edge, tumbling down the side of the cliff and crashing into the sea.

I was exhausted. Damn, I sure have been tired lately. Slowly and mechanically I took down the barricade, walked over to my Ford, carefully stored my sword beneath the rear seat, changed clothes, wiped the mud off my face with an old towel, and drove off, back to the motel. I did not look to see what time it was, but saw Red behind his counter as I drove passed his office. I flashed my headlights and slowly drove to the honeymoon suite.

I knocked softly on the door, calling out "Myoko, It's me Web, let me in." The door cracked open with tearful, red, puffy eyes peering out. "It's all over. You're safe." She guided me toward a very warm bed. I think I was asleep before I fell on the bed fully clothed.

Chapter
THIRTY

It was late morning. The sun was shining through the window. I felt groggy. My muscles were sore and stiff. My hands and face scratched from rolling in the gravel the night before. I thought how good a warm shower would feel. I was naked under the covers. Myoko appeared from the bathroom, fresh as a morning flower, in a traditional silk kimono. I had not moved, and she did not notice I was awake.

She approached my side of the bed, leaned over, looked at my face to see if I was still asleep. I partially opened my eyes and said, "Good morning."

My action and voice startled her, and as she jumped back, she let out a little cry of surprise, "Oh you."

"Do I have anything to wear?" I said. "Or will I have to remain in this bed forever?"

Myoko looked at me with an unsympathetic air and replied. "I washed your undergarments and they are not dry." Then with a soft giggle, "Maybe you could wear one of my larger kimonos. There are no others to see you. It will be only a short time before your clothes are dry."

"Where are the rest of my clothes, my shirt, pants, and jacket? Where are they?" I quizzed.

"You have no patience. Lay back and relax. Your clothes were soiled, and smelled. I cleaned them as best I could, and they are outside airing out the bad scents. They will be ready when the others are dry."

She fumbled through her suitcase, and pulled out a purple kimono, with pink flowers and green grass growing all over the place, threw it over to me saying "Put this on while I check your clothes in the bathroom." Holding out the ugly monstrosity of a garment before me as Myoko left the room, I call out. "Damn it's ugly. I hope it doesn't grow on me." Closing the door behind her, Myoko shouted. "It was a gift, shut up and put it on."

I put the ugly garden curtain on, and looked at myself in the mirror. There was a knock on the door. The loud banging startled me. I instinctively looked around for something to use as a defensive weapon. I picked up a bottle from Myoko's toiletry case, and went to the door. "Who is it?" I said, holding the bottle high. An answer came through the door. "Me, it's Red."

I opened the door, not thinking of the bottle still held high. "My God, were you going to subdue someone with perfume? Going to spritz them into submission?" laughed Red, as he stood holding a breakfast tray that gave off an aroma that stirred a neglected hunger.

My raised arm dropped to my side. Lifting the tray higher, and with a depraved smile on the old Chief's face, he said, "Just thought you two could use something like this. I cooked it myself. It's late and I haven't seen or heard anyone stirring. Are you letting me in, or not? I'm not standing here outside all day, while you lounge in…, whatever that is you're wearing."

Sheepishly, I motioned the old chief in, and closed the door behind him. Setting the food down, he pulled out a large collapsible table from behind the sofa, set it up and placed the food and utensils on it. The coffee pot drew my immediate attention. I filled the two coffee cups and looked at Red, asked if he would join us.

"No" he declined. "It takes a lot of work to keep this place running smooth, and I'm the main crew. Not much time, but I'll see you later this afternoon."

Myoko came out of the bathroom, cheerfully greeting Red, and with an exaggerated sniff of the air purred "What is that delicious aroma," sat down on the sofa, and took the covers off the plates. Red left as we dug into the food. Myoko finished cleaning her plate; she looked up and noticed how I filled out the kimono. She burst into laughter, "That belonged to my adopted Mama Omasati, she was a large woman, but that kimono looked much, much better on her than you."

"Yah. Yah. I hear you." I replied.

After neatly clearing her side of the small table, Myoko said. "Your clothes must be ready; I'll get them while you finished your coffee." Getting up she retrieved my underpants and T-shirt from the bathroom, laying them on the sofa arm as she went outside, and after a minute, returned with my other clothes draped over her arm. I took my clothes into the bathroom, cleaned up, and changed out of that nightmarish robe and into my own comfortable clothes.

I felt like a new man as I stepped back out into the bedroom. Myoko had everything cleaned up, and her suitcases packed. "I thought we would stay here for the weekend?"

"No," she said, "I want to go back to my own place. It needs cleaning and put back in order. If everything is safe now, we must talk ... of you ... who, and what you are. I trust you, but feel that we must reveal ourselves to each other, in surroundings that are more familiar to me. We cannot let anything foreign to us, mask or change the truth. I feel we owe this to each other. We are drawn to each other in a strange and disturbing way."

Myoko teared up, but held back crying to continue. "Your knowledge of my ancestry and the things you say, stir my body and mind, and I can tell that my presence has an effect on you. I do not know if it is my presence, or the memories that I pull from your past. Sometimes I feel that you come from a distant past, and then you are from the present, then from all the periods of time between. I do not know how to view, or approach you. I feel you have not had a happy life. As though it were incomplete, like a last piece of a puzzle, the piece of the puzzle called joy, is missing, and you do not know how or where to look, and you do not know what it looks like, only it's shape. I feel that you are always trying to push things found, into the emptiness of a space, as if to fill it, then feel denied as they fall through or bounce away. Now we must go back to my home, to sort out and find ourselves."

Myoko's words hit hard as they rang true in my mind. Without a word, I picked up Myoko's suitcases and went to the car. As we left, I stopped at the office and left a note for Red, saying that we would come back to see him, and thanking him for everything he did. The clerk said the bill was paid – Red is a good man.

Chapter
THIRTY
ONE

Arriving at Myoko's house, we were surprised at the amount of work needed to put everything back in order. Some of the mess we could not immediately clean up. Myoko washed and cleaned, while I took up the bedroom rug, cutting and ripping it into smaller pieces that would fit in bags, put them outside, for taking somewhere else. I wiped the blood off the bedroom ceiling, sealed and repainted it.

All the bed clothing had to be soaked in an enzyme stain remover, before washing several times in cold water. The bedroom furniture needed washing. It was midnight before we stopped. I asked Myoko that if she would fix us something to eat, I would get rid of the trash bags. I check each item before putting them into the bags to ensure there was no name, address or other means of tracing it. Now it was a matter of loading the bags into my trunk, driving to four or five trash bins, and dumping the bags. Forty-five minutes later, I was back at Myoko's kitchen door. A soft knock and a beaming Myoko left me in. She was in an up mood. She had prepared a lavish meal that was bigger than my appetite.

She had thought I would be very hungry, and from the expression in her face, I could tell she was disappointed. "I thought you would like Hinadori Momijiyaki Irina (chicken cut very thin, with radish greens in a soy sauce), you had mentioned when we were eating with Paul, and that you especially liked it."

"It is very good Myoko" I paused, "But, I'm more tired than hungry. It is very good."

From her face, I could tell that she did not believe me. "I'll help you clean up the dishes, and then we should get some sleep." When we finished the dishes, Myoko went to the bedroom door and turned on the light. Everything was in its place, and the bed turned down, on both sides.

Myoko looked up at me from the top of her eyes, took my hand and started to walk me to the bed. "No, I think I should sleep on the sofa." I said gently. "I'll take the pillow, bring me a blanket. I think it would be best, until we sort out our feeling, and what they mean."

Silently, she got the blanket, and after making me a bed on the sofa, returned to the bedroom. Later, in the silence, I could hear faint sobs coming from the bedroom. I felt like a heel. Rethinking the evening, the lack of appetite, and not assimilating her enthusiasm she must be feeling totally rejected. I did not communicate my true feelings very well. What a dumb insensitive jackass I was. I did not have a good night. I was so consumed thinking what I should have said, and what I should do in the morning, that I never did drift off into a deep sleep.

I awoke to hearing Myoko preparing breakfast in the kitchen. I got up, put on my pants, and neatly folded the bed clothing. Entering the kitchen, I found Myoko cool and distant. From the puffiness of her face I could tell that she also did not sleep well. I said "Good morning Myoko," and in reply, she gestured with her hand to a place at the table, where a cup of fresh coffee sat.

Barely in my chair, breakfast slammed down on the table, in front of me.

"I hope you can find an appetite to get this down. I do not know if this is on your favorite breakfast list or not. You have never mentioned eggs, bacon, or toast to me, so I would not know." She sat down across the table from me and started eating.

I thought I had figured out how to smooth things over this morning, now this blew all that out of the water. "Yes I like this." I said, "And this is not too much." I put a forkful of eggs into my mouth and continued "and this tastes very good."

I looked directly into her eyes. "Myoko" I said. "Your feelings weigh heavy on me. I did not wish to hurt you, make you angry or unhappy. I only wanted to do what I thought was right. I did not want to impose myself on you. I do not want to start anything that you don't want to finish with me."

Myoko stopped eating, looked up at me with a softer face and said. "Eat your eggs before they get cold."

We finished our breakfast in silence, our heads cast down to avoid looking each other in the eyes. "I'll help you with cleaning up the dishes," I said as I stood up and started clearing the table.

"No" Myoko replied so quickly, her rapid outburst startled me. "No, this is not work for a man; it is a woman's ..."

Out of frustration over the present situation, I stopped her mid-sentence with "Damn it - Stop all this nonsense right now. You are not in Japan now. You are in America. You do not have to follow the old customs." I stopped my rambling as Myoko's laughter shattered my shallow train of thought. A sharp pop of a dishtowel on my hip followed her laughter.

I jumped, almost dropping the dishes in my hands. Myoko was still laughing, a little light playful sound, but a laugh begging for retaliation. Maybe a little playful retaliation. With slow deliberate body motions, I placed the dishes in the sink, and then slowly turned to face my attacker. My carefully orchestrated menacing facial expression evoked a more shrill combination of laugh and screams from Myoko's delicate throat and mouth, as she turned from me in mock retreat.

It came to mind that I had not experienced this side of Myoko before, but being caught up in the enthusiasm of the moment prevented me from consciously evaluating this response, and pushed it to the back of my mental catalog of information. I caught up with Myoko, or else she slowed down to wait for me, by the living room door. We collapsed into a tangle of tickling fingers, writhing arms and legs, and a source of noises, grunts, giggles and laughter that were very unintelligible. We might have continued in the pleasurable aerobics on the floor until the point of exhaustion, but our lips found each other.

Time was lost and the world around us became surreal, as we became mentally and physically one. Later, I carried Myoko to her bed turned down, on both sides.

When I awoke for the second time that day, the sun was going down. Turning my head to the side, Myoko came into my view, her head on the pillow, with soft sparkling eyes, a smile, and her normally neat hair, disheveled. I rolled over closer, we gently kissed, and as Myoko lay in my arms, I told her "You are the love of my love, and the life of my life. I will always love, cherish and protect you. I have known ..."

Myoko interrupted "Don't talk, just hold me."

We embraced for a long time before Myoko moved. A nerve shattering feeling shot up my arm. It was numb, and every movement or touch sent new waves of sensation up and down my arm. Sensing my discomfort, Myoko lifted herself off my shoulder, while I slowly dragged my arm after me, easing up to a sitting position on the edge of the bed.

"Oooh" I moan, "you did it. You know how to hurt a guy. Look at my arm, it's numb." Myoko said something in Japanese that I did not understand as she modestly put on a kimono, and with one of her melodic giggles, slapped the side of my arm hard, causing a feeling only experienced by a visit to the dentist. She ran to the bathroom. "I'll get you for that. You'll pay dearly." I shouted. Reaching the bathroom, the door was locked.

Rattling the knob provoked the response "No. You cannot come in. You must wait. It will only take a minute, just one minute."

Thirty minutes later, the door opened, and a smiling, refreshed, and mischievous looking Myoko came through the door declaring, "Your bath is ready. And does the master require a young maiden to wash his back. If you so desire, I am a very good bath attendant. Please, what is your wish most Honorable Master."

"Yes." I said, "This tired old body could use a soothing hot bath, with vigorous scrubbing, followed by relaxing massage. Is the young bath attendant also knowledgeable of such techniques?"

"Yes. Come. Your paradise awaits you." She replied with sparkling eyes and a capricious smile. The theme sound track from *Sayonara*, a hit movie of three years earlier, played softly on the radio.

Chapter
THIRTY
TWO

Sunday came early and noisy. Myoko was shouting for me to wake up. She was in the bathroom yelling, "Web, Web, wake up. Hurry, get up."

I swung my feet out of bed, stretched, and replied, "I'm up. I'm up. What's the matter?"

"I forgot. I have friends visiting. They are friends of my parents. They're coming for lunch. They are very traditional people. They would not understand you, here, like this. They would not understand us, like this."

I looked at the clock. Eight-thirty. "O.K." I shouted back. "I'll straightened up the house while you finish in the bathroom, then I'll get back to the base."

"No, I want you here." She said calmly and softly, as she leaned out the doorway. I laughed as she exposed her face and hair in mid make-up, and said,

"Whatever you want, that's what you'll get." She made a face at me, stuck out her tongue.

She was more Americanized than I realized. We had no time for small talk as we prepared the rooms and ourselves. I was re-checking all the rooms while Myoko fixed us a fast breakfast, rice pudding, fruit, very thin sliced ham, coffee for me and tea for her. I washed the breakfast dishes, while she prepared the luncheon.

"These people must be important to you." I asked.

"Yes, they are Omasati. They took temporary residence so they would be near me, available if needed." Myoko continued talking while preparing the food. "I was to live with them in the United States, but convinced them that I would learn more of this culture and my academics, if I could freely come and go, independently. They were very worried and concerned, but reluctant, and finally agreed to my request and reasoning. They were supposed to be ... like ... an official chaperon for me and now feel uneasy about their approval, a premature approval in their minds. They are looking for a way to negate their decision without offending me. I am lucky this is America and not in some socially restrictive society."

"Yes" I said, thinking of how they were going to view me.

It was eleven-fifteen, when the black Mercedes pulled up in front of the house. Myoko was dressed in a frilly Western styled dress, and her hair fixed in a Japanese style, we were looking out of her living room window, "My god" I said, "They have a chauffeur." She smiled as she passed by me to the door. Myoko met them at her front door. I could hear the greetings and visualized the bowing. I heard Myoko tell the elderly couple that she also invited a friend from the university, and asked them to speak English, for my benefit. She followed them into the living room and introduced me to them as Mr. Drache, and they, as her Aunt Isako and Uncle Oishi Omasati

"Mr. Drache is a consulting friend to Professor Paul Nethrum, the professor with whom I will be working with. Myoko told of the display project we will be developing. When she said that it would center on a replica sword of the White Dragon, of the Kikkawa family, Omasati's poker face cracked a little frown, expressing a worried scowl.

Our introductions were cordial and proper. Myoko reminded Mr. Omasati not to bow at introductions, to which he growled something in Japanese that I could not interpret. I had expected Isako to go into the kitchen with Myoko, but she did not budge from her husband's side. Myoko went to the kitchen, leaving me to fend for myself.

Round one was an intimidating staring contest, followed by round two, the inquisition of why I was visiting, was there a purpose for my presence, and we were entering the third round, concerning what relationship Myoko and I had.

Myoko appeared just in time, announcing that lunch was prepared and ready for serving. During the meal, Myoko dominated and directed the conversation with where her academic studies may lead her. Isako, being a traditional wife, was totally absorbed and amazed at Myoko's independent lifestyle, while Oishi was sizing me up with his stares and questioning, penetrating, steely stares.

Oishi was obviously displeased that Myoko did not indicate the luncheon was over before she cleaned off the table and quickly washed the dishes while still talking. "Now, I'm all done. Could we go to the living room and finish talking?

Myoko and I followed the Omasati's into the living room. We just settled in the easy chairs when the barrage of questions began hitting us. How, when, why did we know each other good enough for me to visit at Myoko's house? Did our introduction follow proper protocol? How, when, and why did I have knowledge of the sword of the White Dragon, and of the Kikkawa family's history?

I sat passively, listening to the questions asked of Myoko, one after another without a pause allowing for an answer. How, when, why was I knowledgeable of the Japanese customs?

Myoko's replies were non-specific, general answers. Her demeanor while standing up to her uncle were not befitting a young woman of traditional Japanese culture.

Uncle Oishi, apparently unable to elicit the information he wanted from Myoko, turned his attention to me. Listening to his inquiries, and with a sense of mutual concern, I calmly told him of my current naval service, previous duty in Iwakuni and Atsugi, my deep interest in the culturally rich history of Japan, and of my readings to satisfy that interest.

When I mentioned the book *Nippon Sun,* he asked. "Do you read Japanese?"

I replied "No." His hardened face softened, and he commented that he did not know that a translated version of *Nippon Sun* existed and asked how I acquired it.

I told him of my visit to the library and the particulars surrounding its purchase. "I would like an opportunity to see your copy Mr. Drache." I asked that he call me Web, and continued to answer his questions, telling him the story of how I met Professor Nethrum, the official versions of the museum intruders, and how Myoko and I had started seeing each other for the benefit of the planned exhibit and how to best honor the Kikkawa family ties to it.

I ended my lengthy spiel with "It is my great pleasure to be in Myoko's company, and I would like your approval, as her official guardians while in the United States, to collaborate with her for the museum, but also to help her learn and understand the customs of this country. I think this would help her to better assimilate her postgraduate pursuits." The Omasati's were not overly enthusiastic about my request, but indicated that they would have to discuss it, and would let Myoko know their decision. After further discussion of the recent Kentai family history, they called their chauffeur, excused themselves and left.

Myoko was totally composed until she saw their black Mercedes drive down the road. She burst with excitement. "I cannot believe how you charmed them. They like you, they like you." Then flying into my arms she said, "You are my knight in shining armor." followed with a long breath-gasping kiss.

Breaking our embrace, I exclaimed. "Damn, I just remembered, we were supposed to meet Paul at the University. I have to call him." I dialed his number, and apologized, telling him that the Omasati's visit took longer than Myoko expected. Paul told me how he, became extremely busy, and it was just as well that we did not come, but he would be available again in two weeks. He would call to make arrangement.

After congratulating ourselves again, on how well the Omasati's visit went, we discussed plans for the upcoming week. We decided that I would come to the university Friday after her classes, then spend the weekend together, to discuss our future and each other.

After thirty more minutes of small talk, I kissed Myoko good night, gathered my things and drove back to the base. The week has been full of contentment, reflection, and anticipation toward Friday.

Chapter
THIRTY
THREE

It was ten o'clock Friday morning when the administrative officer called me regarding an emergency at the university museum. Paul Nethrum called, wanting to talk to me, and the administrative office could not transfer the call to my section of the building. I was to return his call at the university museum as soon as possible.

The lieutenant I worked for came out of his office, and asked me what the emergency was. "We don't have time for personal calls Drache, this is a working office, not some damn resort," he snarled.

I stared at the dumb twit and after a pause said, "I won't know what the emergency is until I call him back, will I? And furthermore, when have you ever heard me on the telephone with a personal call?"

I turned my back to him, and paged through my address book to find Paul's number. While reaching for the telephone to dial his number, I noticed the lieutenant looking over my shoulder attentively. What a dumb shit.

Paul answered on the first ring. "Paul, its Web Drache. What's the emergency?" He replied, "Someone broke into the museum vault. They tore the vault contents apart and took the sword. Why would they want the sword?"

"I don't know Paul." I answered, lying.

Paul continued "Web, the police never found a print, a clue, nothing. Nothing but a note and no one knows what it means. It instructs us to inform the *White Dragon* to meet them at the place of their last encounter, and to follow *Bushido*, whatever that is suppose to mean. Myoko had a bad reaction when I mentioned the note to her. She almost fainted, but said she's feeling better."

I knew what they wanted. They wanted me to follow *Bushido, The Way of the Warrior.* To follow the honor code of the samurai, but I am not bound by those restrictions. "Paul" I said. "Keep Myoko there, keep her there in your office until I arrive, and have security keep a watch on her. Don't let anyone near her, and I mean no one."

"I'm sorry Web, but she said she would be O.K., and went home. What does she have to do with this?" questioned Paul.

"Damn" I shouted. "Paul, get someone out to her house right now. This could be a matter of life and death. Hurry Paul, Hurry. I will explain later. I'm on my way."

"I'll call the Bristol police and have them send a squad car out to her place right away," exclaimed Paul.

"I'll meet you there." I said as I hung up the telephone.

"Drache, your butt's not going anywhere but right here.

You have a job to do and by God you're doing it," said the Lieutenant. I sprung to my feet. The expression on my face must have startled him.

"Don't mess with me." I growled. I knew handling him this way was all wrong. "I'm sorry lieutenant, but a close friend is in extreme trouble. Paul Nethrum is a university professor. He called for my help. You can check it out with the administrative officer."

My sincerity must have softened the old man's heart. "Go, go on. Just make sure you check back in with me with the whole story."

I threw a "Yes Sir," over my shoulder as I ran toward the door. I did not take time to change out of my uniform, but went straight to my car and drove to Bristol.

When I arrived at Myoko's house, Paul and a few officers were inside. Paul saw me driving up and met me at the front door, "The place is a mess Web. What is this all about? How is Myoko involved with these people?"

"The people, who took the sword, want Myoko. They are an old political faction from ancient Japan. They see possession of the sword, even if it is a copy, and Myoko, as their key to assuming power. The emperor's lineage includes Myoko. I guess that's how she knows so much of the sword and its history.

"Why was I kept in the dark on this, and how do you fit into this Web?"

"We don't have time for explanations now. We have to find Myoko." I said and started walking through the house when a policeman stopped me.

"We're doing an investigation pal; you will have to wait

outside till we're done."

Paul held up his hand, "He's O.K. officer. He is the person that alerted us to this being a possible abduction. His name is Web Drache."

The officer waved me through, "Sorry Mr. Drache, just don't interfere with our investigation, and don't touch anything until we're done."

"Fine" I said. Trying to absorb every detail, trying to analyze the information as my eyes swept each room, stopping at each site that did not appear normal. The drawers dumped on the floor, the overturned lamps, photo frame backs ripped from their supports, papers strewn all over the floors. It all brought back memories of the last time they tried to take Myoko. It appeared that the physical abduction took place in the living room, but why ransack the whole house?

If they have the sword they think is authentic, and they have Myoko, what are they looking for? I tried to review everything Myoko and I talked about. "Paul. What documents are needed for a foreign graduate student to register with the university?" I asked.

"Well, I think all they need are their transcripts, birth certificate, proof of their citizenship from their native country, and a letter of introduction from undergraduate school. What are you thinking Web?" asked Paul

"I think they were looking for documentation proving Myoko's blood lines to assure themselves, that she is who they believe her to be." I knew that a confrontation with them was an absolute to return Myoko unharmed. "Paul, I'm going to play a hunch. Will you be home late this evening? Sometime before midnight."

"Sure Web. I'll be home, or anywhere you want me to be." Paul had started to question me but I turned and walked out to my car. My thoughts were on Myoko, what my strategy would have to be. Would I meet them as Web, or the White Dragon?

Chapter
THIRTY
FOUR

It was getting dark as I pulled off the highway, one-half mile down the coast from that bloody overlook. I hid my car in an open area surrounded by shrubs and low trees, and collected my thoughts. After a few minutes of deep thought, my plan was complete.

I changed into my shinobi shozoku, (the all black clothing of the invisible night warrior, in the tradition of the Togakure-ryu ninja), removed my katana (sword), and tanta (knife) from its place of hiding, pocketed my penlight, and followed the water's edge to the meeting place at the overlook.

The evening was fully dark, and fortunately, the heavy overcast concealed the moon and its shining illumination. Cautiously, I made my way up the loose-pebbled surface of the cliff, my mind returned to the earlier events that took place here. I was mentally orienting myself to the topography of the parking area and the surrounding woods when the voices, from the enemy of my sworn allegiance, descended from above. My senses became acutely sensitive and my physical stealth quickly attuned to my immediate environment and demands. The words were becoming clear.

"Remember, Tiaru wants this guy alive. These oriental people are bad, brutal and downright mean. He is planning to torture this nut until he sucks all the information out of him, and then dissect him a joint at a time. This will be gruesome. He will be madder than hell if you do anything more than wound him. Shoot his legs out from under him, or whatever, just don't kill him. Everyone hide in the bushes around this clearing, and keep low. This should be easy with no moon."

I counted six voices in all, so there had to be six or more of them waiting for me. My sword was made ready by raising it out of the scabbard an inch or two, loosened my knife from its sheathing, and made my way around to where I would clear the cliff's edge into cover. The sky was as black as tar; the tangy crisp fall air was slowly blowing from the other side of the clearing. I could smell old beer and cigarette smoke breath. They're close. My feet slipped beneath the leaves covering the ground, finding soft noiseless earth. My totally dilated pupils accommodated full night vision.

A movement by a night-blackened bush drew my attention to a blob of darkness. I eased closer, to an arm's reach away. "Say, you got the time?" I whispered softly.

"Sure, let me." His sentenced stopped short and turned into a quiet gurgle as his thick blood shot from his severed jugular. The leaves crunched under the weight of his automatic pistol, as it fell to the ground.

A terse voice shot out of the darkness "What the hell are you doing, keep quiet."

"O.K., O.K." I whispered back. I wiped my tanta off on the dead man's windbreaker, and eased toward the next voice in the dark.

"Damn it, can't you keep quiet?" came the voice.

"Well I need some help. My gun's jammed." I whispered back.

"You dumb shit; you'll get yourself killed yet. Get over here." Said the second voice.

I made my way over to where the second voice came from. "Here!" I said, holding out my hand. I jerked the hand down as soon as I felt flesh. Grabbing the top of his head with my other hand and pushed his face into the soft ground, smothering out any cries for help. The razor sharp blade of my tanta quickly opened his throat and exposed his life's blood to the night air. I was still holding his face in the smothering ground as I felt his body pulsate, pumping itself dry, then lay still.

I went from one to another, eliminating all but the last two adversaries. My sword never tasted blood. I returned my thoughts to the situation at hand. The two remaining men were standing by the car parked at the side of the road entrance. The driver positioned the car for its headlights to illuminate the center of the clearing, and the majority of the parking area. The shorter man was giving orders. He stood leaning in the driver's door, one foot on the ground and one foot on the door's rocker panel.

The taller man stood at the front of the vehicle, with one foot hiked up on the bumper behind him, leaning on the hood.

The short man was speaking "I don't think he'll show tonight, damn-it. Tiaru will be mad as hell. He will kick the shit out of someone, surer than hell, if he doesn't get his way. I sure feel sorry for the young girl he has stashed. Tim, if he doesn't show in the next thirty minutes, you can round up the men and buy them a drink. We'll have to come back again tomorrow night."

The tall man glanced back toward the car and replied, "Sure boss, but these guys are sure itchy. This ain't their style. All this waiting around really makes them jumpy, what with all those stories we heard about this guy. Shit, what kind of weirdo would go by the name - White Dragon. He must have watched too many ninja movies."

I was at a 90-degree angle to the car, and threw a fist size rock at the taller man, striking him in the head as he finished talking, leaped over the car roof landing on the shorter man, pulling him away from the door and down to the ground. A fast knuckle punch, a shikan-ken, to the throat, immobilized him.

As I stood up, a shot, a small caliber struck me in my left forearm. Falling behind the opened car door, I realized there was no pain, just numbness. My Tanta unsheathed by reflex, and I was looking for the source of the shot.

The man called Tim was backlit by the phosphorous glow of the surf, and incoming waves. His head and revolver outlined, as he was getting up in front of the hood.

A quick flick of my right hand, and my tanta found its mark, in his soft throat. I quickly moved up to him, retrieved my weapon, returning it to its sheath. I threw his gun off into the distance, over the cliff. My left arm was now throbbing with a burning pain. *It could be broken.*

A fast examination showed no exit wound. Bracing myself, I put pressure on the entry wound, and felt the bullet lodged against the bone. I wiped my eyes with my right sleeve, moping up the sweat that ran down off my brow. Putting pressure on the nub of the bullet, I could feel it give. The pain was tooth cracking in their clench, as I rocked it out of the cavity. Pulling out a handkerchief from my chest pocket, I bound it tight around the wound to stem the bleeding.

The no-name short fat man was on his back, coughing and gasping for air, still half out of it. Kneeling down beside him, I quickly disarmed him of a .380 cal. automatic pistol, just like the weapon that Tim had used to shoot me, and a long narrow dagger, keeping both. I thwacked him on the chest with my open palmed hand, knocking all the air out of his lungs. The loud pop and resulting cough of expelling foul air was followed a harsh, raspy sucking sound, as he refilled his rotten lungs with fresh salt-water air. He started to hack, trying to suck in too much air at one time. He had rolled over on his belly, and was getting up on his hands and knees when I shot a shuto, a sword hand configuration of the hand, to the back of his neck. He dropped face first, into dirt with a loud thud.

I heard his laborious breathing, sucking the dusty soil up his nostrils and down his throat. He moaned too much for a fat man, who a short time earlier was eager to see me as a mounted trophy for someone named Tiaru. I attempted to grab him with both hands, but searing pain shot up my left arm. I grabbed his arm with my right hand, and rolled him over on his back. His eyes were trying to focus, and his breathing still labored as he forced words from his mouth. "Where are my men?"

I smiled at him and replied "Dead."

His eyes widened, and he forced more raspy words from his mouth. "All I can see is your face – Who are you?"

I replied with my own raspy sound "I'm that weirdo guy called the White Dragon" and in a more menacing tone asked "Where is this bastard you call Tiaru? And where is he holding the young girl Myoko – Where?" The man called Tim was still making whining, nasal sounding bubbling noises from in front of the car, followed by a weak call for help, then fell silent. This had an obvious effect on the short fat man. His eyes darted from the front of the car back to my eyes. "If she die's, you die. If she lives, you might, depending on what you tell me, and what you do. If you don't talk to me..." I nodded toward the front of the car. "He died slowly, and painfully ... Do you have anything to tell me?"

"Yes, I'll tell you everything I know. I need a drink; throats all torn up. There's a bottle on the front seat."

I yanked him up to a half standing staggering position, and searched the front seat with my right hand until I found the bottle. Handing the bottle to him, I heard myself say, "Here, take a swig and start talking. I'm running out of time and patience."

He tried to pour more booze down his bruised throat than he could swallow. His deep coughing caused him to throw up, while he continued to gulp at the bottle. He stopped gagging and kept a few swallows down. Dropping the bottle on the ground, he looked up at me

"That's better. Now I can breathe ... and talk." I scowled at him. There was a break in the overcast allowing the emerging moon to bath us in its increasingly brighter light. He was studying me in this sudden illumination as he continued talking. "This guy, Tiaru, or how ever you say his name, was introduced to me by an associate of mine. He first hired me to locate this Japanese gal for him, which I did. When his men tried to get her, they bungled the job and he lost her. I had her under sporadic surveillance, and figured out her routine at the university, while this Tiaru was getting information on some damn sword at the university. He became furious when I told him he was stupid for killing his men off, trying to get that toy of a sword, and that little twit of a girl. Neither one is worth a plug nickel to me. Totally worthless."

I interrupted. "Quit stalling, where's the girl?"

"I don't know where she's at." He continued. "All I know is that he's living out near Newport, in some white elephant mansion. He has it leased for the year, throwing parties every weekend, enthralling the upper social stratum of the area. He said he has them eating out of his hands. Maybe he has her stashed there. He mentioned to me one time that there is a dungeon like sub-basement under that rock facade of respectability."

I turn him around gruffly, removing a length of cording from my sash, bound his wrists behind his back, and tied them to his belt. My left arm was throbbing, but I concealed the pain from him. It was best not to show any weakness that might tempt him to try to overcome me. Pulling him over to the passenger side of the car, I opened the door, and pushed him down onto the seat. Taking another cord from my sash, I bound his ankles, pivoted him on the seat to face front and closed the door. Walking around the back of the car, I stopped to check my arm dressing. The handkerchief had worked loose letting the blood seep from the wound. I was worried that the bone might be cracked, weakening it enough to break under stress. I tightened the dressing, and slid into the driver's seat.

Engaging the ignition, the engine roared to life and I maneuvered the car out to the highway. I pulled off the highway and alongside my car. Not trusting my trussed up captive, I shut off the engine.

In my trunk, I located a flat slat and wide tape to make a makeshift splint to strengthen my arm. I also assembled my arsenal of weapons to deal with the unexpected. I picked up the kyoketsu-shogei (a length of cording with a steel ring on one end and a dagger with a secondary blade protruding from the handle at a ninety degree angle) which was hung from the right side of my sash, a kaginawa (a thirty foot thin rope, knotted twelve inches from the end, and a looser twisted roping to ensure rotation of the grappling hook spliced to the end) that was attached next to the kyoketsu-shogei. Then a kusari-fundo (a short length of one-half inch link chain, with weights attached to each end) which was bundled and attached to the left side of my sash. An assortment of shuriken (mixed throwing blades of straight and multi-pointed design) - I selected nine star shaped blades, which I stored in my leggings, and of course, I checked my knife and sword. My absence of two minutes did not bother the bound short fat man.

Chapter
THIRTY
FIVE

As I sat behind the steering wheel, I noticed little expression on his face. He appeared to be deep in thought, and as we drove toward Newport, gave me short apprehensive glances. "Now fat man, where is this mansion?" I asked. He gave me very specific directions taking me to a place commonly known as *mansion road*, and to an isolated turnoff into a secluded estate. I parked the car across the road from the entrance. "Tell me about this place."

The fat man stared at me for a few moments, shook his head, and said, "I've never been inside. I only met Tiaru at this entrance one time." He could see the displeasure on my face. "But, I'll tell you everything I know. He has a large number of Orientals working for him. I do not know the exact number. He belongs to the Jakazua, the Japanese Mafia and must have a real arsenal from the way he talks. As I said before, he mentioned a sub-basement, and walls with hidden doors and passageways. It must be impossible to get in or out without being checked. Oh yes, he also said that an infrared security system, was in and around the building. Really, that's all I know." Telling him to lie down on the front seat until I come back, I left him and made my way across the road, and up the lane toward the gate.

I followed the lane, staying fifteen feet off in the woods. Twice I saw the faint dim source of an infrared light shining towards its reflector. The first sighting put me into a deeper sense of caution and alertness. Each motion was a deliberate move toward my objective, and it came into view.

It was a massive rock portal, spanning the twenty foot wide road with a twenty-five foot rock arch. A bi-fold steel bar gate closed off traffic. There was no guard in the gatehouse, but had an obvious speakerphone attached, facing the gateway, and I could detect electrical insulators, indicating an electrified system. There was no provision for walking traffic. A ten-foot high rock wall topped with three strands of electric wire connected to the gate, and apparently surrounded the perimeter of the estate. A ten-foot bare perimeter hugged the wall, allowed for an open pathway. I cautiously approached the open space, looking in both directions for the telltale faint light, the sign of an infrared system. None was seen, but they could be inside the enclosure. While blending into the shadows of the night, I discretely followed the wall for one hundred feet before finding a tall oak, with a heavy branch, a good thirty feet high, jutting out over the wall.

I quietly scaled the tree to the bough, removed the kaginawa from my sash, and coiled the rope to ensure a maximum throw with no entanglement. Carefully swinging the grappling hook with three feet of slack rope, I released the hook.

It flew out in an arc, the grappling hook wound around the oak limb and as the rope tightened, and recoiled, the grapple rotated snagging the taut line at the other end of the winding.

Tying the free end of the rope to the trunk of the tree, I was in, without using knots, so I could release the tie from the other end. I pulled myself over on the rope, and made my initial penetration into Tiaru's stronghold. Giving the rope as much slack as I could, I whipped the rope counterclockwise, unwinding the twists at the other end, and pulled it free, snapping it back toward me as it released from the tree, to prevent that end from falling and possibly activating an alarm.

A thin growth of trees ringed the inside of the wall. From my high vantage point, I could survey the grounds. I could not see or hear any guard dogs, but could determine the route of the security patrols, and where the manual overrides for the infrared security system were placed. Examining the mansion, I picked out a large, solid looking drainpipe, dropping from the roofline rain gutter down to the ground, embedded in a three-foot wide opening between two decorative rock moldings that jutted out two feet.

I descended to the ground, and crouched behind the tree trunk. My left arm was pulsating in pain and I took a minute to loosen the dressings on the wound. The bleeding had not stopped. The rough bark of the trees was not kind to my feet. I adjusted my tabi (split toed sock/shoes) and rubbed my tired arches. Counting off the seconds, I timed my run to the downspout, avoiding surveillance of the security patrols. My black clothing blended well with the shadow inside the space between the rock moldings.

The exertions of the day had taxed my stamina. I had to rest a few seconds. A security guard stopped on a path not six feet away from me, to light a cigarette. He squatted down, taking his time with his smoke. I could hear his lungs, inhaling and exhaling, watching exhaled smoke drift inland, with the breeze coming in from the sound. I had my kyoketsu-shogei at ready, when the sentry turned on his heel, cleared his throat with his head bent down, and spat onto the grass. His head was rising up, returning to his original squatting position, when his eyes met mine. My two bladed dagger struck his upper chest, locked in his rib cage, knocking out his breath before he could utter a cry of alarm. I pulled him back to me with the attached rope, and dispatched him with my knife when he was within arm's reach. His death rattle did not carry far in the heavy night air. My dagger was wedged in his ribs, and I had a little trouble removing it, then I rolled his body next to and parallel to the wall, in the shadow of small shrubs.

I began my climb to the roof, holding the downspout for balance, and wedging my feet to the inside of the molding for footing. Music and a faint feminine laughter drifted out a second floor window that was too far away from me to see in. I continued climbing the next four stories to the roof.

I started to slip trying to get around the roof's overhang, but managed to pull myself out, over and up to the roof. The damp night air made maneuvering on the slippery metal roofing difficult. The rubber coating on the bottom of the split-toe tabi did not help much. I was walking hand and foot to make my way up the sharp angled roof. I made it to the widow's walk, and unlatched the access door cover, quietly made my entry in and down a wooden ladder to the floor.

The dim spot of light from my penlight lit a stairwell leading down to a door with no light under it. The stairs made a few soft creaks as I eased my weight down slowly using the sides of each step. I maintained a constant pace. The door opened soundlessly and with ease into a dimly lit hallway. Another descending staircase, was halfway down the hallway.

I listened at each door, making my way to the stairs leading down. Each step cautiously followed by the next with a practiced rhythm, until I came to the brightly lit second floor.

Soft classical music, with flirting laughter, came from an open double door, at the head of a sweeping grand staircase, that led into a large ballroom. I heard two voices from within. A heavy, gruff, oriental accented male voice and a light feminine voice with a New England accent.

I crept closer, listening at each passing door, until reaching several large potted shrubberies where I could mask my presence. Peering through the crack behind the door, I could make out the couple, an oriental man around forty, with rough features and black hair, sitting with a young woman looking twenty, blonde, slender, and very polished, dining at an elaborately set dinner, who asked him. "Tiaru Masakado is so hard for me to pronounce, is that your real name?"

"No" Said Masakado. "I took the name of my ancestor, who also claimed his rightful place as emperor of Japan, but was assassinated by a coward member of his own family. I will take his quest and achieve my goal in his name."

"Well," said the woman's voice. "Is there something shorter, or easier, for me to call you?"

"Yes" replied the male, "I told you before to call me Masa. That is what you would call a nickname."

"That sounds so much like a southern pronunciation of master. Do you really want to be called Master?" She replied flirtingly.

"Yes, yes I do," answered the male in a louder voice.

"And when is it that you will be assuming all that power in Japan, Masa? When will you come into all that money?"

"Soon" he said "very soon. Everything is in place. All I need is one remaining symbol of power. An authentic sword of the White Dragon to pull supporters into a coagulated mass of power, and it should be coming to me soon, maybe this very evening."

"I love a strong man who knows what he wants, and goes after it," Purred the blonde. "And you promised me, I could share this with you, in Japan. But, you would have to marry some Japanese woman."

"Yes, but that would only be on paper. She would not be with us. I would put her away somewhere where no one could see her. You would be my companion. You would share in my power; something that would stretch your imagination past the realms of reality. You would not be able to identify the boundaries of its reach. You would never be able to fathom its potential of wealth and fame. It is something only thought of in fairy tales, but it is there, and it is real, and I have only one thing, one person, between the complete key and me. And he has to come to me, because I have what he wants, and he has what I want." He let out a sinister laugh. "But I will keep what he wants, and take what he has. Nothing can stop me from achieving my family's rightful place as ruler of the Far East.

Japan, Korea, China, all the surrounding pitiful little serfdom countries, all will be under my control. I will be bigger, more powerful than anyone else in the world."

"Oh" cooed the blonde, "I love a strong willed man. You are sooo exciting. Just thinking of it gives me goose bumps." Reaching over, she picked up his hand and rubbed her cheek on it. "I'm so glad we met at your ball last night. Why, it was Newport's social event of the year. Everyone tried to meet you, or to catch your eye. I could tell right away you were a very important man who knew what he wanted. That is why I made my jelly-fished fiancée find a way to introduce me to you. After he found out I was staying the evening, how did you calm him? I could see he was furious as your men escorted him out."

"Don't worry about him, he's not excited anymore, and he sure in hell won't bother you or anyone else, ever again."

I knew from the way she was slobbering all over him, I could take care of them later. First, I had to find Myoko. A waiter was bringing a silver platter down the hall.

There must be a service stair, back down that hallway. I waited for him to pass and enter the grand room. As the couple's attention focused on the waiter, I stepped out from behind all those green things, and made my way down the hall, where at the far end, was another set of stairs, the service stairs. I made a fast decent; my tabi's making no noise on the solid steps, down to the first floor. The stair's doorway was open, and I hoped the closed door across the hall was an entrance to the basement.

Checking down the hall, there was no one around. I cracked the door open, and it was the stairs. I softly closed the door behind me, and went down again, to find myself in a wine cellar, isolated from the basement proper by its wire cage.

The lights were dim, but I located a narrow wired door in a wall of the wine cage. I pried the latch open with my knife, and after exiting, pushed the latch and screws back into place, where it would look normal.

Making my way around the basement walls, I looked for an entrance into the subbasement. I made a full circle with no luck. None of the doors opened to stairs. I remembered that fat guy mentioning hidden passageways. I looked around the wall perimeter. Near the wired wine cage was a formal dining table with chairs, with a sideboard and a very large hutch standing next to the wall. I walked over to it, and examined the back. My hand found its back resting on a wooden frame, and roller marks on the floor in front of it. I found the entrance to the subbasement.

My pulse sped up. My arm was not hurting anymore, maybe from the adrenal of my anticipation. I calmed myself and tried to swing the hutch out. *It would not budge. There must be a triggering device.* I rubbed my hands over the details of the hutch front. *Nothing.* My eyes scanned the area for details. Bead board topped with a chair rail covered the bottom half of the basement walls. There was a wide vertical trim board at the end of the paneling next to the hutch and an area of wear, darkened from flesh contact around the top. My fingers found grooves at the back of the trim board.

My fingers gripped tight into the grooves as I pulled the trim board out. I heard a click when the board cleared an inch. Again, I tried swinging the hutch out. It moved smoothly and slowly, with a spring like force trying to pull the hutch back to the wall. It clicked into a locked open position exposing an open stone archway. As I stepped through, I felt my weight depress the stone I stepped on, down until another click released the lock holding the hutch open.

Slowly it closed, putting the space into total darkness. Again, I plunged down the button of my pen light; its beam lit a shaft with a metal spiral staircase leading down into the darkness. I let the steps lead my way down into the black abyss.

The staircase stopped by a massive, metal-strapped door, set into a damp, sweating stone doorway. No light came through the open space under the door or the cracks between the thick boards. I pressed my ear over a large crack.

Soft sobbing came through the crack. My first impulse was to tear down the door and rescue Mykoko, but caution stopped me. I felt around the edges of the door. *Nothing unusual.* I ran my hands over the stone doorway, checking the joints between the rectangular blocks. Nothing. No lock or knob was on the door, just a large iron handle.

Grabbing the handle firmly in my right hand, I slowly pulled the heavy door, trying to keep its momentum to a minimum. The sobbing from the other side of the door grew louder. I swept the room with the beam of my light until it found Myoko, sitting on a dirty, stained mattress, lying on a steel bed.

Her leg chained to its frame.

"Myoko, sshhh – quiet, it's me, Web." I put the beam of light to my face. She stood up, holding out her arms, trying to stifle her crying. Her face was dirty, with streaks below her eyes where the tears washed the grime. She had her bra and panties on, with remnants of her dress draped over her right shoulder. Her eyes were puffy, her body, legs and arms bruised.

I rushed to her, held her in my arms, soothing her sobs with "You're all right, I'm here. I am here. You are O.K. You're O.K. –Sit down, so I can get that chain off your leg."

She stumbled through her words to tell me, - "Tiaru, he told me I had to marry him. If I did not do what he wanted, if I did not please him, he would still marry me on paper, and he would give me to his warriors for a toy, used for whatever they wanted. He is a mad man."

I picked the lock on her leg iron; it snapped open and fell to the floor.

"He said he knows that you are the White Dragon, that he will kill you and take the sword. He is mad. He thinks that possession of the sword, and me, will make him the ruler of Japan. He keeps talking of his family's heritage. He's mad."

I stood up and held her in my arms. "Are you hurt anywhere? Are you able to walk?" I asked.

"Yes" She said, "I'm O.K. I can walk." She started sobbing again, and I told her she must be quiet for us to get out of the house. We walked out of the room and up the circular stairs. Stepping on the stone clicked the hutch lock mechanism open; it swung open slowly as I pushed. We made our way around the table and chairs, toward the wine cage when I noticed an open doorway in the wall opposite us that I did not see earlier. I had a funny feeling in my gut. I urged Myoko on "Hurry Myoko, hurry."

The lights popped on. Six men armed with automatic rifles surrounded us, and standing in the wine cage door was Tiaru. "What have we here? Small birds that fled their cage, and I am the cat that found them. Yummy. Yummy. Cats like to eat small tender birds, especially young sweet birds like Myoko. However, cats love to play with tougher game, like you Web Drache. I will enjoy playing with you. I will enjoy watching you die, painfully, begging for a quick death – You must take me for a fool, Mr. Drache. You are a pitiful excuse for a Jonin, a Master," Then laughing, "or even a White Dragon. You are a boy, playing a game, and you do not even know the rules. I make the rules, and you will beg me to let you know what they are. Take them back down below for our entertainment."

When he had stopped puffing himself up with his self importance, the slender blonde stepped up from back in the wine cage, and stood by his side, looked at Myoko and me, and said. "Is that horrid thing what you have to marry? Oh God, that is revolting. Just the thought of you with anything like that is disgusting. That makes me sick."

The armed men closed in on us. I could do nothing.

One of the goons pushed Myoko hard on the back of her head, causing her to fall to the rough, coarse floor, and from the corner of my eye, I saw a rifle butt coming, flying toward my head – everything went black.

Chapter
THIRTY
SIX

A splitting headache woke me. Tied in a wooden chair, my restraints were fashioned after an old torture technique. My arms bound at wrist and elbow to the chair's flat arms. A noose was tight around my neck, ran down the back of the chair, and tied to my feet back under the chair. Ropes were around my chest and waist, binding me to the chair back.

My head pulled back, I was in pain. My black clothing ripped off and lay in a pile to the side. Lanterns spaced out on the floor cast upward shadows, giving the room an eerie, surreal look. I was naked. They had removed the dressing from my wound. I raised my head. A foot came crashing down on my groin. I yelled out in pain. In that space between consciousness and unconsciousness, I heard a rough coarse voice laughing. "Now a Samurai or a Ninja does not faint from a little pain. Look at this little baby dragon's eyes roll back in his head. Poor thing shrinks from pain. Help him."

Cool water thrown into my face revived me. I glanced over

to the left, to the bed. A dirty rag gagged Myoko. She lay on the bed, tied. The blonde was poking her in the upper arm, hitting the top of her head, and down her body, wherever she thought Myoko might be sensitive to pain, with a long wooden pointer. Myoko made shrill noises through her nose. Tiaru walked over in between Myoko and me, obstructing my view of her.

Looking down at me, he asked. "Do you have anything to say?"

My throat was painful, felt gravelly. "May every Japanese foot in the world have the opportunity to rest on the top of your head." I knew that was as bad of an insult there was to a person like Tiaru, stuck in the old traditions. His cane whipped cracking down on my wound, ripping it open and exposing the bone. "Oh, look at that. His scratch is bleeding. You two men, come over with your cigarettes, and stop his boo boo hurt and bleeding."

Two men came into focus, came closer, one on each side of me, holding their cigarettes out in front of them. The first character held the burning end of his smoke in my open wound, pulled it out, puffed a few times, and crushed it out in another spot on my left arm. The demon on my right was holding the burning tobacco next to my skin in several places, while Tiaru was carefully examining my silent sword. I screamed in pain, "You bastards must eat dung. You're like shit rollers, looking for a place to lay their eggs." Tiaru snarled at me, came closer, my sword raised for a strike. His swing knocked over a lantern. Loose bedding draped across a chair caught fire.

The blade came down to the side of my head, it came down flat, and as my mind retreated to place of resolve, I heard

Myoko writhing on the bed, trying to escape her pain. I heard Tiaru order one of his men to get the other sword. "I will dissect this worthless specimen, and use his guts for fish bait."

Everything went black. There was no pain. It was peaceful and quiet. Then, lo and behold. The damn mist returned. The old man floated toward me, and that familiar dragon head, a tatso-gashira, raised his ugly head from the mist, their eyes locked on mine, coming closer.

"Web Drache, you disappoint me. You did not properly follow your teachings. You, blood of my blood could have failed. We have returned for your final lesson. Call it a bonus post graduate session." He smiled. That was the first time he ever smiled at me. "We have come to you and we are one." In my darkness, I could feel that old, long forgotten shiver, the rush of energy flowing through my body, that growl, strong, loud, and ear splitting, coursed through that rock chamber below the basement of the mansion. My eyes snapped opened, the dungeon filled with a cloudy mist, and a loud roaring growl bounced off the walls, feeding me with renewed energy. I stood up, the ropes binding me snapped apart, falling from my body, the shattered wooden chair fell to the floor in shambles. I reached my hand out to my sword. Tiaru and his henchmen were dumbstruck, frozen in their tracks. My sword started to sing, glowing in the dim light, burning Tiaru's hand. As he threw the sword to rid himself of its burning pain, it flew into my extended hand. The rifles were resting on a rack at the far side of the room, but Tiaru and his men did not reach them. It would have done them no good, even if they could have closed the distance to them, before the singing sword found their flesh. Their screams were short lived. The sounds of pain and fear that started in their throats never had a chance to leave their mouths. Five bodies were laying in eight pieces on the floor, a model of the eight main islands of Japan, like small stepping-stones, spread out to the door, in an ocean of red blood, pointing the way out. The room filled with acrid smoke from burning synthetic cloth.

A whimpering drew my attention to the corner by the cot. The blonde was cowering in the corner, covering her head, begging me not to kill her. Begging to keep the monster away from her. Begging "I'm sorry, I'm sorry, I never meant to hurt anybody. Please don't hurt me." Myoko was unconscious. I forgot about the blonde. Myoko's bindings fell away when touched with the edge of my blade.

I slipped on the shredded pieces of my black uniform. I picked Myoko up off the bed, and carried her out of the smoke filled room, up into the basement, through the wine cage, and up the stairs. People were leaving, looking around asking, "What was that noise? What happened? Was there an explosion? Did anyone call the fire department?" The corridor filled with guests, trying to force their way out the main doors, trying to escape to the outside and fresh air.

The sixth henchman sent to retrieve the phony sword saw me in the hallway. I set Myoko down, propping her up against the wall, and stood waiting for him to come closer. He raised the sword in a typical two-handed grip when my singing sword cut him in two at the waist.

His sword, locked in his hand in a death grip, flew back

into an electrical outlet. I picked up Myoko again, heard the outlet sizzle and pop, as it shorted out, and continued to a set of French doors, in the wall of a room adjacent to the main doors. In the confusion and smoke, no one noticed me carrying Myoko out the doors, and down to the front gate.

I put Myoko down beside the lane, and looked for a switch to open the gate. Pushing a button in a stand along the left side of the road, the gate folded back. Myoko became conscious and propped herself up on her elbows, shaking her head. She uttered a soft cry of fear as I approached, recognized me and started crying. I got her to her feet, out the gate, and across the road to my car. She asked me. "What happened? Where are we?"

"Everything is all right," and comforted her with "you're with me, and we have left the mansion. We're going home."

We approached the car and I saw the short fat guy in the road, his feet and arms still bound. Tire tracks ran across his clothing. I put Myoko into the passenger seat, and went over to check him. He was dead. Returning to the car, I examined Myoko closer. She had bleeding puncture wounds in her arms and legs, but I could not find any serious injury.

Myoko's gaze fixed on my eyes. She pulled me to her in a tight embrace. "Please don't leave me alone, never again, not for a moment," she begged in my ear.

I pulled her arms from around my neck. "I must go back, I have to finish what was started," and moved away, to return to the mansion.

She begged me to stay with her. "Please, please do not leave me, not now." Hearing a loud explosion, I looked up. The whole place was on fire, people were screaming. The blonde came staggering down the lane, her clothes on fire. She fell to the ground under the gates arch, and lay still.

I stood watching the mansion burn, the people running to escape the flames and confusion. I heard the fire engine's siren; I turned back to the car, got in, and drove off with Myoko at my side. While driving, my thoughts began to jell. "Did all this really happen, or was my latest encounter a dream my subconscious conjured up to rationalize what actually happened?" Myoko snuggled tight against me and my thoughts returned to her.

It was two o'clock in the morning when we walked through Myoko's front door. Remembering that Paul would be waiting for a phone call, I dialed his number. He answered on the first ring. "Yes, Paul Nethrum."

"Paul, this is Web. It's all over. Myoko is safe and at home. The sword is in a house that burned down over by Newport. I do not know if it recoverable. I will talk to you tomorrow, and fill you in on all the details. Good night."

"Web, Web" was coming out of the telephone as I rested it back on the cradle.

The house was still a mess. I looked at Myoko. She was trying to straighten her hair. "That must be a woman's reflexual thing," I laughed, leading Myoko into the bedroom. We lay down on the bed just the way we were. I do not know about Myoko, but I immediately fell into a deep sleep with pleasant dreams of consents and blessings, from and old man, a young woman, and an ugly dragon.

Morning sounds woke me from a dream come true.

Reaching over for Myoko found emptiness that immediately yanked the pit of my stomach up to my throat. The past events that led up to last night's confrontation-soured optimism. "Myoko! Myoko!" was screaming out of me. I was fully awake now - what is wrong with me, how insecure can one become, telling myself, *there must be a logical reason for her absence.*

Forcing myself out of bed, I searched for an explanation. The bathroom was empty. The kitchen was empty - *wait, on the table is an envelope.* Getting closer, the name Web became clearly visible. *Hah, she went to the store for breakfast - to surprise me.* The envelope was not sealed. Slipping the single sheet of paper out of the envelope, I read words that strangled my mind and soul.

> **"Dear Web,**
>   **My Great Grandfather visited me last night in a dream, cautioning me against our consuming love, telling me that you and I are of the same blood, and are trying to live a life that cannot be, a forbidden union.**
>   **He commanded me to return to Iwakuni, to take control of the Kikkawa Dynasty, restoring it to the glory of ancient times. I must go to sort out what I believe, what is the truth, and what I must do. If I do not return, please know my love will always be with you, no matter what my decision."**

"OLD MAN, OLD MAN, once again you intrude on my life." I screamed. "We will have our day of reckoning - you need me more than I need you. You WILL come to me, and you will HAVE to return Myoko to me. You WILL repair all the damage you and your nightmares have done to me. I am no good to you as a vegetable in some mental institution."

The door opened and Myoko stepped in carrying a grocery bag. "What is all this yelling and commotion?" Seeing the opened letter in my hand, she paused. "Oh Web! I was hoping to return and destroy that paper before you found it. It was written in haste, before I could rationalize what was revealed to me last night in my sleep. I..."

Placing my open hand over her mouth, I interrupted. "Myoko! Reading this, I thought you were lost to me. In my mind, you were coerced to return to Iwakuni, removed forever from my sight and love. You are..." My pent up emotions released themselves as I pulled Myoko to me, embracing her. "You are not leaving me to return to Iwakuni, are you?"

She returned my embrace, kissing me, while mumbling, "Not today. Maybe someday, - but not today."

We found our way back to the bedroom, breakfast forgotten. The grocery bag was still sitting on the kitchen table.

THE
END

About The Author

Charles Schwend served 20 years in the U.S. Navy, retiring as a Chief Petty Officer. Some of the many military positions held were: B-26 (JD-1) crewmember; Foreign National Recruiter under the U.S. State Department; U.S. Navy and U.S. Coast Guard Recruiter for the Far East; U.S. Navy Liaison to the U.S. Army; Casualty Control, Cruiser-Destroyer Force, Atlantic Fleet, etc. Journalism major at SIU-E. Co-founded the Highland Writer's Group. Retired from the State of Illinois. Leisure activities include: writing; beekeeping; wine making; and mushroom cultivation.

LaVergne, TN USA
15 March 2010
175937LV00003B/1/P